THE ADVENTURES OF JACK BRENIN

BOOK THREE

SILVER HILL

THE ADVENTURES OF JACK BRENIN
BOOK THREE

SILVER HILL

CATHERINE COOPER

ILLUSTRATIONS BY
RON COOPER and CATHERINE COOPER

infiniteideas

First published in 2011 by
Infinite Ideas Limited
36 St Giles
Oxford
OX1 3LD
United Kingdom
www.infideas.com

A CIP catalogue record for this book is available from the British Library

ISBN 978–1–906821–74–6
Brand and product names are trademarks or registered trademarks of their
respective owners.

Cover designed by D.R.ink
Typeset by Nicki Averill
Printed and bound in Great Britain by CPI Antony Rowe,
Chippenham and Eastbourne

For Camelin
You know who you are!

THE MAP
OF
GLASRUHEN VILLAGE

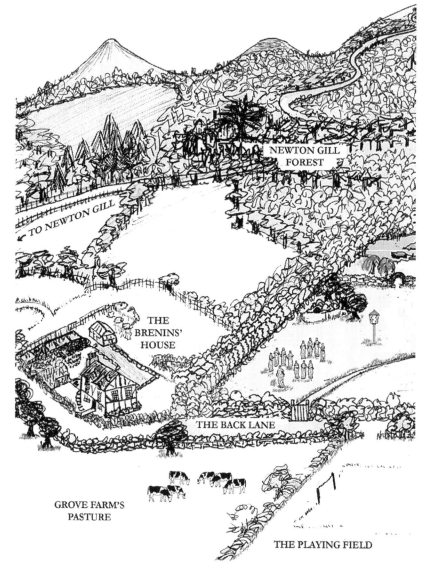

NEWTON GILL
FOREST

TO NEWTON GILL

THE
BRENINS'
HOUSE

THE BACK LANE

GROVE FARM'S
PASTURE

THE PLAYING FIELD

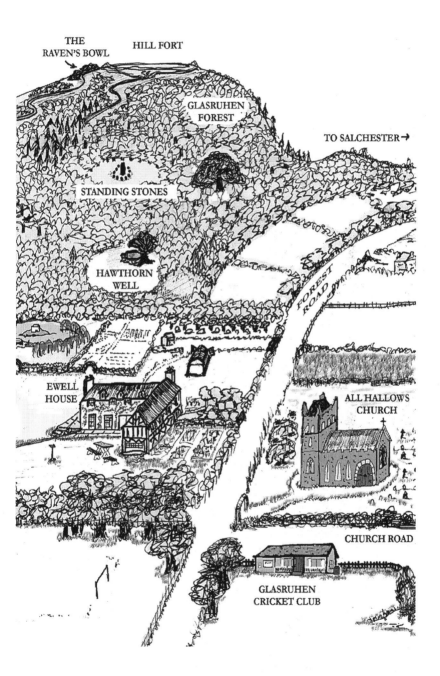

THE RAVEN'S BOWL

HILL FORT

GLASRUHEN FOREST

TO SALCHESTER →

STANDING STONES

HAWTHORN WELL

FOREST ROAD

EWELL HOUSE

ALL HALLOWS CHURCH

CHURCH ROAD

GLASRUHEN CRICKET CLUB

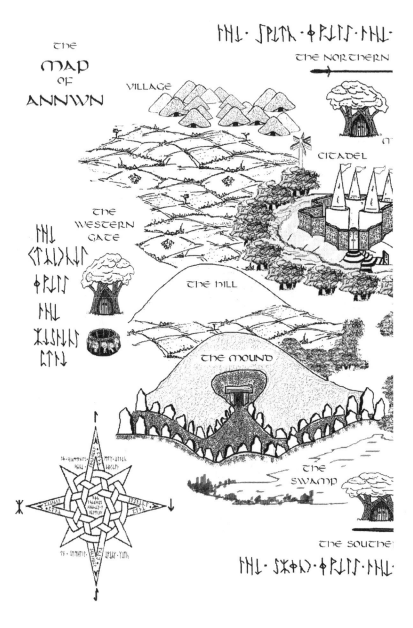

THE · SPER · Ϸ ELIS · HIL ·

THE NORTHERN

THE
MAP
OF
ANNWN

VILLAGE

CITADEL

THE
WESTERN
GATE

THE HILL

THE
CTAD⟩IN
ϷELIS
HIL
XISHIX
CTN

THE MOUND

THE
SWAMP

THE SOUTHE

THE · SXϷN · Ϸ ELIS · HIL ·

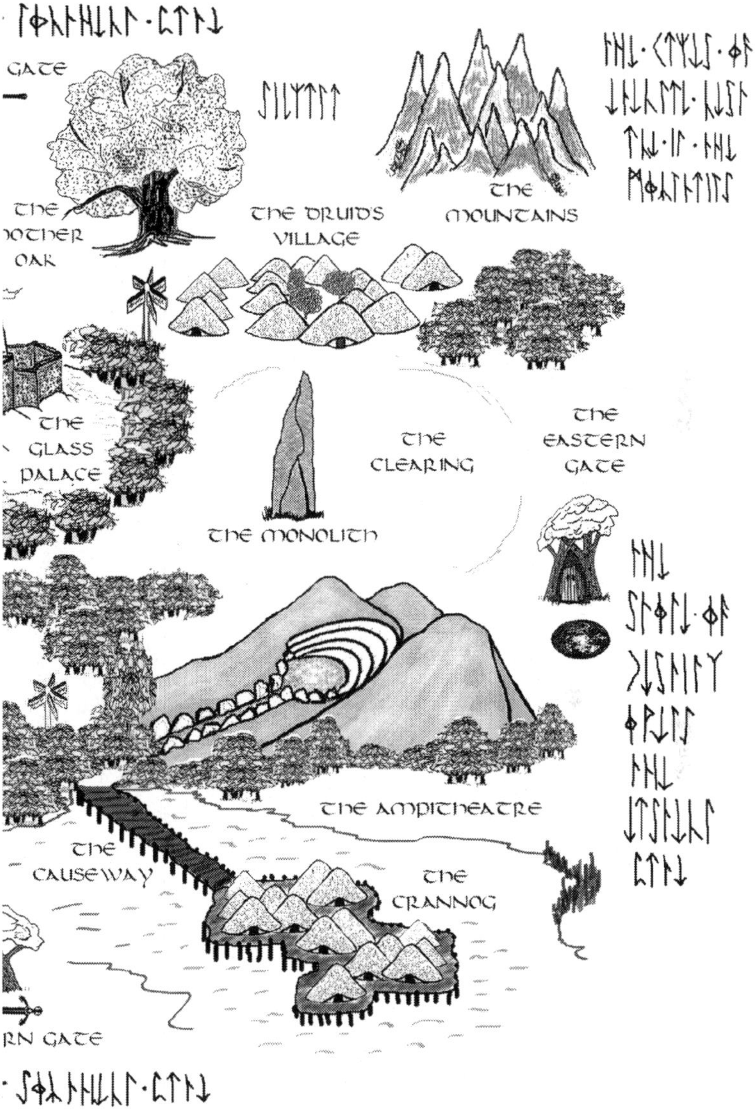
GATE
THE DRUID'S VILLAGE
THE MOUNTAINS
THE GLASS PALACE
THE CLEARING
THE EASTERN GATE
THE MONOLITH
THE AMPITHEATRE
THE CAUSEWAY
THE CRANNOG
GATE

THE MAP OF
SILVER HILL AND THE CRAGS OF STONYTO

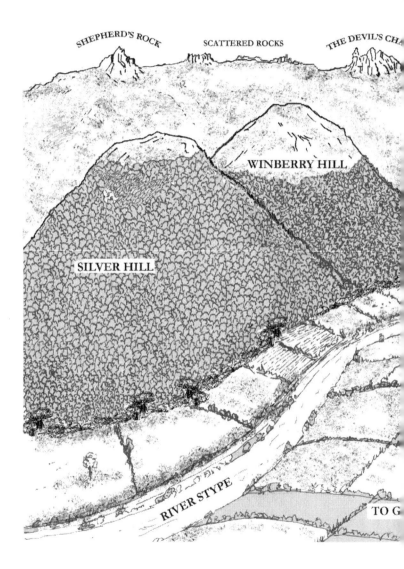

SHEPHERD'S ROCK SCATTERED ROCKS THE DEVIL'S CH

WINBERRY HILL

SILVER HILL

RIVER STYPE

TO G

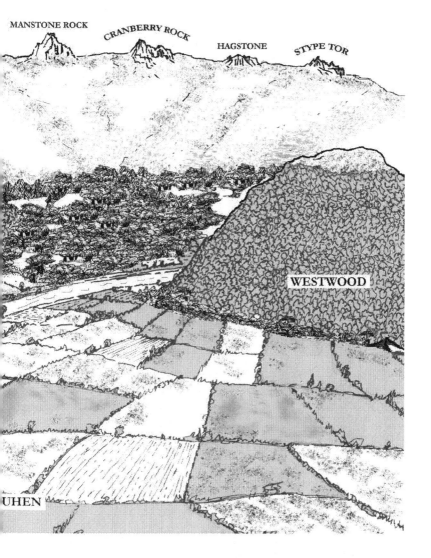

IDGE

MANSTONE ROCK

CRANBERRY ROCK

HAGSTONE

STYPE TOR

WESTWOOD

UHEN

CONTENTS

PROLOGUE

Jack aimed the wand at his big toe and read the spell out again. He added his own sound effect as the single blue spark left the tip.

'Kerpow!'

Long white hairs sprouted from nowhere. Soon his entire toe was covered.

'Look Orin! Do you like my hairy toe?'

Orin scampered down from her cage and examined Jack's foot.

'You could try green hair next,' she squeaked excitedly.

'I'd better see if I can remove this lot first.'

Jack gave his hairy toe one last look before trying the reversal spell. As two blue sparks hit his toe the white hair disappeared. Jack sighed deeply as he flipped through the pages of his Book of Shadows.

'This chapter tells me how to change the shape of my nose or ears, how to make warts appear and disappear, how to grow hair on different parts of my body but it doesn't tell me how I can get rid of these spots.'

He went over to the mirror and examined his face. Seven days ago he'd had a spotty rash but now he looked like some strange creature with pale mottled skin. He was covered from head to foot in calamine lotion, which Nora insisted he had to use. Each itchy spot had been individually dabbed with a fingertip of the pink lotion, which had thankfully dried white. Nora said it would stop the itching, and it had, but it wasn't speeding up his recovery. She'd refused to try any kind of magic to get rid of his chickenpox. Once Camelin knew he was *highly contagious* he'd decided not to fly over. The only message he'd written to Jack in his Book of Shadows had read...

CU W
the
pox
hav gon

... that was a week ago, and since then he'd not even tapped on his window.

Jack had felt too ill to even move for the first couple of days but now he was getting restless. Being confined to his bedroom until the blisters had gone wasn't easy. The good thing was that he'd had plenty of time to explore the different chapters in his Book of Shadows and to write to Elan. He'd told her about the planting of the Hamadryad saplings, their rapid growth and how excited the Gnarles in Newton Gill Forest had been when he'd returned Allana to them. He'd sung his solo for them, the one he was going to sing at the end of term concert if he was better in time. Jack looked at his calendar and counted the days left 'til the end of term. He needed to be better soon. He smiled when he saw the big red circle around yesterday's date when he should have gone to visit his new secondary school. He'd been worrying about it for weeks and now he'd missed it. The chickenpox had given him the best excuse in the world not to go but being ill had stopped him going out altogether.

He wasn't exactly bored, but the days seemed endless and empty. After all the recent excitement and adventure it was hard having to act like an ordinary boy all the time. He longed to fly again and was missing Elan and Camelin. Elan had written and asked him how he felt but she'd not given him any real news. He'd spent hours reliving their adventures in Annwn, but the more he thought about it, the more he longed to return. A loud tap on his bedroom door made him jump.

'Look who's here to see you,' said Grandad as he peered into the room.

It wasn't hard to guess as Jack only had the one visitor. He smiled as Nora came in and put a basket down on his bed.

'And how are you feeling today?'

'I think I'm well enough to go out,' Jack replied hopefully.

Nora inspected Jack's spots and shook her head.

'You might be able to pay us a visit in a couple of days but you won't be going back to school until next week.'

'When will I be able to fly again? I promised Charkle I'd help him look for his family.'

'Flying is out of the question until you're completely better.'

Jack sighed and sat down heavily on the bed making Nora's basket wobble. She steadied it and smiled as she opened the lid.

'I've got a surprise for you. I've brought you something to read, it might come in handy for when you go dragon hunting.'

Jack watched as Nora carefully unwrapped a rectangular package. She handed him one of her handmade books. It was red with an ornate clasp and decorated corners. The binding felt hard and almost scaly.

'It's my Dragon Lore book. It took me years to collect all the information inside and even longer to find a dragon skin to bind it with.'

'Dragon skin!'

'Yes, real dragon skin. Take good care of it Jack and learn all you can, I've got a feeling that if Charkle is to find his family he's going to need all the help he can get.'

'I'll look after it, I promise.'

'I'll leave you in peace so you can study the book. You can return it on Friday. Your blisters should have gone by then.'

As soon as Nora closed the door, Jack opened the book and began to read. His spine tingled as he turned the pages. He could feel a new adventure was about to begin.

SECRETS

'Let's have a look at you,' said Grandad as he inspected Jack's spots. 'Do they still itch?'

'Not all of them. I can go over to Ewell House today, can't I?'

'Nora seemed to think some fresh air might do you good. She also said something about you having a book to return.'

Jack nodded and stood still as Grandad dabbed all his spots with calamine lotion.

'There you go, get yourself dressed. You can have your breakfast downstairs today then get straight off to Nora's. She said you could stay for lunch if you wanted to but if you don't feel well enough you can come back.

I'm not going anywhere.'

Jack waited until Grandad closed his bedroom door then did a victory dance around the room before feeding Orin.

'Do you want to come too?'

Orin shook her head and started squeaking. Jack held up his hand for her to stop.

'Hang on, let me get my wand. Now, what did you say?'

'They're too busy to play with me.'

'Who are?'

'Fergus and Berry, the last time we were there they told me off for following them and said I wasn't allowed in the herborium.'

'What do you think they're up to?'

'They wouldn't tell me. They just said it was important.'

'Does Nora know?'

'They made me promise not to tell her. They said it was a secret and the less I knew about it the better.'

'That doesn't sound right. I wonder what Motley's asked them to do?'

'I don't think it was Motley. He's been doing an important job for Nora with the rest of the Night Guard. Fergus and Berry were cross because he wouldn't let them go along. They were grumbling about being left out. Fergus said it's because they're the youngest and smallest. I know they were given some jobs to do and told to guard the house but I don't think Motley said anything about the herborium.'

'Are you sure you don't want to come?'

'I don't want to see them. Berry said to mind my own business and Fergus told me to stay away.'

'Don't worry. I'll try to find out what's going on. I think I might know who's behind all this.'

Jack was grateful there was a shortcut to Ewell House. It meant that no one would see him with a spotty, blotchy face. As he walked through the hedge at the bottom of Grandad's garden he breathed in deeply. The trees and air smelt good. He couldn't wait to tell Camelin everything he'd learnt about dragons from Nora's book. He wasn't sure how it was going to help them look for Charkle's family but at least he felt prepared. In fact, he couldn't wait to begin.

Even though Jack was eager to see Camelin again,

he didn't rush. It felt so good to be out and about. The bright sunlight almost blinded him as he stepped out of the shady tunnel. Before going up to the house he went round to the back of the rockery and put his head into Camelin's secret cave.

'Saige! Are you there?'

A load croak came from a pile of leaves at the back.

'I've got a question for you.'

Jack waited until Saige hopped to the opening.

'How many chickenpox spots have I got?'

The little green frog didn't answer straight away and Jack was about to ask her again when she croaked the answer.

'Four hundred and twenty-eight.'

'Four hundred and twenty-eight! Wow! Are you sure?'

Saige turned and hopped back to the leaves repeating the answer each time she leapt.

'Four hundred and twenty-eight, four hundred and twenty-eight, four hundred and twenty-eight.'

As Jack stood up a familiar voice came from a nearby tree.

'Four hundred and twenty-eight what?'

'Chickenpox spots.'

'Well don't come near me I don't want any of them.'

'I'm not contagious anymore.'

'You don't look too good, you're all blotchy.'

'It's only lotion. Besides, Nora said ravens don't catch chickenpox.'

'You might give me ravenpox. That'd be much worse than chickenpox.'

'There's no such thing as ravenpox.'

'We're both raven boys, you don't know what we could catch.'

Jack decided to change the subject.

'What have Fergus and Berry been up to in the herborium?'

'Shhh! Don't shout so loud.'

'I wasn't shouting, I just asked you a question.'

Camelin glided down to the top of the rockery. He nodded his head towards the trees and glowered before hopping down to the cave.

'Perhaps we ought to go and visit Saige, see how she's getting on.'

'I've just been. She was fine.'

Camelin pecked Jack's shoe.

'Ow! What was that for?'

'I think we need to visit Saige. Now.'

Jack realised Camelin had something to say that he didn't want the trees to hear. He bent down and shuffled into the cave behind Camelin.

'What's up?'

'I don't want anyone to know about Fergus and Berry. They've been doing a little job for me.'

'Job?'

'A very important job, I've been very busy this week.'

'Too busy to write? You didn't answer any of my messages.'

'I couldn't.'

'It wouldn't have taken long. Just a *hello* would have been nice.'

'I told you I couldn't. I haven't had my wand all week, not since you got the spots.'

'Did Nora find out about the dustbin you materialised in your loft? Does she know how many sweets you ate?'

'One hundred and sixty-two,' croaked Saige.

Camelin strutted over to the back of the cave and addressed the pile of leaves.

'I don't need reminding, couldn't you just hop off somewhere for a while? This is a private conversation.'

'So, did Nora find out?'

'No.'

'What happened to your wand then?'

'She took it away. I got told off good and proper about not using magic for my own benefit.'

'What on earth did you do?'

'I *bigged* one of her buns.'

'What d'you mean *bigged*?'

'I know how to make things bigger. I thought it would be a good idea to make one of Nora's little buns cake sized.'

'And?'

'I went a big too far. If I'd stopped on two lots of the bigging spell and eaten it, Nora would never have known, but I did it one more time and it exploded all over the kitchen. She knew what I'd done straight away. I didn't have time to get rid of the evidence, there was bun everywhere. She told me she didn't want to hear any excuses and took my wand away. I wasn't even allowed to clear it up. I can't have it back 'til I can be trusted again or until we have wand practice together.'

Jack tried not to laugh but the thought of the gigantic exploding bun was too much. Camelin frowned.

'It's not funny.'

'I'm sorry, but I did warn you not to misuse your wand.'

'You sound just like Nora.'

'You still haven't told me what Fergus and Berry are doing in the herborium.'

'It's a secret and if you don't know you can't tell.'

'I can keep a secret.'

'And Nora's good at getting them out of you. And if you thought it was something she ought to know you might go and tell her anyway.'

Jack didn't know what to say. He knew Camelin was right.

'How long have Fergus and Berry been doing this important job for you?'

'Ten days,' croaked Saige.

Camelin shook his feathers and looked very annoyed.

'You won't keep asking questions when Nora's there will you? I never know when Saige is going to be around.'

'Ten days? Is she right?'

'Of course she's right, she's always right. But how did you know about Fergus and Berry? Nora didn't say anything to you, did she?'

'No, it wasn't Nora. They upset Orin and I said I'd try to find out what they were up to.'

'Well now you know. It's a secret mission, and

that's all you're going to find out.'

'Can we go up to the house now? I've got a book to return to Nora.'

'What kind of a book?'

'It's the one about Dragon Lore.'

'The one that's covered in real dragon skin?'

'That's the one.'

'She lent you that?'

'Yes. Why?'

'It's one of the books she keeps under lock and key, it's very precious. Did you read it all?'

'I did. There's all kinds of amazing information inside.'

'Like what?'

'I know why all the blue dragons are extinct.'

'The dragonors?'

'The very same.'

'So what happened?'

'The book says the dragonors were very bad tempered and liked to eat people. They're the ones you read about in all the old stories. The ones the knights used to fight. In fact, the knights were so successful they killed them all.'

'Did the book tell you the cover is made from dragonair skin?'

'No, I was going to ask Nora where she got it from.'

'It came from a really famous fire-breathing dragon called Wygrym Sharp Claw the Dangerous.'

'So how did Nora get its skin?'

'They moult. Every hundred years they grow a new skin and wriggle out of the old one. Nora found it in one of their caves and brought it home. She said it's the best thing to bind books with, it's strong and doesn't rip, but best of all it's fireproof. So if it didn't tell you any of that what did it say?'

'Well I'm not sure I should tell you, Nora might want me to keep the information a secret. I'll ask her first to see if it's alright.'

Camelin humphed loudly.

'I don't suppose it told you anything useful like how we're going to find Charkle's family or even how many dragons are left.'

'Four,' croaked Saige as she jumped past them.

Jack and Camelin stared at the little frog.

'How many dragonettes are left?' Jack asked slowly.

'Three,' Saige replied.

Jack shook his head.

'That's not good news. What do we do now? Do we tell Charkle there's only two other dragonettes left?'

'They might not even be his family'

'We need to ask Nora, she'll know what to do.'

Jack and Camelin made their way up to the house in silence. This new information was something they'd not been prepared for.

'What's the matter?' asked Nora as she came out of the kitchen. 'Are you feeling unwell again Jack?'

'I'm fine, but we've just had some information and we don't know what to do with it.'

'Oh dear, that doesn't sound too good. What was it?'

Camelin flew up onto the back of the stool but didn't say anything. Nora looked at Jack.

'Saige just told us that there are only four dragons left and only three of them are dragonettes.'

'Oh my goodness! Charkle had such high hopes he was going to find his whole family.'

'The ones left might not even be his family,' croaked Camelin.

Nora looked concerned.

'It also means there's a dragonair out there

17

somewhere. You'd have thought I'd have heard about it by now. I wonder where it could be?'

'The dragonettes must be somewhere too,' added Jack.

'I need to think about this. Don't you two worry about it, leave it with me. But we're going to have to tell Charkle. It's going to be a big disappointment for him but he needs to know. For now, until I've had time to think, it's going to have to be our secret. Agreed?'

'Agreed,' Jack and Camelin replied.

Jack took off his backpack and began to open the top.

'I've brought your book back.'

'Did you read it all?'

'I did, it was fascinating. Am I allowed to tell Camelin about the Dragon Lore.'

'If he's interested,' replied Nora as she looked at Camelin.

'I'm interested but I'd rather have some wand practice with Jack.'

Nora shook her head.

'That wand stays locked up in my herborium until I know you can be trusted again.'

At the word herborium Jack's eyebrows shot up. Camelin frowned.

'Well can we transform and go flying?'

'Jack isn't well enough yet, maybe tomorrow but definitely not today.'

Camelin sighed.

'It's no fun around here.'

'Why don't you both go down to the lake. I'll call you when it's lunchtime.' Jack picked up his wand and set off across the grass as Camelin flew on ahead. Jack saw him land in the willow tree by the water's edge.

'Shall I tell you about the Dragon Lore?' asked Jack as he looked up at Camelin.

'Naw, not now, I've got something to do. I'll be back in a bit. But don't tell Nora.'

Jack watched Camelin fly around the lake to the kitchen garden. He wondered what he could be up to now. For want of anything else to do Jack started drawing in the soft earth with his wand. He stopped when he heard a scampering sound. When he looked up, Fergus and Berry were peeking around the trunk of the willow tree.

'Hello, you two.'

'Hello to you Jack Brenin. We're looking for Camelin,' said Fergus.

'I was sure he flew into this tree,' squeaked Berry.

'He did,' Jack assured him.

Berry turned to Fergus.

'See, I told you it was Camelin.'

'But he told us to meet him behind the shed in the kitchen garden,' replied Fergus.

'And he didn't turn up. I knew I'd seen him fly into this tree,' Berry said crossly.

'He was here, but now he's gone,' explained Jack.

'Where?' asked Fergus and Berry together.

'He didn't say but he said he'd be back soon. Why don't you stay and wait for him?'

Berry and Fergus nodded and perched on the nearest root. Jack smiled as he looked from one to the other. They were almost identical. Both had a silvery brown coat and protruding front teeth and were smaller than the rest of the Night Guard. Jack could only tell them apart because Berry was smooth and sleek while Fergus always looked tousled.

'So,' began Jack, 'what's all this I hear about you two doing a very important job for Camelin?'

Fergus nudged Berry who was about to speak.

'It must be important if he gave it to you two.'

'Oh it is,' replied Berry. 'He's promised to *big* us in return.'

'You were told not to say anything,' grumbled Fergus. 'You want to be *bigged* don't you?'

'*Bigged?*' asked Jack.

'It's a secret. He told us not to tell Nora, but I'm sure it's alright to tell you. Camelin promised to make us bigger so we'll be like the rest of the Night Guard. We're always being left out because we're the smallest, or the youngest, or some other excuse Motley comes up with,' explained Berry.

'He's going to use his bigging spell if we get his wand back for him,' added Fergus.

Jack looked worried.

'Is that wise? Don't you know what happened to the cake he bigged?'

Both rats shook their heads.

'It exploded!'

Fergus and Berry exchanged looks and gulped.

'Exploded!' gasped Berry.

'Yes, splattered all over the kitchen. That's why Nora locked his wand up.'

'He didn't tell us that,' grumbled Fergus.

'I'm not sure I want to be bigged,' squeaked Berry.

'What exactly did Camelin ask you to do?'

Fergus sighed and began to explain.

'Nora locked Camelin's wand up in the cupboard on the wall. Camelin can't get to it because there's nothing to perch on so he asked us to get into the dresser drawer and find the spare key for the lock. We were going to get his wand out and put a twig in its place so Nora wouldn't know he'd got it back. Then he was going to big us both.'

Berry nodded in agreement and continued explaining.

'We made a hole in the back of the dresser and got into the drawer but there are lots of keys. We've been trying as many as we could when Nora's been visiting you.'

'And you didn't find the right key.'

'No,' replied Fergus. 'None of them would turn in the lock. I said to Camelin that Nora might have put a spell on the lock but he said she wouldn't have, it's the only cupboard in the whole house he can't get into, which is why she put it in there in the first place.'

'Have you tried them all?'

Berry shook his head.

'Not yet, but Camelin said it didn't matter if we couldn't find the spare key. He's sure Nora's special key is in the drawer too.'

'Special key?' asked Jack.

'It's supposed to open anything,' replied Berry. 'But how could just one key open any lock?'

Fergus shook his head and rolled his eyes.

'Because it's special, it's a magic key.'

'There's nothing special in that drawer. We should know, we've been in and out of it for the last ten days,' said Berry.

A flapping of wings made them all look up.

'I thought I told you two to meet me by the shed in the kitchen garden,' grumbled Camelin as he landed on a branch. 'What are you doing here?'

Fergus and Berry didn't reply.

'Are you two listening? You can go and do that special job for me at lunchtime. You won't be disturbed for at least an hour.'

Fergus coughed and stood on his haunches.

'If you don't mind we've decided not to be bigged after all.'

Camelin glowered at Jack.

'You told them, didn't you?'

'It was only fair they knew what happened to the bun.'

'I thought you were my friend?'

'I am but you wouldn't want to hurt Fergus and Berry would you?'

Camelin shook his head.

'But I want my wand back.'

'I think you're going to have to wait until Nora

says you can have it.'

Camelin let out an exasperated sigh.

'Life's not fair, especially when you're a raven.'

Berry looked relieved.

'We'll be off now,' said Fergus, and without waiting for a reply they both scampered away.

Jack felt a bit guilty. The willow tree would have heard the whole conversation and it wouldn't be long before Nora found out what Camelin was up too. Unless she knew already, keeping any kind of secret from Nora was difficult. If she did know, he doubted she'd have left the spare key in the drawer. It was also unlikely she'd keep her special key in a place where it could easily be found.

Camelin sighed.

'You can tell me about the book now. I've got nothing better to do until lunchtime.'

Jack found a comfortable spot, lay on his back and began to tell Camelin all about dragons.

HOWLING HILL

After lunch Nora decided Jack ought to go home. She said he wasn't to overdo it on his first day out. He hadn't realised how tired he was until he got back and immediately fell asleep. He'd slept again after supper. When it came to bedtime Jack was wide awake. He lay in bed trying to feel sleepy but his mind was racing. Too many thoughts about dragons were filling his head. He heard the hall clock chime eleven. It wasn't long before Grandad climbed the stairs and started getting ready for bed. When the house was quiet, Jack reached over to his bedside table for his Book of Shadows, picked up his wand and created a light from the tip so he could see to write to Elan.

Half an hour later, he'd written three pages. He watched the ink disappear and shut his book. He didn't expect an answer tonight. Before he put his wand away Jack tiptoed over to Orin's cage.

'Are you asleep?' he whispered.

The curtain twitched before Orin poked her head out.

'I thought you were in bed.'

'I've been watching Timmery.'

'What's he doing?'

'Flying back and forth past the window.'

Jack dimmed his wand, opened the curtains and peered into the darkness.

'There he is. Did you see him?'

'What do you think he's doing?'

'Maybe Nora asked him to keep a lookout.'

Jack watched as Timmery came over and tried to hover in front of the window. He could do it with ease as a hummingbird, but it didn't work when he was a bat and it looked as if he was doing a strange kind of jerky dance. Jack waved.

'Can I come in?' Timmery squeaked in a muffled high-pitched voice.

Jack opened the window and the little bat flew in and landed on top of Orin's cage.

'What's wrong?' asked Jack. 'Isn't Charkle with you?'

Timmery sighed.

'Such terrible news, terrible news. Charkle's with Nora, he knows all about what Saige told you. He's been crying for so long he's run out of steam.'

'Oh dear, I knew he'd be upset.'

'It didn't help when Camelin said the two dragonettes might not even be anyone from his family.'

'Poor Charkle.'

'Nora sent him to bed.'

'Charkle?'

'No, Camelin. She wasn't pleased with him. He's been in a lot of trouble lately, which is why I couldn't ask him to come over tonight.'

'Come over for what?'

'We've got to do something to help poor Charkle.'

'I'm sorry Timmery, I know I promised to help, but I can't until Nora says I'm well enough.'

'I need you to help me tonight.'

'But I can't fly.'

'You don't have to go anywhere. I got to thinking, and when I saw your light on I thought I'd talk to you myself, with no one else around. I don't know why we didn't think of it before.'

'Think about what?'

'Asking the Book of Shadows. I would have suggested it to Nora but I didn't want to disturb her when she was trying to comfort Charkle, but then I thought if you were awake I could ask you to help. Please Jack, say you will. It would be wonderful if you could.'

'Of course I'll help, but ask what?'

'You know the story we heard in Annwn, The Dragon of Howling Hill?'

'I do remember, it was brilliant, but what's that got to do with Charkle's family?'

'I want you to ask where Howling Hill is.'

'But it was only a story, it's not real.'

'What if it is real? The storyteller told everyone about the Glasruhen Giant and that's a true story. It wasn't quite the same as Nora's version but we all know a giant used to live on the hill. If we could find Howling Hill it'd be a start and there might be a dragon under it, like it said in the story. I could at least take Charkle to look. It would cheer him up and give him something to do.'

'I'll ask but I'm not sure we'll get an answer.'

'But you'll try?'

'Of course I will.'

Jack put his Book of Shadows on the bed. Orin scampered onto the bedspread and Timmery flitted onto Jack's shoulder. He concentrated hard and put his hand on the front of the book. He spoke softly so he wouldn't wake Grandad.

'Where is Howling Hill?'

Jack removed his hand and they waited expectantly. Nothing happened.

'Maybe it was the wrong question. I'll try asking it another way.'

Jack thought again before once more placing his hand on the front of his book.

'Is there a place called Howling Hill?'

Again they waited and again the book remained firmly shut.

'I'm sorry Timmery – I don't know what else to ask.'

'Maybe it used to be called something else?' squeaked Orin.

Jack smiled.

'You might be right. We could ask the question the other way round, not about the hill but about the dragon.'

'Oh that's wonderful, Jack. I knew you'd be able to help.'

'You can thank Orin not me and we haven't got an answer yet.'

Jack put his hand on the cover.

'Where should we look for dragons?'

As soon as Jack removed his hand, the book flew open and the pages turned rapidly. When they eventually stopped they were looking at two blank pages. Just as Jack was beginning to think the book had made a mistake, the faint outline of a map slowly appeared. He watched in fascination as a river, trees and hills gradually took shape. It was the strangest looking map Jack had ever seen, and there was something vital missing: there wasn't any writing. He looked sadly at Timmery.

'I'm sorry, this map's not going to be any help at all. It could be anywhere.'

'Ask about the wood,' suggested Timmery.

Jack put the tip of his wand on the small wood in the middle of the map.

'Where is this wood?'

No writing appeared, but instead, much to Jack's surprise, the map began to rise from the page and the pictures began to grow. A long narrow hilltop rose rapidly, its stony ridge was covered in strange rock formations. Two large wooded hills popped up out of the farmland that lay between two rivers. Colour flooded the landscape. Jack was speechless. It all looked so real. He reached over and touched the top of the larger hill but his finger went straight through the image. As he looked closer at the valley and the wider of the two rivers, he got the strangest feeling.

'I think I've been here before.'

'Can you remember where it is?' asked Timmery excitedly.

'I think it's Westwood.'

Jack got his magnifying glass out of his drawer and examined the landscape more closely.

'Look! There's the cave where we found Finnola Fytche. It *is* Westwood.'

Timmery looked really disappointed.

'But we already know Charkle's family aren't there any more.'

'But that's only one small part of this map. They could be anywhere, it's a big area and we didn't get a chance to have a good look around last time we were there.'

'You're right,' piped Timmery. 'What are those two hills called?'

'The one behind Westwood is Silver Hill and the other one is Winberry Hill. I don't know what the long ridge is called. I've only been there once. But there's the Gelston River; Camelin and I followed it on my first long flight.'

'Oooh! I'm so excited,' Timmery squeaked as he flittered around the room. 'I can't wait to get started.'

'There's no guarantee we'll find any dragons. I think we need to speak to Nora before we start getting excited.'

A creak on the landing sent Orin scampering back to her cage. Jack doused the light from the tip of his wand and was in bed pretending to be asleep by the time his bedroom door opened a fraction. In their excitement they must have been making more noise than Jack had realised. Jack lay very still and it wasn't long before his bedroom door closed again and Grandad went back to bed.

'Timmery,' whispered Jack, but there was no reply. He hoped the little bat wasn't going to raise Charkle's hopes too high.

It was late when Jack woke. He couldn't stop yawning as he dressed. He was about to go downstairs when his Book of Shadows began vibrating. It seemed ages since he'd had a message. Jack doubted it was from Camelin, he couldn't see Nora letting him have his wand back so soon. He hoped it was from Elan, he was dying to hear all the news from Annwn. He grabbed his own wand and opened to the first page. The words, faint at first, began to darken as the message appeared. He was slightly disappointed when he saw that it was from Nora.

I've got something important to attend to today and I'm not sure
what time I'm going to be back.
Before I go, I'll call in and ask your grandad if you can spend the afternoon at Ewell House doing an important job for me.
I'll leave instructions for you on the kitchen table.
Gerda, Medric and Camelin will need feeding too if I'm not back by teatime.

He wanted to know where Nora was going but he knew it was pointless to ask. If she'd wanted him to know she'd have told him. Jack hadn't seen much of Medric or Gerda since they'd returned from Annwn and now he'd got a good excuse to row over to the island and say hello. He wondered what job Nora wanted him to do, maybe she was just giving him an excuse to spend the afternoon with Camelin. Either way it meant he'd be able to go out. He got his wand and wrote back.

I'll be there.

'I had a visitor this morning,' Grandad told Jack as they ate lunch. 'Nora came to see me.'

Jack tried to look surprised, as Grandad spoke.

'She's had to go and see Elan and doesn't know how long she'll be gone.'

At this news Jack nearly choked on his sausage.

'Is Elan ill? Has she got chickenpox too?'

'Nora didn't say, she just said it was important and asked if you'd be able to do a job for her in the herborium. She said she'd leave you instructions on the kitchen table. Now, if you don't feel up to it I can go or I'll come with you if you don't want to go on your own.'

'I'll be fine,' Jack assured Grandad.

'Are you sure?'

Jack nodded.

'Off you go then and get yourself ready, I'll see to the washing up.'

Once Jack was back in his room he checked his Book of Shadows. There were no new messages and still no reply from Elan. He wondered if Nora really had gone to see her. If she had she'd be in Annwn by now. Jack sighed. It was going to be a long wait until he was allowed to go back, October was three months away.

Jack looked in the mirror. Although his face was still covered in scabs he didn't feel ill any more. He wasn't too happy about going back to school looking the way he did but he wanted to sing in the concert. If he could prove to both Nora and Grandad that he was well enough to look after things at Ewell House, he knew he'd be allowed to go to school in the morning.

He put his Book of Shadows into his backpack but before he packed his wand he went over to Orin's cage.

'Do you want to come with me today?'

Orin shook her head.

'Everyone will be too busy to play and you've got jobs to do too.'

'I'll tell you everything when I get back.'

Orin nodded and climbed sleepily into the hammock Jack had made for her and settled down for an afternoon snooze.

'I'm off now Grandad,' Jack called as he made his way downstairs.

'If you have any problems come back and get me. And if Nora's not back by teatime, can you make sure her birds are fed.'

Jack nodded.

'Just be careful with the geese they've got a nasty peck when they feel inclined.'

'I will. I'm sure everything's going to be fine.'

Jack thought the only problem he might have would be making sure Camelin didn't help himself to too much food. The rest was going to be easy.

'Couldn't you have got here sooner? I've been on my own for hours,' grumbled Camelin as Jack stepped into Nora's garden. 'You know, you don't look too good with all those scabby things on your face. Can't you put that white stuff on again and cover them up?'

'Nora said I didn't need to use it once they stopped itching, they'll drop off soon enough now.'

'Well don't go dropping them anywhere near me. They're yucky.'

Jack ignored this, and asked, 'Do you know where Nora's gone?'

'Annwn, she said it was important and she had to see Elan.'

'Aren't you curious to know what's going on?'

'Nope, I hope she's gone for ages so we'll have all afternoon to do things.'

'Things? You mean the jobs Nora's left for me to do?'

'Jobs! What jobs?'

'Nora said she's left me a note on the kitchen table. I think we'd better go and see what it says before we plan anything else.'

Camelin left Jack to walk through the garden alone and flew on ahead. As Jack entered the kitchen Camelin was grumbling to himself. There was a piece of paper on the table.

'What's it say?' asked Jack.

'There's nothing on it,' announced Camelin.

Jack picked it up. As soon as his hand touched the paper Nora's small neat handwriting appeared.

You'll need to take all the ingredients I've listed on the back of this note to the herborium. I've left you some more instructions in there along with the key to the cupboard where my special herb extracts are kept. I've been making a potion but I didn't have time to wait until it was cool and it's at a critical stage. The recipe is half done, it needs finishing this afternoon or it will be ruined. I've written on the recipe where you need to start. When you've added all the ingredients ask your Book of Shadows to show you the spell for making Dragon's Brew into Dragon's Breath.

'I'm afraid the *things* you've got planned will have to wait, Nora wants me to finish off a potion she's been brewing. I've got to sort it out this afternoon or it'll be ruined.'

'Oh that's great! You get to use your wand unsupervised but I don't.'

'It doesn't say anything here about me using my wand.'

'Don't you know anything? Potions always need some kind of magic and magic means using a wand.'

Jack ignored Camelin's remark.

'Are you going to help?'

'Nope.'

Jack turned Nora's note over.

'I've got a list of things to take down to the herborium. You could give me a hand.'

Camelin didn't reply, he *tutted* when Jack took his wand from his bag and grumbled to himself as Jack collected the ingredients. There was a big pile on the table by the time Jack got to the end of the list, too much to carry in one journey. He looked around for something to put them in. Nora's picnic basket was by the stove.

'Perfect,' said Jack as he picked it up and started to pack the ingredients inside. 'I'll see you later then?'

'Suppose so, you will try and hurry up won't you? I've got important things to do too but I need some help.'

'I'll help you when I've finished Nora's potion.'

Camelin shuffled from foot to foot.

'D'you mean it?'

Jack nodded.

'Aw, thanks Jack, you're a real pal. Give me a shout when you're done.'

THE CUPBOARD

Jack struggled into the herborium with the basket. A small cauldron stood on a tripod at one end of the table and Jack peeked inside as he passed. It was almost full of bright green goo, a bit like the compound Nora had put on his hands the first time they'd met. There were two pieces of paper on the table, weighted down with one of the candlesticks. As before, when Jack picked them up, Nora's writing appeared. On one was a recipe for the potion and the other the instructions. The ingredients and quantities had been listed along with the order they should be added to the cauldron. Half way down the page, Nora had written *START HERE*.

Jack read down to the bottom and found Camelin was right, he would have to use his wand.

For the dragon's brew recipe first make half a cauldron of green pea stew and let it bubble for six hours.

GREEN PEA STEW

3 cups of green peas
1 carrot
10 black peppercorns
9 cups of water
1 pinch of salt
18 parsley leaves

Whilst the pea stew is bubbling gather half a cup of fresh morning dew from nettle leaves and add it to the pot. Bring the mixture back to the boil then simmer.

Add the following
1 cup of rotting haricot beans
5 burdock leaves, 3 dill flower heads and 3 bay leaves
Next mulch up a small jug full of meadow hay and add whilst hot. Grind together one scale from a dragon skin and 3 lapis lazuli pearls and add to the cauldron.
When the mixture is thick stir it with a hawthorn stick to add the smell of rotting flesh.

Start Here

* When the mixture is cool add all the following.
6 teaspoons of ginger
1 teaspoon of mace
the zest of 4 lemons
2 crushed fennel stalks
3 whole garlic bulbs
13 feverfew leaves
and 36 shelled and ground hazelnuts

Stir again with the stick, then tap the bottle of dragon-wort pollen three times over the potion so the pollen covers the top. Then crush 1 large dragon-wort leaf between your palms and sprinkle on top of mixture.
This might not smell too good but once the mixture stops bubbling the smell will go.

USE A GLOWING WAND FOR THE SPELL - NO SPARKS

He blew out a long, slow breath. He couldn't believe Nora trusted him enough to make a real potion. He felt his spine tingle. This was better than being cooped up in his room. He'd do his best not to let her down but he couldn't help wondering what Nora was going to do with a whole cauldron full of Dragon's Brew.

Once the contents of the basket were on the table, Jack arranged them in the same order as Nora's list. Four of the jars had fine powder inside. Some he'd heard of but others he hadn't. The one labelled mace was a bright reddish colour, the garlic and ginger a warm yellow and the fennel dark green. One by one Jack checked off the ingredients. All but the dragon-wort leaf and dragon-wort pollen were now ready on the table. These must be the special herb extracts Nora kept locked in the cupboard. They didn't sound like the kind of things anyone would keep in the kitchen, not even Nora. He went back to the kitchen and collected his book. All he needed now was the cupboard key. He looked around but there was nothing on the table or the dresser. On his return to the herborium he searched everywhere but the key was nowhere to be found. In desperation he took his wand and asked loudly, 'Where is the key to the cupboard?'

To his amazement the top drawer of the dresser began to rattle and shake violently before it finally shot open. It was full of old keys of various shapes and sizes. Some were made of brass, others were almost black and a couple looked quite rusty. This must be the drawer Fergus and Berry had been looking in for Camelin. It was only then that Jack realised he didn't even know which cupboard he was supposed to be opening. He stared dismally at the array of keys.

'I need some help,' Jack announced to the drawer.

Two muffled high-pitched voices came from behind the dresser. Jack couldn't make out what was being said but he thought he might know who the voices belonged to. He bent down and peered into the drawer. Berry's head was peeking through a hole in the back.

'What are you doing behind there? I thought you weren't helping Camelin any more?'

'We're not,' replied Fergus as he appeared from the back of the dresser and scampered around Jack's feet, 'We're hiding from him.'

'We heard him say he wasn't coming to the herborium with you so we thought it would be the safest place to be,' explained Berry as he wriggled through the hole he'd been looking through.

'I can't find the key to Nora's special herb cupboard. She said in her note she'd left it out for me but I can't see it.'

Fergus nimbly ran up the dresser and joined Berry in the drawer.

'Which cupboard did you want?'

'That's the problem, I don't know. Nora said I needed to get into the cupboard where her special herb extracts are kept. I need a whole dragon-wort leaf and some of its pollen to finish off the potion she's been making.'

'That would be the third cupboard,' squeaked Berry excitedly as he scampered over to the other side of the room. 'Nora has three cupboards for herbs.'

'But which one is the third?'

'Nora labels the keys,' explained Fergus, 'and there are letters on the doors, go and look.'

Jack bent over as Berry stood on his hind legs and pointed up towards a faint letter F on the first door. The next door had a faint letter S and the last door had a T.

'First, Second and Third!' exclaimed Jack. 'That's brilliant but it still doesn't help me get it open.'

'You could try using your wand,' suggested Fergus.

Jack waited until Berry was well clear of the cupboard before pointing his wand at the third door. The tip glowed and Jack concentrated hard.

'Open!' he commanded and watched as a beam of soft green light travelled from the tip of his wand and disappeared through the keyhole.

Fergus scurried across and tried the handle but it wouldn't open.

'Why don't you try,' suggested Berry. 'You're stronger than us.'

Jack twisted and turned the handle but the door remained firmly shut.

'You'll just have to find Nora's special key, it's in the drawer somewhere. You know, it's the one we've been looking for all week for Camelin,' said Berry.

Jack went back to the drawer. There were so many keys he'd be hours if he had to try every one in the lock.

'Camelin says it opens anything,' continued Berry.

Jack concentrated hard.

'Which key opens any lock?' he asked and willed as much force down his wand as he could.

A loud jingling and clicking came from the contents of the drawer. The keys seemed to have a life of their own and began shuffling around. They formed themselves into a pyramid and only became still when one of the dullest looking keys was poking out at the top.

'There's nothing special about that one,' said Fergus.

'We've got nothing to lose,' said Jack as he carefully picked out the key from the pile. There was a loud clatter as the pyramid instantly collapsed. Jack inspected the key closely. It no longer looked dull or ordinary. Tiny sparks danced across the metal making his hand tingle.

'Look!' he said as he showed Fergus and Berry.

The rats looked at the key and then looked at each other.

'Can't you see the sparks?' asked Jack.

Fergus and Berry bent their heads closer to the key.

'Looks dull to me,' announced Berry, and Fergus nodded in agreement.

Jack held the key up to the light but it no longer sparkled, it must have been a trick of the light or maybe he'd imagined it.

'Oh well! I might as well try it,' he said as he bent down in front of the cupboard.

The end of the key looked too big for the small hole in the door but the nearer Jack got, the less dull the key became. The tingling sensation once more ran through his fingertips. Tiny sparks began to dance across the metal again. The tip shrank before his eyes, and slipped into the keyhole. It was a perfect fit and almost seemed to turn itself in the lock. Fergus and Berry cheered when the door swung open.

'You did it, Jack, you did it. You're so clever with your magic,' squeaked Berry.

Jack pulled the key out of the lock. It looked dull and ordinary again.

'I don't think we'll tell Camelin about this, do you?'

Both rats shook their heads vigorously.

'I think I'll keep this safe until Nora gets back. At least I can get on with the potion now.'

Jack slipped the key into his pocket and looked through the neatly labelled bottles and jars inside the cupboard.

'Here it is: dragon-wort pollen and these must be the leaves.'

Jack took out a small green bottle with a glass stopper and a long brown paper package that had been neatly tied up with string.

'We'll help,' Fergus offered. 'We're good at counting seeds and berries.

Jack took the stoppers out of the various bottles and jars before grating the zest from the lemons. The air in the herborium began to smell wonderful and as the rats breathed in each new aroma their little noses twitched excitedly. He was grateful Fergus and Berry were able to

crack the hazelnuts with their sharp teeth. After half an
hour, all the ingredients from Nora's kitchen had been
added to the mixture in the cauldron. The goo wasn't so

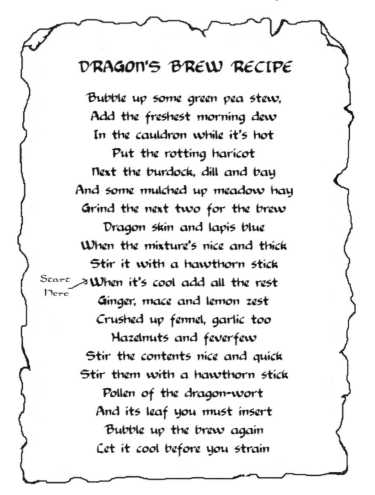

DRAGON'S BREW RECIPE

Bubble up some green pea stew,
Add the freshest morning dew
In the cauldron while it's hot
Put the rotting haricot
Next the burdock, dill and bay
And some mulched up meadow hay
Grind the next two for the brew
Dragon skin and lapis blue
When the mixture's nice and thick
Stir it with a hawthorn stick
Start Here → When it's cool add all the rest
Ginger, mace and lemon zest
Crushed up fennel, garlic too
Hazelnuts and feverfew
Stir the contents nice and quick
Stir them with a hawthorn stick
Pollen of the dragon-wort
And its leaf you must insert
Bubble up the brew again
Let it cool before you strain

green any more. Jack looked around for the hawthorn stick Nora had left, so he could stir the liquid. He pulled a face as he stirred, something didn't smell too good. He wondered if he'd done something wrong until he remembered to check Nora's instruction page.

'It's the stick that smells,' he explained to Fergus and Berry, who'd gone to the other end of the table. 'It says here it smells of rotting flesh.'

'What do you think Nora's going to use it for?' asked Berry.

'I've no idea, she just asked me to make it. I hope I'm doing it right.'

'It might be better when the dragon-wort's gone in,' suggested Fergus.

'Well here goes,' announced Jack. 'The last two ingredients, I'd better do this bit.'

As he pulled the stopper from the bottle the whole room filled with the smell of rotten eggs. He quickly put the stopper back.

'Ugh!' cried Berry as he leapt off the table and scurried out of the open door. Fergus and Jack weren't far behind him. 'What is that stuff? I didn't know pollen could smell like that!'

'We'll stay out here till you've finished,' said Berry.

Jack took a deep breath before entering the herborium again. He opened the bottle, held it over the cauldron and carefully tapped the side three times as the instructions said to do. The tiny grains of orange pollen spread rapidly over the surface but didn't sink. By the time Jack got the stopper back in, his eyes were watering. He took the bottle over to the cupboard and replaced it before taking a few gulps of fresh air by the open door.

'Nearly done,' he spluttered to Berry and Fergus.

The leaf didn't smell too good either, but not as bad as the pollen. Even though it was dried and wrinkled it was a flame red colour. Jack turned it over and found the back was covered in small green spots. After reading Nora's notes again, he crushed the leaf between his hands and rubbed it into a fine powder. He sprinkled it evenly into the cauldron and watched to see what would happen. It filled the gaps between the pollen and also floated on top of the mixture. All he had left to do now was to find the spell and turn the Dragon's Brew into Dragon's Breath. The bad smell had almost gone so Jack decided to clear away before asking his Book of Shadows for the spell. He repacked the picnic basket first and put it outside the door. Fergus and Berry weren't anywhere to be seen.

'Not much more to do,' Jack called.

He wrapped the dragon-wort leaves up in the paper and retied the string before returning the package

SPELL TO TURN DRAGON'S BREW

INTO DRAGON'S BREATH

Point your wand straight at the brew
and keep a steady glow from the wand tip.
No sparks or the mixture might explode.
Be prepared for a nasty smell

MAKE THE BREW INSIDE THE POT
BUBBLE SO IT'S NICE AND HOT
MIX IT UP SO VERY WELL
TO ACHIEVE THE PROPER SMELL
DRAGON'S BREATH FROM DRAGON'S BREW
MAKE IT INTO GREEN SHAMPOO.

When the smell goes the mixture
will stop bubbling and the spell will be complete.

to the cupboard. He took the key out of his pocket and examined it closely. It was still the same size as the small keyhole. It tingled in his hand again as he turned it in the lock. Once the key was safely back in his pocket he went over to the table and put his hand on the front of his book and asked for the spell.

'How do I make this brew into Dragon's Breath?'

The book jolted into action, the pages flew open and turned rapidly until the spell he'd asked for appeared. Above and below the spell were instructions, written in red ink.

Jack read everything twice before he picked up his wand. He put his left hand over his nose in case the smell was as bad as it had been before and then repeated the words. He tried to make sure he kept a steady glow from the tip of his wand as he pointed it at the mixture inside the cauldron. A bright yellow plume came out of the pot. It rose to the ceiling then spread around the room. The smell was dreadful. As the mixture swirled around, the pollen and crushed leaf disappeared. Once the last speck of orange had gone the contents of the cauldron started to bubble. Jack was finding it hard to breathe. He had to use the hand protecting his nose to wipe his streaming eyes. He began to cough which made his wand wobble. The mixture rose to the top of the cauldron and began to bubble over the sides. Jack needed both hands to steady his wand. His nostrils filled with the pungent smell and his eyes streamed making it hard to see if he'd got the potion under control again. Just when he thought he wasn't going to be able to stay inside the herborium a moment longer the mixture stopped bubbling and the air suddenly cleared. Jack dashed to the open door and breathed in great gulps of fresh air. When his eyes had stopped streaming he looked back inside the herborium. There was a green mess on the table where some of the potion had run down the side of the cauldron but everything else seemed to be alright. The yellow cloud was gone. Fergus and Berry joined him at the doorway.

'I think it's safe to go in now,' said Jack as he wiped his eyes again.

Fergus and Berry leapt onto the table and sniffed the spilt potion. Jack hesitated before looking into the cauldron.

'I wonder what it's for?'

'What what's for?' croaked a familiar voice as Camelin flew in through the open door and landed on the table. He immediately started to cough and choke.

'What's that smell?'

'That's nothing. You should have been here five minutes ago.'

'But where's it come from?'

'It's the important job Nora wanted me to do.'

Camelin took a look inside the cauldron.

'Ugh! Are you sure you've done it right? It doesn't look too good to me, not something I'd want to drink!'

'I don't think it's for drinking, at least I hope not!'

Camelin shuffled to the other end of the table.

'Are you ready to help me now?'

'I was going to give you a shout as soon as I'd put all these things away in the kitchen.'

'Aw, leave them 'til later, I need you to help me in here.'

Jack smiled, he thought he knew what Camelin was about to say next, and maybe Fergus and Berry thought the same since they were nowhere to be seen. It came as a surprise when Camelin pushed a small key towards him.

'Nora left this so it must be alright for you to use it. You can get my wand out now. It's the key, look, it says THE Cupboard on the label.'

Jack looked at the key carefully. He put his hand in his pocket and felt the shape of the key inside. They were identical. He tried not to let Camelin see his smile.

'That's OK, I'll open the cupboard for you,' said Jack as he picked up the key.

'You will! Aw Jack, that's great, you're a real pal.'

Jack started walking towards the three small cupboards.

'Where are you going? It's this way,' croaked Camelin.

'I think you'll find your key opens this door,' said Jack as he bent down and unlocked the cupboard with the faint letter T on the front.

'But it says THE Cupboard, and Nora left it out.'

'Nora left it for me, and I think you'll find *THE* is Nora's abbreviation for *Third Herb Extract* cupboard.'

Camelin humphed loudly.

'You mean it's not my key?'

'No, it's not.'

'But what about my wand?'

'Only Nora can decide when you're ready to have it back.'

'It's all right for you, you've got yours. Can you try and magic it open?'

'I don't think so.'

'You're no fun any more. That wand's gone to your head.'

Before Jack could reply Camelin took off, swerved past him and disappeared through the open door.

'Oh dear!' said Jack, as Fergus and Berry came out from behind the dresser. 'I didn't mean to upset him.'

'He's been like that all week,' explained Berry.

'He'll be fine when it's teatime,' squeaked Fergus.

Jack laughed. He knew the little rat was right. He wondered how long Nora was going to be. He didn't want to feed Camelin too early but there was no reason why he couldn't take Medric and Gerda's food to them now.

'I'm going over to the island. Do you two want to come?'

Both rats shook their heads.

'Things to do,' said Fergus, as he stood to attention. 'Things to do.'

Jack smiled. He knew Fergus was mimicking Motley.

'We've been left a list of jobs too, so we'd better get on with them, or we'll be in trouble again if they're not done by the time Motley and the others get back,' explained Berry.

'See you later,' said Jack, but there was no reply, the two little rats had already gone.

The bucket of grain was heavier than Jack had imagined it would be. He struggled with it to the edge of the lake and eventually managed to get it into the boat without spilling too much. He sat down under the willow tree for a few moments to get his breath back. He'd never rowed a boat before and it looked a long way to the island.

Jack tried to push the boat into the water, he heaved and shoved but the boat wouldn't move. Maybe he ought to go and get Grandad but he didn't want to admit defeat so easily. He held up his wand and then hesitated. He'd been told to use it wisely and he didn't know if transporting a bucket of grain across the lake would count as a good use of magic. Maybe he could just use his wand to help him get the boat into the water and start rowing once he was afloat. He looked around to make sure no one was watching, stepped into the boat and pointed his wand towards the front. He focused his thoughts into a request, 'I need help to get the boat to the island.'

The boat began to rock violently from side to side. Jack wished he'd sat down before he'd spoken. He staggered to gain his balance and ended up banging his knee on the bucket. There was a sudden jolt as the boat left the shore and hit the water. Jack didn't have time to pick up the oars, he just managed to grab the seat and steady himself before the little boat began speeding towards the middle of the lake.

'Slow down!' he yelled. 'Slow down!'

He really must think very carefully before he used his wand again and make sure he gave better instructions. The boat slowed gracefully and ran ashore onto the sloping bank of the island's soft earth. Jack breathed a sigh of relief, his hands hurt and his knuckles were white from clinging onto the seat. His legs were shaking as he climbed onto the island. He'd thought either Gerda or Medric would have been there to meet him but neither goose appeared. He didn't want to go over to the shelter without being invited so he called as loudly as he could.

'Hello! It's Jack, I've brought your supper.'

Medric's head shot out of the shelter.

'Shhh!'

'Sorry!' whispered Jack. 'I didn't mean to disturb you.'

'It's not me it's Gerda. Loud noises when you're laying aren't good.'

'Sorry, do you want me to take the eggs back for Nora?'

Medric lowered his neck and shook his tail feathers. Jack realised he'd said the wrong thing.

'I most certainly do not want you to take any of Gerda's eggs, these eggs aren't for eating they're for hatching.'

'Hatching!'

'Yes, hatching, don't you know anything?'

'Nora didn't tell me. I'm sorry. I was only trying to help. I've brought your supper.'

'Supper! It's a bit early for supper.'

'I know but I've got to go home for mine soon so I thought I'd bring it over now and say hello.'

'You'd better come inside after you've put it out.'

It was harder lifting the bucket of grain out of the boat than it had been getting it in. Jack tipped the contents onto the bare earth where Nora usually put it, returned the empty bucket to the boat then made his way to the shelter. He knocked on the side of the open door.

'Come in, come in,' said Medric.

Jack was worried he might tread on the eggs but when he entered the shelter he found that the straw from around the entrance had gone. It had been piled into the far corner and shaped into a circular mound, on top of which sat Gerda.

'Do you want to come and have a quick look?' she asked as she slowly raised her body.

Jack could see a clutch of large white eggs.

'Ten,' Medric informed him. 'Better sit down my dear, you don't want them getting cold.'

'When will they hatch?' asked Jack as he watched Gerda settle herself gently back onto the nest.

'Not for a while yet,' replied Medric as he started hustling Jack towards the doorway.

'Well I'd better go. I don't want to disturb you.'

'Fine, fine,' said Medric as he waddled out of the shelter. 'Gerda's looking forward to hearing the splatter of webbed feet. We'll invite you over when they've hatched.'

'Thank you, I'd like that,' replied Jack before saying goodbye.

When he reached the boat he turned to wave but Medric had already gone back inside. He wondered if Camelin knew about Gerda's eggs. As he climbed into the boat he thought carefully about what he was going to instruct the boat to do. 'Return me slowly to the shore,' was the best he could come up with.

The journey back was much better. Jack trailed one hand over the side and dangled it in the water as he enjoyed the view. He thought he saw a movement in the willow tree and a black shape he recognised. As the small boat ran ashore Camelin swooped out of the tree and landed by the water's edge. He waddled over and waited until Jack had secured the boat and removed the bucket before speaking.

'Using magic again? I thought we had to use our wands wisely?'

Jack didn't want to get into an argument and he knew it was useless to try to explain.

'Do you want dinner too?'

'Now you're talking,' replied Camelin as he flew past Jack. 'Race you to the kitchen.'

Jack had no intention of racing. He returned the bucket to the shed and then peeked into the herborium. He sniffed the air. The nasty smell had gone so he checked the potion. Everything looked alright, as far as he could tell, so he closed the door and started to make his way towards the kitchen. A rapid fluttering of wings above his head made him look up. Before Jack could say or do anything, Timmery flew past him and crashed into the wall. He spiralled down to the grass and lay there, not moving.

'Timmery!' yelled Jack.

'Never mind that, where's my dinner,' grumbled Camelin from inside.

Jack carefully picked up the little bat. He could feel his heart beating but he still wasn't moving.

'Ooh! What you got there?'

'It's Timmery. He's knocked himself out on the wall.'

'What's he doing out at this time of day, he knows he can't see anything when it's sunny.'

'I don't know. What do you think we should do?'

'Have dinner?'

Jack ignored Camelin and tried to make Timmery comfortable. The little bat began to stir.

'Are you alright?' asked Jack.

'Oh dear! Oh dear!' piped Timmery.

'What can I do? Have you broken anything?'

'I don't think so. I couldn't see but I had to come and tell Nora, we've got a problem and it's all my fault. Oh dear! What to do? What to do?'

'Nora's not here. Can I help?'

'It's Charkle, he's gone.'

'Gone!' exclaimed Jack.

'I told him about the map and now he's not in the belfry. I can't find him anywhere. He's gone and it's all my fault.'

DECISIONS

Jack felt worried. He knew he was partly to blame. If only he'd told Timmery not to say anything to Charkle about Howling Hill until they'd spoken to Nora he might not have disappeared.

'Try not to worry,' Jack told Timmery. 'Maybe he's already back at the belfry. Do you want Camelin to fly over and have a look?'

Timmery nodded.

'I'm not going anywhere 'til I've had some food,' grumbled Camelin.

'You might as well go and take a look and by the time you get back I'll have your tea ready.'

Camelin glowered at Jack before flying off towards the church tower. When he'd gone Jack looked at Nora's list. He prepared the food for the bird table first then put Camelin's in his dish. When he'd finished he sat down next to Timmery. He looked very forlorn and was using his wings to shield the bright sunlight from his eyes. Jack pulled the curtains closed so he'd be able to see a bit better.

'Tell me what happened after you left my room last night.'

'I went back to the belfry and Charkle wasn't there but I didn't worry because I knew he was with Nora. He came back about dawn. He was very upset and I thought if I told him about Howling Hill it would cheer him up. I told him everything, about the questions, your book and the map. He was really excited. By the time we'd finished talking it was sunrise so I said we'd go and have a look together tonight and went to sleep. When I woke up, he'd gone.'

'Nora's gone too and I don't know how long she's going to be away.'

'Gone where?'

'Annwn.'

Timmery looked upset. Jack didn't feel happy either. He wished Nora was here. He didn't think Camelin would find the little dragonette at the church; he suspected Charkle had gone back to the Westwood Roost.

'Did he say anything at all to you?'

'Not really, it was getting light and I was sleepy. I was just glad he wasn't upset any more. We've got to do something. You will help won't you Jack?'

'I will. I'm trying to decide what Nora would do. Would she wait for him to come back or would she go look for him?'

'Well he's not at home,' Camelin informed them as he landed on the table in front of his bowl. 'Is this it? Don't I get something a bit more exciting than cheese and pickles? Can't we have a take away?'

'No,' said Jack so forcefully that it made Camelin jump. 'Nora didn't leave me any money for a take away.'

'What are we going to do?' squeaked Timmery.

Jack gently stroked the fur on the top of Timmery's head.

'Try not to worry. I'm sure he'll be fine. I'll go and feed the birds and when I get back we'll decide what to do. While I'm gone you can tell Camelin all about last night.'

Jack took his time putting the seed onto the bird table. He needed time to think. He wondered if he ought to send Nora a message. But she'd left him in charge and that meant taking responsibility. Whatever she'd gone to do in Annwn must have been important. He didn't know if she'd want to be bothered by something like this. Charkle could show up at any time and then he'd feel stupid if he'd caused a fuss over nothing. On the other hand, Charkle might be lost or in trouble. Jack suddenly felt very alone. He knew he couldn't ask Grandad for help. He was going to have to make a decision on his own, and hopefully it would be the right one.

'We need a plan,' Jack announced when he got back to the kitchen.

Camelin and Timmery waited expectantly but Jack didn't know what to say. He placed his Book of Shadows on the table, lowered his hand and was about to ask for help when the book began to vibrate. Camelin hopped over to Jack.

'It's a message. Open the book and see what it says.'

Jack turned to the first page and watched the name appear.

'Look, it's from Nora,' continued Camelin as he peered over Jack's arm.

'What's it say?' asked Timmery. 'Is she coming back soon?'

'I'm afraid not,' replied Jack. 'She says she's got to stay in Annwn a bit longer to help Elan and she hopes to be back in a couple of days. I'm to sort out everyone's food but I don't have to do anything else to the potion. She says she'll strain it when she gets home.'

Timmery fluttered around Jack's head.

'Oh dear! Oh dear! What are we going to do? Can you ask Nora?'

'No,' said Camelin. 'She'll be cross if she has to come back.'

Jack wasn't sure Nora would be cross but there must be a big problem in Annwn or she wouldn't be staying. He wrote a short reply then closed the book decisively. It was time for him to take charge.

'We're going to go and look for Charkle,' Jack announced. 'Tonight.'

'Tonight!' exclaimed Camelin. 'But how?'

'You'll have to watch Grandad's house and when all the lights go out it'll be safe for you to come over. I'll leave the window open so you can get in. We'll transform and fly over to Westwood and see if we can find Charkle.'

Camelin's beak fell open.

'You said you'd never go on a midnight flight again.'

'I meant with you, this is different, you're coming with me and we've got something very important to do.'

'It was important last time,' grumbled Camelin.

'This is different, I know where we're going and why, last time you didn't tell me anything until it was too late.'

'What's Nora going to say if she finds out? You promised her: no more adventures.'

'I've already asked her.'

'When?'

'When I was ill. I asked if I could help Timmery and Charkle find the dragonettes when I was better and she said yes. I'm better now so I'm allowed to help.'

'Bet she didn't mean you could go out in the middle of the night.'

'Probably not, but this is an emergency and Nora isn't here to ask. We're just going to have to try to make sure we don't get into any trouble. OK?'

'OK.'

'I can come too, can't I?' asked Timmery.

'Of course you can,' said Jack.

Camelin humphed, 'I've told you before, it's too far for a bat.'

Timmery peered at Jack.

'Is it really too far?'

Jack nodded.

'But you can cling onto my back, I don't mind.'

Camelin frowned and grumbled to himself.

'Don't see why he has to come.'

'Timmery needs to come along in case we have to look inside any of the caves.'

Jack waited for Camelin to respond but he didn't.

'That's settled then, you'll come over tonight as soon as the lights go out. I'd better get off now or I'm going to be late for my tea.'

'Bet it's not cheese and pickles,' croaked Camelin.

Jack didn't reply. He was sure Camelin would find an opportunity to eat something exciting before he saw him again. He ran down to the hedge and didn't stop running until he reached Grandad's house.

Jack excused himself early and went up to bed. He'd told Grandad he felt a bit tired, which wasn't far from the truth. He'd done more that afternoon than he'd done for a week. His main concern was trying to get some sleep before it was time to fly over to the Westwood Roost but his mind was in turmoil. Too many questions kept popping into his head, questions he couldn't answer. What if he was too tired to go to school in the morning? He desperately wanted to sing the solo at the concert. If he wasn't there, someone else would take his place. What if Grandad found him gone? How could he explain? Even if he told the truth Grandad wouldn't believe him. What if they got into trouble? No one would know where he'd gone, and worse still, he couldn't tell anyone what he was planning to do. In the end he decided to write a note and leave it with Orin. If they did get into trouble at least Grandad would know where to start looking.

'Do you understand what to do if I don't come back?' he asked her.

She nodded and repeated Jack's instructions.

'Keep the letter safe so no one sees it but if you're not back by breakfast I'm to put it on your pillow where Grandad will find it.'

'That's the best I can do in case there's a problem,' said Jack sleepily.

He put his pyjamas on, opened the window and got into bed.

Jack's room was in total darkness when he woke up. There was also a nasty smell. He wondered if some of the potion mixture had splashed onto his T-shirt. He sniffed the air as the smell grew more pungent. It was then he heard a deep snore. He moved his foot underneath the sheet until he found a heavy lump near the bottom.

'Wake up!' he whispered.

Jack waited but the snoring continued. He pushed Camelin with his foot and gently rocked him but instead of waking him it had the opposite effect. The snoring got louder. Finally Jack pushed him hard. He heard the fluttering of wings as Camelin rolled off the end of the bed.

'What you do that for?'

'You were snoring, loudly. You'll wake Grandad.'

The smell of fried onions reached Jack's nose.

'Is that you making that awful smell?'

'You fed me!'

Jack sniffed.

'It smells like burger and chips to me!'

'Well cheese and pickles don't fill you up, not when you've got a long flight to make.'

Jack got up and opened the window wider to let in some fresh air.

'Why didn't you wake me?'

'I got fed up waiting for the lights to go out so I came over early. It's lonely over there on my own.'

'I thought Timmery was with you?'

Camelin snorted.

'Can't get any rest while he's there, it's just talk, talk, talk.'

'You should have woken me.'

'You were asleep and I wanted to see what a proper bed was like. Nora doesn't let me on them at home.'

'I can't imagine why!'

Jack reached for his wand and shone a light towards his clock.

'We'd better transform and collect Timmery, it's nearly midnight already. It'll take us at least an hour to get there and maybe longer to get back if I'm tired. I haven't flown for a couple of weeks. We need to get something straight before we set off – when I say it's time to come back I mean it. And if I say no to anything, I mean that too.'

'You get more and more like Nora every day,'

Camelin grumbled as he and Jack touched foreheads.

There was a blinding flash. Jack shook himself once he'd stepped out of his pyjamas. It felt good to be a raven again.

'Ready?'

'Ready.'

'I don't suppose Charkle's back?' asked Jack as they landed inside the bell tower.

Timmery flitted round their heads.

'He isn't. I do hope he's alright.'

'Climb on,' Jack told Timmery.

Jack didn't want to admit it but he wasn't exactly sure how to get back to the Westwood Roost. He knew the general direction but in the dark everything looked different and there wasn't even a moon tonight. He knew they didn't have enough time to get lost.

'What are we waiting for?' asked Camelin.

Jack was relieved when Camelin took off from the bell tower. All he had to do now was follow.

As they flew over the fields Jack peered down but

he couldn't see any of the familiar landmarks. After a while he began to enjoy the flight. The weight of responsibility seemed to lift from his shoulders, he felt carefree and elated. He tried to bring his thoughts back to their problem but the raven part of him took over.

'Whee!' he croaked as a sudden impulse overtook him and he flew past Camelin on his back.

'Thought you couldn't do that?'

'There's nothing to fly into here.'

Jack became aware of Timmery flitting round his head.

'I thought you were having a ride?'

'I thought so too but I wasn't holding on tightly enough. Do you think you could warn me the next time you're going to turn over?'

'Sorry, I don't know what got into me.'

Camelin sniggered.

'Come on, race you.'

It wasn't a fair race. Camelin didn't wait until Timmery had reattached himself. Jack knew he wouldn't be able to beat Camelin but it did feel good to speed through the air. Occasionally Camelin flew upwards in a wide arc and did a triple loop-the-loop.

After a while Jack's bones began to ache. He hoped it wasn't much further. He'd been concentrating so hard on flying he'd not taken much notice of the landscape but even in the dark, he could see they were approaching a long stony ridge. Strange rock formations stood jagged and black on the horizon. He suddenly realised it was the same one his Book of Shadows had shown him. Jack felt a shudder run down his back. The place hadn't looked too bad in his bedroom but now, as they flew towards it, he suddenly felt threatened.

'What's that place?' he called to Camelin. 'Over there on the horizon.'

'They're the crags of Stonytop Ridge. You don't want to go up there after dark, especially on a moonless night.'

'Why not?'

'Don't you know anything? Some of those rocks aren't what they seem to be.'

'How would I know, I've never heard of Stonytop Ridge before.'

Jack heard Timmery's shrill voice in the still night air:

'When lightning flashes in a thunderstorm,
On Stonytop Ridge a Hag is born.'

Jack shuddered again. He didn't like the look of the crags or the sound of Stonytop at all. He looked at the sky, it might be dark but at least there was no sign of a storm.

Camelin flew alongside.

'It's Hag country, all round here. That rhyme's as old as the crags themselves. Some say they come to life on stormy nights. There'll be a crash of thunder, a flash of lightning, an ear-splitting crack, then bang! One minute you're looking at a rock, the next it's a Hag. All the bits of shattered stone up there are the remains of rocks that have exploded.'

Jack didn't doubt there was some truth to what Camelin was saying. He knew mountaintops and ridges weren't safe places to be in any kind of a thunderstorm, moon or no moon.

'Do you think it's true?'

'Don't know, but it's where Hags go when they all get together, especially on moonless nights. You'd have a problem telling the difference between some of those rocks and Hags in the dark.'

Jack shuddered as he remembered their encounter with Finnola Fytche.

'We'd better stay well away. The one Hag we've already met was one too many for me.'

Jack was glad Camelin didn't disagree.

'Are we nearly there?' asked Timmery.

'We are,' shouted Camelin as he tilted his wings and began his descent. 'Westwood Roost here we come!'

Jack could see the mouth of the cave as they came into land. Its gaping black mouth looked menacing. They were on their own this time: no magic, no Nora or Elan to help. Jack desperately tried to think of a plan. Neither he nor Camelin could see in the dark. He didn't want to ask Timmery to go inside but it was the only solution. With any luck, if Camelin were right, Finnola Fytche wouldn't be at home. She'd be out among the crags on the Ridge, doing whatever Hags did when they got together.

'Would you mind taking a look around inside,' Jack asked Timmery.

'Of course he wouldn't mind, that's what we brought him for isn't it? Aren't you forgetting how brave he is?' mocked Camelin.

'He doesn't have to go in if he doesn't want to,' said Jack firmly.

'I'm fine,' piped Timmery as he flitted around the entrance. 'I'll stay close to the roof and be in and out before you know it.'

'You'd probably better not call out to Charkle, just in case anyone's home. We don't know what might happen if we disturb a Hag, do we?' said Jack.

It wasn't long before Timmery was back.

'Anything?' asked Jack.

'Not a thing. It smells awful inside, not the kind of place bats would want to roost, or dragonettes either. I don't know how anyone could live in all that mess.'

'Me neither,' agreed Jack looking meaningfully at Camelin.

'My loft doesn't smell.'

Jack's eyes began to water as the faint odour of rotting cabbage wafted from the cave.

'That wasn't me, I don't like boiled cabbage,' Camelin snapped as Timmery opened his mouth to speak.

Jack wanted to laugh but managed to control himself.

'This is serious and we don't have much time.'

'Why don't we get up higher so we can have a better look around?' suggested Camelin.

Jack looked over to the crags. They looked even darker and more forbidding from the ground.

'I'm not happy about going up there tonight.'

'What about Winberry Hill?' said Timmery.

Jack didn't have time to consider, Camelin was already airborne.

'Come on you two, what you waiting for? Follow me.'

Jack turned so Timmery could climb onto his back.

'It's alright Jack, I'll fly, it's not far and we can keep a look out as we go.'

'How far can you see in the dark?'

'Quite a long way.'

Jack and Timmery flew after Camelin but Jack didn't hurry to catch up. He was still thinking. He tried to imagine where he'd go if he was Charkle. It made no sense to go back to the Westwood Roost – they all knew Charkle's family wasn't there. Timmery said he'd told him about the map and the questions they'd asked.

'What would I do?' Jack asked himself. A sudden thought hit him like a thunderbolt, it was obvious: Charkle would be looking for Howling Hill. With any luck, he'd be around here somewhere.

'He's not here,' announced Camelin as Jack landed.

'Are you eating something?' asked Jack.

'You bet, you've got to try them,' replied Camelin as he bent over and delicately pulled some berries from a small bush. 'Don't tell me you didn't know it was winberry season? Why do you think they call it Winberry Hill?'

Jack knew he shouldn't get distracted but he could smell the juice from the winberries. The temptation was too great and he too began plucking the large black berries from the bushes.

'Have you two nearly finished?' asked Timmery.

'I'm sorry,' said Jack, 'I don't know what got into me.'

'About thirty winberries!' laughed Camelin.

Timmery flew round their heads.

'Where do you think we should start looking?'

'Why don't we call him,' suggested Jack.

'I thought we'd agreed not to,' grumbled Camelin. 'Can't you make your mind up?'

'What if we use the call of the raven owl? Charkle's got amazing hearing. He'll know it's us straight away. It'll be easier for him to come and find us, especially now we're on top of a hill.'

'Ooh, you're so clever Jack,' called Timmery as he fluttered about.

A strange sound made Camelin's head jerk up, 'What was that?'

'It's me,' squeaked Timmery, 'I'm doing the call of the raven owl.'

'Oh no, you're not. That's nothing like it.'

Camelin threw his head back and hooted as loudly as he could. Jack joined in and Timmery too. They stopped, listened and peered into the darkness.

'Let's try again,' suggested Jack.

'Without him this time,' grumbled Camelin as he

nodded towards Timmery. 'He's putting me off.'

Timmery looked a bit hurt but nodded.

'Ready?' asked Jack.

'Ready.'

They both hooted long and loud. This time the sound bounced back from the other hill. When Jack's breath ran out he stopped the call, dropped his head and scanned the sky.

'Look!' he croaked excitedly. 'Look, over near the top of the other hill, there's something small flying towards us.'

Camelin jigged around Jack.

'It's him isn't it? We've found him.'

'I think he's found us,' replied Jack. 'I'm sure it's Charkle, I do hope he's not too upset.'

They watched as the tiny shape flew towards them. When it was overhead it did a triple loop-the-loop.

'It is Charkle!' cried Timmery.

Jack was amazed. The little dragonette seemed to be in high spirits.

'Where've you been?' asked Timmery.

'We've been really worried,' said Jack.

Charkle began speaking so quickly it was hard to understand what he was saying.

'Come and see, come and see,' he chirruped as he flew

excitedly above their heads. 'I've found it, Howling Hill, it's real. I heard the dragon howling. Oh do come and see.'

'Where?' Timmery asked excitedly.

'Over on the other hill. You've got to come, Norris and Snook might be on the other side of the door.'

'A door?' asked Jack.

'Yes, a tiny door, it doesn't open but you can look through the keyhole.'

'And what about the dragon?' asked Timmery.

'It's a long way off but you can hear it roar and howl.'

Jack looked worried. They'd only come out to find Charkle. He wasn't prepared for dragon hunting. He'd read Nora's book so he knew that dragonettes weren't capable of howling or roaring loudly. If there really was a dragon on the other side of the door it wasn't going to be Norris or Snook, it was going to be something considerably larger.

'We can't go through the door tonight. We need to get back to Glasruhen,' Jack told them.

He could see the look of disappointment on Charkle's face, even in the dark.

'But I thought you'd be pleased, I might have found some of my family and you won't even come and have a look.'

Jack felt bad. Charkle looked so disappointed.

'There's nothing we can do tonight but as long as we don't take too long we can go and have a look through the keyhole. After all, it's on our way home. Once we've had a look we'll have to go back. Grandad will be really worried if he finds I'm not there and I need to go to school in the morning.'

Charkle flew over and landed on Jack's shoulder. His long pointed tail swayed from side to side. He could tell the little dragonette was very excited.

'Oh! Jack Brenin, I know there's a dragon somewhere behind the door I can smell dragon's breath from here.'

Jack didn't want to disappoint Charkle again but he suspected it was Nora's potion he could smell.

'Are we going or not?' grumbled Camelin.

'We are,' piped Charkle. 'Follow me.'

Charkle took off and Timmery followed. Camelin glowered and hunched his wings. 'Who said he could go first?' he mumbled.

'Come on,' Jack coaxed, 'the sooner we get over to Silver Hill, the sooner we can get back. Let's go and see what Charkle's so excited about.'

THROUGH THE KEYHOLE

Soon, Silver Hill loomed below them. Its twin peaks looked out of place in the landscape and although Jack knew its slopes were covered in trees, in the dark they looked bare and barren. He could just see the outlines of what must once have been ancient forts on both hilltops. Charkle flittered downwards towards the slope of the smaller hillside and disappeared into a crevice.

'It's down here on this ledge,' he called. 'You'll have to be careful it's not very wide.'

Camelin landed first and skipped daintily to where Charkle hovered.

'Come and look Jack,' said Charkle. 'I know there's a dragon somewhere behind the door.'

'I can't see a door,' replied Jack as he scanned the rock face.

'Camelin's stood in front of it,' explained Charkle. 'It's only small.'

As Camelin stepped to one side Jack could make out the faint outline of a doorway.

'Is it a Spriggan door?' he asked.

'Naw, Spriggans don't have much use for doors,' replied Camelin.

'It's about the right size for a dragonette,' piped Timmery excitedly. 'Perhaps you should knock and see if anyone answers.'

'I've tried that, and I've shouted through the keyhole,' said Charkle. 'That's when I heard the roaring and growling.'

'This door's too small for a big dragon,' said Jack.

'Move over,' grumbled Camelin as he bent over and put his eye to the keyhole. 'Let me see.'

'Oooh listen!' cried Charkle excitedly. 'There it is again.'

Jack listened intently but he couldn't hear anything. Then a distinct low rumbling began in the distance. As the sound grew, the ledge on which they stood began to vibrate.

'What can you see?' Jack asked Camelin.

'It's a monster with great big eyes coming towards the door and…'

Camelin's words were lost as a thunderous noise filled the crevice. It seemed to bounce off the rocks and echo around inside Jack's head.

'Oh my poor ears,' said Charkle from underneath his wings. 'Now do you believe me? That's a dragon if ever I heard one. It might know where my family went. We need to get the door open. We need to and go and look for it.'

'… it was really big and long and moved really quickly,' gulped Camelin. 'I thought it was going to come straight through the door.'

Jack could see Camelin was shaken. He was too. He wasn't in any hurry to open the door and find out what was on the other side. He needed to ask his Book of Shadows more questions before they made any rash decisions. Nora had made them promise they wouldn't have any more unplanned adventures. Once they stepped through the door into the unknown he'd have a problem explaining why he'd gone, but if they planned it carefully, he wouldn't have broken his promise. After all, she'd said he was allowed to help Charkle. They could easily find the door again when they were better prepared.

Jack looked at the horizon. It was still dark. With any luck if they set off now they'd be home before dawn. He tried to work out how much sleep he'd be able to have before it was time to get up for school. He knew it wasn't going to be enough. He didn't know how he was going to convince Charkle to come back with them. Jack decided a firm command would be best.

'Time to go. We'll make plans tomorrow and come back when we can.'

Much to Jack's surprise Camelin took off without any argument.

'Follow me everyone,' he croaked.

'Do you both want to climb on?' Jack asked Charkle and Timmery.

'No need,' replied Charkle, 'we've been getting around just fine. Watch!'

Timmery grabbed the pointed end of Charkle's tail and wrapped himself around it.

'Dragonettes can fly for hours without getting tired,' he explained.

'Isn't it hard work with Timmery on your tail?'

'Not at all, dragonette's tails are really strong and besides, Timmery doesn't weigh much at all.'

Without another word Charkle sped off after Camelin. Jack was amazed by how fast the little dragon could fly, even with Timmery suspended from the end of his tail.

Jack found the flight back difficult. He could see Camelin trying hard to keep up with Charkle but in the end even he had to drop back. Jack smiled as Charkle did a triple loop-the-loop. He wondered if the little dragonette knew Camelin wasn't able to keep up and was showing off on purpose. Charkle circled above Jack's head before flying alongside.

'We'll get back if you don't mind, it's nearly dawn. See you tomorrow.'

'See you tomorrow,' Jack called as Charkle sped away.

Jack peered at the sky. It was dark now, but he knew Charkle was right, it would soon be light. He wished he could fly faster and be home sooner. All he wanted to do was climb into bed and sleep.

Thankfully it wasn't long before the familiar sight of Glasruhen Hill appeared. As they flew over the summit the sky began to lighten. Jack needed to be back in bed before the sun came over the horizon. He brought his wings down powerfully, summoned every ounce of energy he had left and caught up with Camelin.

'As soon as we get back I have to go to bed. I'll come round tomorrow after school.'

'Fine, but what about my breakfast?'

'I'm sure you'll find something.'

Jack could hear Camelin grumbling as he followed him through his open bedroom window.

The blinding flash as they transformed woke Orin.

'I'm sorry I've got to go to bed, I'll tell you everything later,' Jack told her as he yawned deeply. He could hardly keep his eyes open as he got back into his pyjamas. He was vaguely aware of Camelin whispering to Orin as he crawled into bed. Exhaustion overtook him as his head hit the pillow.

'Here you are sleepyhead,' said Grandad as he put a glass of milk by the side of Jack's bed. 'Feeling any better today?'

Jack felt groggy but he wasn't about to say that to

Grandad. He needed to get ready for school.

'I'm fine, I'll come down for breakfast.'

'Breakfast! It's lunchtime!'

'But I've got to go back to school. If I don't, they won't let me sing in the concert.'

'Don't you worry about that, getting better is more important. Let's have a look at your spots before we make any decisions.'

Grandad drew the curtains and came back to inspect Jack.

'Well I never, they've gone!'

Jack shot out of bed and looked in the mirror. His face was clear. He pulled up his pyjama top. There wasn't anything on his chest or back either.

'That's amazing,' said Grandad. 'Looks like someone magicked them away in the night.'

Jack wondered if Camelin had somehow got his wand back and done something to him but that was unlikely. It must have happened when they'd transformed. The main thing was that he felt well, looked fine and knew Grandad couldn't keep him at home any longer.

'Can I go back for the afternoon?'

'I don't see why not. Get yourself ready, we'll have some lunch and then I'll walk down to the school gate with you.'

Once Grandad had gone Jack picked up Orin and hugged her.

Jack dressed quickly, found his wand and started to tell Orin about the night's events.

'We found Charkle.'

'I know, Camelin told me all about it, he stayed for ages after you'd gone to sleep. The dragon sounded scary, it's a good job Camelin was able to stop it from breaking the door down.'

Jack laughed.

'Is that what he told you?'

'You mean there wasn't a dragon?'

'I don't know what it was but it made the ledge we were standing on shake. We need to go and find out what it was for Charkle's sake. I'd better get a move on or I'm going to be late.'

'I think you had a message in your book this morning, I heard a buzzing.'

'Why didn't you wake me up?'

'Camelin told me not to disturb you.'

Jack lay on the floor and wriggled under his bed until he could reach the book. He'd pushed it right to the back where he hoped it wouldn't be seen. As he pulled it out it vibrated rapidly in his hands. He flipped the cover to reveal the first page and saw Elan's name appear at the top.

We have a big problem here in Annwn and need
Charkle's help.
Ask him to go through Glasruhen Gate tonight at dusk.
Nora says he'll find the portal in the forest by the
standing stones
and she'll meet him on the other side of the
Western Gate.

Jack was disappointed. He'd waited all this time for a message and when it had come it wasn't really for him and didn't tell him anything. What was the big problem? Why did they need Charkle's help and not his or Camelin's? Worse still Elan hadn't said when Nora might be back. Jack decided to ask and quickly wrote back.

What's wrong?

He waited for what seemed like an age for the answer to appear.

Nora and Charkle will come back tomorrow night.
She'll explain everything then.
Hopefully Charkle will be able to help and the problem
will be solved.

Jack sighed. Elan still hadn't told him what was happening in Annwn. He wouldn't be able to deliver the message himself, he'd have to ask Camelin to go and see Charkle later. It would mean the little dragonette wasn't going to be able to go back to Howling Hill for a while. In a way Jack was relieved, it meant he didn't have to go back either, at least not until Nora got back. She'd know what they ought to do. For now Jack was going to put any thoughts of dragon hunting far from his mind, he had a concert to think about.

'I'll see you later,' he told Orin as he grabbed his school bag and set off downstairs.

Jack had been expecting lessons so it was a big surprise when he was told the choir and orchestra were rehearsing all afternoon. His teacher had been overjoyed to see him and Jack was secretly pleased when she'd told him no one else could have sung the solo as well as he could. They'd all been given last minute instructions about the dress rehearsal, which they'd be performing to the rest of the school the following afternoon. The concert would be the day after on the school field, as long as it didn't rain.

On his way back to Grandad's Jack wondered if Nora would be back in time to hear him sing. She'd not said anything about it all the time he'd been ill. He really did want her to be there. He was lost in thought when he met Grandad on the back lane.

'You can come straight home I've been over to Ewell House and fed all the birds.'

'Oh... er...thanks,' replied Jack. It was the last thing he'd expected to happen and try as he might he couldn't think of a reason for going back to Nora's that he could give Grandad. Grandad carried on talking but Jack wasn't really paying attention until he was asked a direct question.

'Did you check the kitchen before you left yesterday afternoon?'

'Yes, why?'

'You had to have seen it with your own eyes to believe it, I don't know how it got in but that raven was in there. Didn't want to come out either. I had to chase him with the broom. He must have hopped in there without you noticing.'

Jack didn't know whether to laugh or not. The thought of Camelin being chased around his own kitchen and not being able to complain bitterly about it would have been a sight to see. Then it occurred to Jack he'd probably hear all about it later. That was, if he was able to think of a reason to go back.

'Sorry. Had he done any damage?'

'Not that I could see. He didn't seem too interested in the bird seed I put out for him you'd have thought a big bird like that would have been hungry.'

Jack had to pretend to cough as he fought to keep himself from laughing. While Grandad chatted on about watering Nora's plants in the herb garden, Jack had a thought, a reason for going back to Ewell House.

'Did you check the herborium?' he asked Grandad.

'I only fed the birds, why?'

'Nora left me instructions to do a job for her and I left it all in the herborium. Would you mind if I went and checked, just to make sure everything's alright?'

'You can go over after tea. I'll come with you if you like.'

'It's OK, I'll be fine.'

As they reached the gate, Jack heard a rustling from one of the trees in the field opposite. He thought he knew who it might be. When he looked up he could see Camelin perched on one of the lower branches. He didn't look at all pleased. Jack tried to look sorry but it didn't seem to have any effect. He heard several loud *caws* and *humphs* before Camelin flapped his wings noisily and took off in the direction of the shops.

'I'm really sorry,' Jack told Camelin when he arrived at Ewell House.

'Bird seed! Doesn't your Grandad know anything about ravens?'

'I didn't know he was coming round until he'd already done it.'

'I'll have you know I've had to go to the burger bar again. And this time it was your fault.'

'I didn't think you'd starve. I brought you a cheese sandwich, just in case, but if you don't want it...'

'Aw Jack, you're a pal, I've always got room for a cheese sandwich.'

Jack pulled out a neatly wrapped package from his pocket. It was a bit misshapen but he was sure Camelin wouldn't mind. Within seconds it was gone.

'Now, we've got things to discuss,' croaked Camelin.

'We do, I've had a message from Elan.'

'A message! Nora's not coming back early is she?'

'No why?'

'Er… I've got a job to do before she gets back.'

'What kind of a job.'

'Well Nora paid a little visit to my loft and saw the dustbin.'

'Did she find out what you'd done?'

'No she said she was pleased I was being responsible and was glad I'd decided to get a dustbin and have a good tidy up.'

'And did you?'

'I didn't. How was I to know she'd come and check?'

'Was this before or after she confiscated your wand?'

'After, but before she left, she said I'd got to tidy it all up by the time she got back or there'd be trouble.'

'And you haven't.'

'I haven't. I thought I might have got my wand back by now. You could give me a hand and magic it all clean and tidy.'

'I haven't brought my wand with me. I only came to tell you about Elan's message.'

'I'm going to have to do it all by beak. You've no

idea how much tidying up there'll be.'

Jack smiled. He knew exactly how much rubbish Camelin had in his loft.

'Elan has asked me to get a message to Charkle. They've got a problem in Annwn and need his help.'

'His help! Not ours? What's he got that we haven't?'

'I don't know but they want him to fly through Glasruhen Gate tonight at dusk and Nora will meet him on the other side.'

'I suppose you want me to take the message.'

'Please.'

'Where's the gateway?'

'By the standing stones.'

'Alright but when I get back we'll talk about my bit of business.'

'When you get back I'll be at home.'

'See you later then.'

Before Jack could say anything else, Camelin was airborne. It suddenly crossed his mind that the *business* Camelin had mentioned might be something other than opening the cupboard in the herborium or tidying up the loft. No doubt he'd find out later.

VISITORS

Jack watched for Camelin from his bedroom window. There was no sign of him and Jack had no way of checking if he'd delivered Elan's message to Charkle. In a couple of hours it would be dusk and Nora would be waiting in Annwn by the Western Gateway. He opened the window wider and waved in the hope that Camelin would see him and fly over. Jack sighed before picking up his wand and Book of Shadows. At least there were plenty of things to learn from his book while he waited. He was about to ask it a question when Orin gave an excited squeak.

'What is it?' asked Jack.

'It's Fergus, on the window ledge, look!'

As Jack turned he saw Fergus, then Berry climbing in through the open window. Jack wondered if they'd come to apologise to Orin but neither of them spoke. Seconds later the two young rats were joined by Motley.

'Are the rest of the Night Guard with you?' Jack asked.

'No, no, no, certainly not, wouldn't do to take them away from their duties. No, we're here on business. Something I need to get to the bottom of and these two youngsters seem to think you know something about it.'

Jack tried not to laugh as Motley marched up and down in front of the two smaller rats. They both hung their heads so Jack presumed they'd done something wrong. Motley stopped in front of Fergus.

'It wouldn't go amiss if you spent a bit more time grooming, you don't get sleek fur like mine in two minutes you know.'

Fergus hung his head even lower. Jack felt sorry for the little rat. He knew what it was like to have unruly hair; no matter how long he spent at the mirror his hair never looked good. When Motley finished inspecting Fergus and Berry, he turned back to Jack, cleared his throat and thrust out his chest before continuing.

'We, the rest of the Night Guard that is, are on a very important mission for Nora. I left these two youngsters in charge at the house, I gave them some important jobs to do, jobs I wanted doing. They now tell me they've been helping Camelin find a missing key. When questioned further, I find, not only have they not done the jobs I gave them, but they went and cleared up the mess in Camelin's loft instead.'

Motley stood to attention, narrowed his eyes and stared at Jack.

'I know they were helping Camelin to look for a key, but I didn't know anything about them helping him tidy the loft,' said Jack.

'Help! Help! They tell me they were left to do it all on their own and it was such a mess it's taken them hours. They also tell me that Camelin promised you'd give them some biscuits, gingerbread ones to be precise, in exchange for all the work they'd done. Is that true? I came back to check on the jobs they should have done and found them on their way here. Have you got gingerbread for them? Have you been encouraging some of my junior Night Guard to neglect their duties?'

Jack looked at Fergus and Berry. He felt very sorry for them.

'I had no idea about the loft clearing or about the biscuits.'

Motley turned to Fergus and Berry and started tapping his foot.

'What have you got to say for yourselves now?'

'Camelin promised Jack would have some biscuits for us, didn't he Fergus?' Berry said so quietly Jack could hardly make out what he was saying. Fergus nodded in agreement.

'I don't think you should be cross with Fergus and Berry,' said Jack. 'It's all Camelin's fault. If you wait here I'll try and sort out the payment. I'll go and ask Grandad if he's got any biscuits.'

Motley nodded his head and the two little rats looked very relieved. Jack went down to the kitchen and looked in the biscuit tin but it was empty. The kitchen door was open and Jack could see Grandad in the garden hoeing his potatoes. Jack went to join him.

'Are there any biscuits Grandad?'

'Got your appetite back have you?'

'I wondered if there were any gingerbreads, only the tin's empty.'

Grandad stopped hoeing for a moment.

'The new packets of biscuits are on the second shelf in the pantry. Be a good lad and put them in the tin, maybe you could make me a cup of tea and bring me out a couple of shortbreads too, this is thirsty work. Help yourself to what you want.'

Jack thanked his Grandad and went back to the house. He was relieved he'd be able to sort out the payment for Fergus and Berry without too much trouble. He went back to the kitchen and found three packets of biscuits and tipped them into the tin. He shook the crumbs from the packets into a dish then picked out all the broken biscuits to add to the crumbs. The dish was quite full when he'd finished. Before he went back upstairs he put the kettle on.

'Help yourselves,' said Jack as he put the dish of broken biscuits on the bedside table. He smiled as he saw Orin bound across to the bed. She had a liking for biscuits too. 'I won't be long, I've just got to go and make Grandad a cup of tea.'

Jack was longer than he'd planned to be. Grandad needed some help tying up his tomato plants. By the time he got back to his room the light was beginning to fade. When he put the light on there was a hurried movement as three little rats darted behind the curtain.

'It's only me, you can come out.'

Jack smiled as Fergus and Berry peeked out from behind the curtain. Orin scampered onto the bed.

'I thought you'd have gone by now,' said Jack then realised that was probably a bit rude.

'Motley told us to stay here until you got back to thank you for the biscuits and the others say thank you too,' explained Berry.

'Others?'

'Yes,' continued Fergus, 'Motley sent each one of the Night Guard up in turn so they could share the biscuits.'

Jack looked at the dish, it was nearly empty.

'No wonder there's not much left!'

'There'll be even less soon, Raggs hasn't been yet,' Fergus mumbled as he looked longingly at the plate.

Jack heard a scampering on the ivy outside. Raggs, the old ship's rat, appeared on the windowsill with his long whiskers twitching.

'Oh, something smells good!'

'Please help yourself,' said Jack.

'So kind, we didn't get anything like this on board

ship you know, only had hard biscuits then, good for keeping your teeth sharp but no taste or flavour.'

'Can you stay a while?' asked Jack.

'Should be on my way but I'm getting old now and it would be good to rest my weary bones for a while. Motley's had us out every night since you got back from Annwn. Watching the boundaries you know.'

'What for?' asked Jack.

'Intruders. Nora wants us to make sure there are no strangers around.'

'Oooh! Tell us more,' squeaked Berry excitedly. 'We never get to hear what's going on.'

Raggs picked a crumb from his pale grey fur before peering closely at the two younger rats.

'Not my place to tell, you know. I don't want to get into trouble for passing on confidential information to juniors.'

'Could you tell me?' asked Jack.

'Well that's a different matter entirely. Nora said if she wasn't around we were to come and find you and tell you everything and you'd know what to do. Something to do with a strange sounding word that starts with *vesp...*'

'Vespula!' gasped Jack. 'I know exactly who you've been looking out for, you don't need to worry, I know all about Velindur. Does Nora think he might come here? I thought she'd released him a long way from Glasruhen.'

'Whoever he is he told her he'd have his revenge. We've been watching out for anyone we don't know in the area who might be trying to cause trouble.'

'And have you seen anyone?'

'Nothing suspicious but I could tell you what everyone else has been doing in Glasruhen.'

'What's Vespula?' asked Fergus.

Raggs coughed.

'I don't think you need to be worrying about that. Let the rest of us take care of it.'

'See,' said Fergus, 'I told you they don't tell us anything, but we know secrets too. We know what Camelin's gone looking for, don't we Berry.'

'You do!' said Jack.

'We do,' confirmed Berry.

'Would you like to tell us?'

'Maybe we shouldn't, we don't want to get into any more trouble,' replied Fergus.

'We could trade,' said Jack. 'Some more biscuits for information?'

Fergus and Berry both sniffed the air and looked at the dish. Fergus whispered in Berry's ear.'

Raggs looked crossly at the two younger rats.

'Spit it out lad. Don't you know it's rude to whisper? If you can't say it to all of us don't say it at all.'

'I er... er I'd like some more biscuit and I can tell you what Camelin's doing even if Berry doesn't want to.'

'No I can help tell too,' squeaked Berry.

'So,' began Jack, 'what's Camelin been doing?'

Fergus took a step closer to the dish.

'He's looking for a Dorysk.'

'Whatever, for?'

Fergus lowered his voice to a whisper and began speaking rapidly.

'He needs one to go through the keyhole but he's gone to find one first so he knows where it is and then he's going to ask you to magic some pins so he can bribe him and ask you to go Dorysk hunting but he'll already know where to find one.'

That was too much information for Jack to make sense of.

'You mean he's gone to find a Dorysk?'

Both rats nodded.

'Then he's going to pretend he doesn't know where it is and get me to go Dorysk hunting with him?'

'Exactly,' said Fergus. 'Can we have some more now?'

'Yes, help yourselves.'

'Why would he want a Dorysk to go through a keyhole?' asked Raggs who'd finally finished nibbling his biscuit and was busy cleaning his whiskers.

'Because he wants his wand back,' said Berry.

'I'm not sure it's the keyhole in the herborium that Camelin is thinking about,' said Jack thoughtfully.

'I know where the Dorysk is,' announced Raggs.

'You do!' replied Jack.

'He's in the fairy mound.'

'What's a fairy mound?'

'Any mound you find between oak, ash and thorn trees belongs to fairy folk. A family of badgers used to share this one but they moved out, they found it too noisy on feast nights. When fairies get together they can make quite a racket, you know, and fairy music's not to everyone's taste. The badgers didn't like it.'

'And you know where this fairy mound is?'

'Oh yes, it's at the end of the back lane, the Dorysk likes the fairies and joins in when they're feasting and they don't seem to mind. They never let us rats inside the mound though. I've offered to tell them some of my stories but they just laugh. They don't stay in one place too long and can disappear in the blink of an eye.'

'You've all been really helpful,' said Jack. 'Thank you.'

'Well, must be off, I'll take these young whipper-snappers with me too,' said Raggs as he hustled Fergus and Berry towards the open window.

When they'd gone, Jack sat on the end of the bed and had a think.

'Is it the keyhole on Silver Hill?' asked Orin.

'I think it might be, but I really don't want to have to fly over there again tonight. Not if I don't have to.'

Jack was deep in thought when a flutter of wings startled him. Camelin swooped in through the open window and landed on the floor. Camelin spoke before Jack could say anything.

'Can I smell biscuits?'

'There's a dish on the table,' answered Jack.

'Ooh I love biscuits!' Camelin replied as he hopped round to the table. 'Where are they?'

'On the plate,' said Jack.

Camelin gave Jack a black look.

'There's none left!'

Jack looked at Orin, who was busy grooming her fur.'

'Fergus and Berry must have eaten them.'

'All of them!'

'No, the rest of the Night Guard had some too.'

'Why didn't you tell them to save me some?'

'Because someone promised they could have them.'

'Not everyone, only Fergus and Berry.'

'If you'd got here earlier you could have had some.'

Camelin began searching the floor.

'Not even a crumb,' he grumbled.

'Fergus and Berry did two jobs for you so they had twice as much as everyone else.'

'That's not fair.'

'Oh yes it was,' said Jack firmly, 'it wasn't easy getting them some biscuits. You should have asked me first before you promised them something.'

'Wasn't time, had things to do.'

'What kind of things?'

'Just things. Can we get down to business now?'

Jack sighed.

'I suppose so but I'm tired and was going to have an early night. You did give Charkle the message didn't you?'

'I did, he's getting ready to fly over to the standing stones, he'll be in Annwn in no time. That's why we haven't got any time to waste. I've got a plan.'

Jack smiled. He wanted to hear what Camelin had to say.

'A plan? What kind of a plan?'

'Well, I got to thinking, if we go and find ourselves a Dorysk, and we've got something he really wants, we could persuade him to shrink down and come over to Silver Hill with us tonight. He could go and have a look through the keyhole and if Norris and Snook are there, we'd have a nice surprise for Charkle when he comes back.'

Jack hadn't realised Camelin's plan was for Charkle but he really was very tired.

'Can't we go another night?'

'Nope, I want to show Nora that I can do something really good and then she'll let me have my wand back.'

'So you've got an ulterior motive?'

Camelin didn't answer straight away. He busied himself crumb hunting again around Jack's bed.

'You will come won't you? I'd rather know what's on the other side of the door before we go through it.'

Jack agreed that it made sense to send the Dorysk in for a look. Whatever was behind the door wouldn't notice a tiny creature. The more information they had before Nora came back the better.

'I'll tell you what,' said Jack slowly as he pretended to think, 'if I find a Dorysk first you can go over to Silver Hill and I'll go to bed and if you find one first I'll come with you, agreed?'

Camelin chuckled to himself.

'Agreed, but you know you've lost don't you? I'm the best Dorysk hunter there is.'

'I won't be able to go far from the house. Is it alright if I just look down the back lane?'

'That's fine but how will you know when I've found one?'

Jack tried not to laugh.

'You can make the sound of the raven owl and if I find one first I'll do the same. We can meet back here.'

'Better get ready for a long flight,' chuckled Camelin. 'See you soon.'

Jack watched as he flew off in the direction of the cricket ground, then he began to worry. He knew where to go and look but catching the Dorysk might not be as easy as he'd hoped. Even if he could capture one, he'd no idea how he was going to persuade him to fly over to Silver Hill with Camelin.

THE PIN MILLIONAIRE

As soon as Camelin was out of sight Jack consulted his Book of Shadows for a *materialisation spell*. He intended to create something very special, something he could use to tempt the Dorysk out of the fairy mound. Jack didn't know much about collecting things. He didn't know if anyone who already had over a million pins would really want any more. He tried to imagine something unusual, something the Dorysk could boast about. Most pins looked much the same. Then Jack remembered the notice board at the Cricket Club. All the posters had been held in place with drawing pins. A thousand drawing pins in a clear pot might interest the Dorysk. It would certainly be very unusual. The Dorysk could put it on his mantelpiece and show it off, it would be a talking point for anyone who visited.

Jack closed his eyes and imagined the pot of pins. He raised his wand slowly until it was above his head then drew a large circle.

'*Exsisto*,' he commanded and pointed his wand forcefully at the floor.

A sudden thump and rattling made Jack open his eyes. There at his feet was a small transparent pot crammed full of bright shiny drawing pins.

'Brilliant!' exclaimed Jack as picked up the pot and examined it before putting it in his pocket. 'I'm off now Orin, won't be long. I've got a Dorysk to catch.'

Jack peeped through the crack in the living room door. Grandad was asleep in his chair. He usually slept for a couple of hours after dinner every night. He didn't think Grandad would wake up but just in case he wrote a note to say where he'd gone and put it on the kitchen table.

'*Tego texi tectum*,' he whispered as he touched the paper with his wand.

The writing disappeared. It would only reappear if Grandad picked the paper up. It was a clever spell, one he'd looked up after he'd found Nora's note. Jack had remembered it easily because he liked the sound of the words. He was fascinated by all the information he found in his Book of Shadows and didn't seem to have any problem remembering anything he'd read. Jack stood and listened before going out of the back door. Grandad was snoring loudly and with any luck he'd be back before he woke.

As soon as Jack was through the gate he ran to the end of the back lane. It came to an abrupt end. Jack stood in front of a small hedge. A signpost pointed across a field towards the road, which led to Newton Gill. There was a well-made stile next to it that Jack climbed over. To his right was a small wood. The information Raggs had given him was correct. Inside the field were three old trees, a tall ash, a stout oak and an overgrown thorn. Jack looked around for the fairy mound. The grass was tall and a mass of poppies covered the whole area. As they swayed gently in the breeze, Jack thought he could see the top of a small grassy hummock in the middle. This had to be the fairy mound. He ran over and stood in front of a badly made tunnel that disappeared into the earth. Anyone who happened to stumble across it would immediately think it was an old badger sett. Jack looked to see if anyone was around. When he was sure he was alone he took out his wand and made the tip glow brightly. The light was invisible in the daylight but once he pointed his wand into the tunnel the whole inside lit up. Jack knew straight away that this was the right place. He could see a small green door with an arched top. Two large black hinges held the door in place and a large silver doorknob glinted in the light from his wand. Jack didn't know whether to knock and ask for the Dorysk in person or tap on the door and hide until the Dorysk answered. He reached inside then hesitated, he was sure he could see a face in the doorknob. Maybe it was his reflection? As he leant further in, the doorknob quivered. For a moment the silver looked molten. Jack jumped when two pointed ears popped out of the side, a tuft of hair, a small nose and a wide mouth followed. The head stared at Jack and then smiled. When the head spoke Jack nearly dropped his wand.

'You've missed the last feast and the next one isn't 'til full moon. Goodbye.'

'No wait,' cried Jack, 'I'm looking for the Dorysk, is he in?'

'You've come to the wrong door. Goodbye.'

'Please, don't go, it's important.'

'I'm the one who decides what's important and like I told you, no feast, no entry, no Dorysk. Goodbye.'

'Won't you tell me where to find the Dorysk

before you go? I really do need to talk to him. I was told he lived here.'

'Not here he doesn't, lives next door, but he won't come out if he knows you're there, he's always worried about being caught. You're going to have to be very clever to catch him.'

Jack looked around to see if there was another fairy mound close by.

'Could you tell me which direction I need to go and how far it might be?'

The head's mouth opened wide and it began laughing so hard it gasped for breath.

'It's next door, right next door, in the next tunnel. That's a good one – how far!'

'Thank you,' said Jack once the head had composed itself. 'Do you know if he's in?'

'No idea, you'll have to go and find out. Now I really have to go. Goodbye.'

Jack knew their conversation was over when the ears, nose and mouth disappeared and the head once more became a doorknob. He put out the light from his wand and carried on around the mound. On the opposite side he found another tunnel. The door was well hidden under ivy and brambles. Jack decided to try to tempt the Dorysk out and then pounce. He took the pot of drawing pins and rattled it several times before placing it in front of the entrance. He went and lay on top of the hummock and waited. He hoped the Dorysk was at home and would soon come to investigate the noise. Jack heard a scraping and a scuffling from inside the mound followed by a sniffing sound. The Dorysk scurried out of the tunnel and bumped straight into the pot of pins. As he fell backwards Jack pounced.

'Got you!'

'Oh please, please don't hurt me. I haven't told anyone, please don't hurt me.'

Jack held the Dorysk up so he could see him better. The Dorysk peered back but Jack doubted he could see much because he wasn't wearing his glasses.

'I'm not going to hurt you,' said Jack as reassuringly as he could.

'What are you?'

'It's me, Jack Brenin, I met you in the woods with Camelin.'

'You're not Jack Brenin, you're an impostor. The Jack Brenin I met had feathers. You're a spy, I know you are. You've come to test me. The nasty Bogie sent you didn't he?'

'I haven't spoken to Peabody for a while.'

'No, not Peabody, Pyecroft. Oh me, oh my! I

don't know what came over me! I'm really not myself. Dorysk's don't give information out to strangers.'

'I am Jack Brenin, I'm a raven boy, like Camelin.'

'How do I know you're telling me the truth? I can't even see what you look like.'

'Where are your glasses?'

'No, no! Ask me anything but that question, you've only got one question but please don't ask me that.'

Jack could see that the Dorysk was upset.

'What's wrong?'

'No, no! I can't answer that question either. Oh me, oh my. What to do? What to do?'

'I can magic you a pair of glasses if it would help.'

'You can? Glasses that won't break?'

'Yes, I think I can do that.'

'Oh, I'd be most grateful if you could.'

Jack put the Dorysk on the ground, trying to remember what his other glasses had looked like and waved his wand. There was a loud crackling sound, which made the Dorysk jump. His little paws shot up to his face.

'You did it! Oh how wonderful! I can see again.'

'Try breaking them, let's see if it worked.'

The Dorysk took the glasses off and put them on the grass. He quickly picked them up again.

119

'No, no, I can't, what if they break?'

'I'll mend them.'

'You do it. I couldn't bear to break my own glasses.'

Jack put his foot on the small pair of round-rimmed spectacles. He felt them scrunch under his trainer but when he lifted his foot again, the glass instantly rearranged itself into frames that had already straightened. Jack bent over, picked up the pair of glasses and handed them back to the Dorysk.

'Oh thank you, a thousand times thank you, I've not been able to see much at all without them. How can I ever repay you?'

The Dorysk took a step back so he could bow to Jack and hit his heel on the pot of pins.

'Oh my, what have we here?' the Dorysk said excitedly.

'A thousand flat headed pins.'

'And what would someone have to do to own a pot of pins like this?'

Jack took a deep breath and was about to explain the problem but he remembered he still hadn't had his own question answered.

'Why did the Bogie take your glasses?'

The Dorysk looked cautiously around.

'Bend down so I can whisper,' he told Jack.

Jack lay on the hummock. The Dorysk again looked around.

'I found out some top-secret information and to stop me telling anyone the nasty Bogie came and stole my glasses. He said if I told anyone he'd break them and I'd never be able to see again.'

'Don't you worry, I know a *sticking spell*. If Pyecroft comes back and tries to take this pair he won't be able to get them off your head.'

'Really?'

'Really.'

Jack waved his wand and used the same spell Nora had used on the cauldron when they'd been in Annwn.

'There you are. No one will ever be able to take or break your glasses again.'

'You are so kind. Can I do anything in return for you?'

'Well,' began Jack, 'we have a little problem and we could do with your help. We need you to use your incredible shrinking powers to go through a keyhole and do a bit of finding out for us.'

'*Us?*'

'Well there's me and Camelin and I suppose Charkle and Timmery, but they don't know what we're planning. We need to know what's behind a small door

121

on Silver Hill before we open it.'

'Information gathering's what we Dorysks do best but it's a long way to Silver Hill.'

'I can get you a lift. Camelin will fly you over there.'

'It's a deal then. And what information would you like for the pot of pins?'

Jack didn't like to ask the Dorysk for the secret he'd found out, it just didn't seem fair, even though he was dying to know.

'Perhaps I can save my question for another time, would that be alright?'

'Oh fine, fine, just let me know. You can ask me what you want whenever you want, Jack Brenin, in return for these wonderful pins. But please don't tell anyone where you found me, I like to keep my whereabouts a secret. I don't want everyone knowing where I live.'

'I promise, and in return perhaps you'd keep a secret for me and not tell Camelin I came calling!'

'It's a deal. I'll just go and put these somewhere safe.'

Jack hadn't realised the pot would be so big and heavy for the small Dorysk.

'Here let me help,' said Jack, as the Dorysk struggled to pick it up. 'Would you like me to make it a bit smaller for you?'

'Oh no! It's perfect as it is, I can manage. I've got it now.'

The Dorysk heaved the pot up and once it was securely in his front paws he scurried back down the hole. Jack had no doubt he'd come back. It wasn't long before the small prickly creature reappeared at the entrance, looking very pleased with himself, though a little out of breath.

'Can you shrink yourself down so you could fit in my pocket?' asked Jack.

'Here we go,' said the Dorysk as he squeezed his eyes tightly shut, hunched his shoulders and began shrinking. It wasn't long before a small brown mouse, wearing a pair of tiny spectacles stood next to Jack's foot.

Jack put his hand out so the Dorysk could climb on and be lowered into his pocket.

'Hold on tight, I need to get home as quickly as possible,' Jack said before he began running across the field towards the stile.

When he got back to the kitchen he found the note hadn't been moved and he picked it up and put it in the bin. Jack peeped into the front room and was relieved to see Grandad was still asleep. He took the stairs two at a time and as soon as he got into his room

he opened the window wide and made the call of the
raven owl as loudly as he could.

It seemed ages before Camelin appeared in the
distance. Jack knew he'd be grumpy when he arrived.

'Look what I've found!'

'You used your wand didn't you?'

'He caught me fair and square,' squeaked the
Dorysk.

'How do I know that's not just an ordinary mouse
you've magicked a pair of glasses onto?'

If only Camelin knew how close to the truth he was
he wouldn't have been pleased but Jack didn't need to
defend himself as the Dorysk began transforming again.

'Now, I believe you want my help? Something
about a flight over to Silver Hill and a bit of information
gathering?'

The Dorysk started walking towards Camelin.

'Oh no you don't, you're not getting on my back
with all those prickles.'

Camelin looked pleadingly at Jack.

'Could you manage something small?' Jack asked.

'Something very small and not at all prickly,' added Camelin.

The Dorysk squeezed his eyes shut, there was a loud pop and he was nowhere to be seen.

'You let him escape,' grumbled Camelin. 'You should have held onto him while he transformed, he could be miles away by now.'

'Shhh!' said Jack trying to listen. 'He's over there.'

A tiny flea, wearing a minute pair of glasses, was jumping up and down on the end of Jack's bed, trying to attract their attention. Jack laughed.

'Is he small enough now?'

'I suppose so,' said Camelin as he shuffled over to the bed. 'Climb on but don't you go wriggling around, sit nice and still. We'll be at Silver Hill in no time. There's no amateur flyers to hold us up tonight.'

Jack ignored Camelin's last comment. He was just grateful he didn't have to make the journey.

Camelin hopped onto the windowsill.

'Leave the window open and we'll come back and tell you what we find out.'

'Okay,' sighed Jack, 'but if it can wait 'til morning I'd be grateful. I really do need a good night's sleep.'

125

It was a warm night. The breeze from the open window wafted over Jack as he lay on his bed and it wasn't long before he drifted off.

Jack woke with a start when something heavy landed on his bed. It was dark so he reached for his wand and made a dim light appear at the tip.

'It's me, wake up!' said Camelin.

'I can see it's you and I am awake,' Jack replied sleepily. 'I presume it's important. What did the Dorysk find out?'

'I've no idea. He got straight on my back, ordered me to fly back here and refused to talk to anyone but you. And if he thinks he's getting on my back again as a flea he's wrong, he's made me itch all over.'

Jack didn't see the Dorysk at first and then a small shape in the middle of his bed began to grow. Soon his familiar prickly form appeared. He began speaking so quickly and so loudly that Jack worried he might wake Grandad.

'Shhh! You're going to have to whisper. What's

wrong?'

'Oh dreadful news, dreadful!'

'Did you see a monster?'

The Dorysk shook his head.

'You'd better start at the beginning,' said Jack, 'and tell us everything.'

The Dorysk sat on his haunches, took a deep breath and began.

'I thought it would be dark inside the mountain but it wasn't. There are crystals all over the walls, and lots of light everywhere. I transformed into a moth and flew down the passage until I came to a room. That's when I heard it.'

'The monster?' asked Camelin.

'No, I didn't see a monster. I heard two Spriggans planning the menu in honour of Chief Knuckle's forthcoming visit.'

'What's so bad about that?' asked Camelin.

'It's what they're planning to cook. Roast dragon is on the menu. Two roasted dragonettes to be precise, tomorrow night.'

Jack felt sick. His stomach churned. He had so many questions he wanted to ask but couldn't find his voice.

'Why tomorrow?' asked Camelin. 'Why now?'

The Dorysk sighed deeply.

'The Spriggans were talking about the celebrations. One of them called it the *Candleless Feast* but I don't know what all that's about. What I did find out was that the dragonettes aren't needed in the mines any more. Now they've got the new lights they're obsolete as candle lighters and from what the Spriggans were saying they're a real delicacy to eat.'

Jack was beginning to piece together the situation. It meant the two dragonettes were in grave danger. It was going to be up to him to find a way to save them. They couldn't rely on Nora's help because she might not get back from Annwn in time.

'We'll have to get into Silver Hill tonight,' said Jack thinking aloud.

'Tonight!' grumbled Camelin, 'but we've only just got back.'

'I thought you said you were doing this for Charkle. He's not going to be very happy when he comes back and finds the only two other dragonettes left on earth have been roasted for a Spriggan Feast. We've got to go back and rescue them right now.'

TO THE RESCUE

No one spoke. Jack's mind was racing. He knew that making the right decision now was crucial. If he got it wrong he could put everyone in danger. He thought about the two dragonettes. Whether they knew it or not they were in trouble, and without help they'd be roasted for the feast.

Jack took a deep breath and looked pleadingly at the Dorysk.

'I've got a plan but we're going to need your help again.'

The Dorysk bowed low to Jack and touched his glasses.

'For you, Jack Brenin, I would do anything.'

Camelin coughed.

'That's a bit over the top isn't it? You don't even know what he wants you to do.'

Jack ignored Camelin and began outlining his plan to the Dorysk.

'I'm going to need you to go back through the keyhole once we get to Silver Hill. When you've found out exactly where the dragonettes are being kept, you come back and tell us. We'll go in through the door and rescue them.'

The Dorysk nodded.

'And just how are you planning to get through the door?' asked Camelin.

Jack didn't want to say anything about Nora's special key but he didn't want to lie either.

'I'll take my wand. It means I'll have to fly with it in my beak but I don't think we're going to be able to rescue the dragonettes without a bit of magic.'

Camelin seemed to be happy with the answer.

'If you're going to be able to open the door why don't I go and get Timmery, he can go in first with the Dorysk. When they've found the dragonettes Timmery can come back and lead us in. He's so brave, he won't mind.'

'That's a brilliant idea.'

Camelin looked surprised.

'It is?'

'Definitely. Do you think you can find him quickly?'

Camelin shuffled over to the open window and set off towards the church. Once he'd gone Jack turned to the Dorysk.

'When we get there I'm going to open the door.'

'You might need more than magic, depending on what kind of a door it is, and I didn't see a key. The only thing on the other side of the door was a Bogie hat.'

'A Bogie hat?'

'Yes. You can smell Bogie as soon as you're in the tunnel. They'll use any door they can find but I don't think it started out as a Bogie door, it's too well made. You find all kinds of doors in all sorts of places, some big, some small. Some belong to the Fair Folk and some the not so Fair Folk. This one might even be a dwindling door.'

'What's a dwindling door?'

'It's a special kind of door the Druids used to make long ago. You don't see many of them these days. They were put in important places that weren't used very often. If a stranger or unwelcome guest got through the door the Druids would know because each time it was opened without permission it got smaller. If this is a dwindling door you might need a special key to open it.'

'I've got a special key, it's magical key but I don't want Camelin to know about it.'

'I can keep secrets when I have to. I'll never trade that piece of information to anyone, I promise.'

Jack was very grateful to the little Dorysk. He went over to the chair where he'd left his trousers, fished in the pocket and pulled out the ordinary looking key. It was the same shape and size it had been the last time he'd used it in the herborium. To transport it over to Silver Hill he'd need to shrink it even more and put it around his neck. Jack couldn't see any keyhole small enough in his room. He was contemplating looking in his Book of Shadows for help when he remembered something he'd got in his memory box. He opened the bottom drawer of the dresser and removed an old leather casket. Jack looked at it for a few seconds and ran his hand over the leather before lifting the lid. He rummaged inside until he found a small silver heart on a chain. In the middle of the heart was an open keyhole. It had belonged to his mum and was one of his most treasured possessions. His hand trembled. The key sparkled from inside. Tiny lights danced across the dull metal until the whole key shone. As he moved it towards the locket his fingertips tingled. The key began to shrink until it was a perfect fit. Jack undid the chain and slipped the key onto it before putting it back round his neck. It was smaller than the gold chain he wore, which held his acorn, but he knew it would be safe when he transformed and it was lost from sight in his feathers. Jack had only just replaced the box when Timmery flitted into the room.

'Let me introduce you two,' whispered Jack, but before he could get any further, Camelin flew in, landed heavily on the bed and made the Dorysk bounce up and down several times before he managed to regain his balance.

'Dorysk ... Timmery ... Timmery ... Dorysk,' said Camelin grumpily, 'you both know Jack and you both know me. Now can we get on?'

'Thanks,' said Jack. 'And you're right, we ought to get going.'

'Oh I do love adventures,' said Timmery. 'I'm honoured to be included.'

'I wish I could come with you,' whispered Orin.

'I'm sorry,' said Jack. 'A Spriggan tunnel is no place for any white rat.'

'I know,' sighed Orin. 'You will be careful won't you?'

Jack stroked her head to reassure her before turning to Camelin.

'Ready?'

'Ready.'

'Close your eyes everyone,' said Jack before touching his forehead against Camelin's.

Once he'd shaken himself free of his pyjamas he turned to Timmery.

'Hop on.'

'Oh no you don't,' interrupted Camelin. 'I'll take Timmery, you can have the Dorysk. He wriggles about too much. We'll see how you like it when you feel itchy all over and can't have a good scratch.'

Camelin had already left with Timmery and didn't see the Dorysk shape-shift into another tiny bat. Jack tried not to laugh.

'Our secret,' the Dorysk said as he climbed onto Jack's back. 'We won't tell the grumpy one!'

Jack set off at speed after Camelin into the moonless night with his wand securely held in his beak.

'Ow! Watch what you're doing with that,' Camelin grumbled as Jack landed bedside him on the narrow ledge in front of the small door.

'Sorry, I've never flown with anything in my beak before.'

The Dorysk wriggled out of Jack's feathers and by the time he jumped onto the ledge he was a flea again. Jack looked around. There was a small path leading down the hillside. He gripped the end of his wand with his claws and made a light glow from the tip so they'd be able to see.

'Look Camelin, down there, it's wider on the path, come and help me transform, then I can get the door open.'

Jack and Camelin hopped down to the lower level. For a split second the whole of Silver Hill lit up. Jack was grateful it was a dark night and no one was around, he wasn't happy about being naked. He picked up his wand and ran back up the path leaving Camelin to follow. By the time Camelin reached the door Jack had already removed the silver chain and used Nora's special key to unlock it.

'You're getting a bit good with that wand,' said Camelin. 'I've got a lot of catching up to do when I get mine back.'

Jack removed the key and slipped the chain back over his head when Camelin wasn't looking. Thankfully the door opened inwards but it squeaked noisily. Jack closed it behind them as quietly as he could. The hat the Dorysk had seen earlier was still on the hook, but to Jack's delight, hanging underneath it was a coat. It wasn't the best fit but at least Jack didn't feel so exposed with it on, especially when he realised it wasn't pitch black inside. As the Dorysk had said, a soft glowing light filled the warm tunnel. There was an inviting smell of cooking too, which hadn't gone unnoticed.

'Barbecue!' croaked Camelin excitedly.

'You don't think we're too late do you?' said Jack.

'Too late for what?' asked Timmery.

Jack turned and frowned at Camelin.

'You didn't tell Timmery, did you? You could have told him everything on the way over.'

'Needed all my breath for flying, don't do small talk.'

Jack sighed and shook his head. He had far more important things to worry about than being cross with Camelin. He quickly told Timmery everything the Dorysk had seen and heard. By the time Jack finished, Camelin had already made his way to the end of the

136

tunnel. His beak was open and Jack knew he was enjoying the lovely smells.

'You don't think that's roast dragon do you?' Jack asked him again.

'Naw, that's sheep. Spriggans will nab one if they can. If it's an important feast they'll have more than one down there.'

'But I thought the feast was tomorrow night,' gasped Jack.

'That's what they said,' confirmed the Dorysk. 'Let me go see what I can find out.'

'Can you see in this light?' Jack asked Timmery.

'No problem at all, it's only like dusk or dawn, not too bright at all, I can see just fine.'

'That's a relief,' grumbled Camelin. 'After I brought you all this way it'd be such a shame if you had to wait outside in the dark.'

'This is getting us nowhere fast,' said Jack. 'We need to act quickly and get back to Glasruhen as soon as we can, preferably with two dragonettes.'

'I'll send Timmery back as soon as we find them,' the Dorysk said as he changed into the form of a moth. They were both soon lost from sight as they flitted off down the tunnel.

Jack leant against the wall. He'd thought of a plan

while they'd been flying but he wasn't sure it would work. He knew he couldn't do it on his own and was going to need Camelin's help.

'How much weight can you carry in your beak?' Jack asked as innocently as he could.

'Lots, I can lift Nora's small cauldron when it's empty.'

'So, do you think you could fly with a dragonette in your beak?'

'No need, why would you want to carry a dragonette when it can already fly?'

'You'd have to if it was sealed inside a lantern like Charkle was.'

'You mean … we're going to … that's brilliant … but can you fly all the way back to Glasruhen with a dragonette, a lantern and your wand in your beak too?'

This was the question Jack had been asking himself. It was the only problem he could see with his plan. He didn't know if he had the strength to fly all the way back with an extra passenger. The only way he'd find out was if they successfully rescued the dragonettes.

They seemed to wait in the tunnel for ages. Jack was worried about Pyecroft showing up and demanding his coat back but the only sound they heard was a low rumbling coming from deep within the hillside.

'They're all eating,' grumbled Camelin. 'I can't smell cooking any more.'

Jack sniffed the air. He was sure Camelin was right as he knew more about food and how it was cooked than Jack did but he was more worried about the Dorysk and Timmery than his stomach.

'Do you think they're alright? They seem to have been gone ages.'

'They'll be fine, how couldn't they be? A shape-shifter and such a brave bat...'

'Oh, so kind, so kind,' came a voice from the mouth of the tunnel. 'Now, are you two ready? The coast is clear and the Dorysk has found the dragonettes. The good news is they've not been roasted. The bad news is they're in the Spriggans' larder, in a big cauldron full of marinade.'

'Are they hurt?' asked Jack. 'Did you ask them their names?'

'I didn't see them or have time to talk to them but when I left the Dorysk was explaining about the rescue, so maybe he's asked them.'

'What kind of marinade?' asked Camelin.

Jack glowered at him.

'Are you coming or would you rather stay here?'

'Just asking, a raven's allowed to ask the odd question isn't he?'

'Lead the way Timmery, we're coming.'

Jack was grateful the little bat had such a good sense of direction. The tunnels twisted and turned downwards. The small lights on the sides of the tunnels gave out a warm glow and made it easy for them to follow Timmery. Even though Jack could see where he was going he knew he wouldn't be able to find his way back without a guide. Timmery didn't even hesitate when they came to a junction. It meant they were able to move deeper into the hill quickly and quietly. Eventually Timmery stopped outside the doorway of a well-lit room.

'It's too bright for me in there. I'll wait out here and keep watch. This is the larder, the others are inside.'

Jack cautiously crept into the room. He was surprised to see rows of tables, all laden with food. He turned and gave Camelin a warning look.

'Over here,' called the Dorysk.

Jack looked around and saw the Dorysk fluttering above a large cauldron, which sat by the hearth. Jack ran over and looked inside. To his relief the two dragonettes looked alright, considering their circumstances. Their cages had been tied to the cauldron rings and were immersed in the mixture. They were having difficulty keeping their heads above the surface.

'Don't worry,' Jack told them. 'We've come to rescue you. I'll have you out of there in no time. I'm Jack Brenin and this is Camelin.'

'We know,' one of the dragonettes managed to say as it struggled to keep its head out of the marinade. 'We're very grateful you've come… they were going to…'

'It's alright,' interrupted Jack. 'We'll talk later, but what are your names?'

'I'm Norris and this is Snook,' the other dragonette replied.

'Won't Charkle be pleased,' said Camelin as he hopped around the cauldron. 'Now I'll be able to have my wand back.'

'Charkle!' cried both dragonettes.

Jack felt so happy for the two brothers.

'Yes, Charkle. He's safe and we've heard a lot about you two, but let's save all that for later, we need to get you out of here. We've got a long flight ahead of us once we get out of the tunnels.'

'So what's the plan?' asked Camelin.

'We all need to get away from here as quickly as possible,' explained Jack. 'Timmery can lead and the Dorysk can bring up the rear, in case we need to use Plan B, but first I need to get you two out of this cauldron and find something to tie onto the ends of these ropes or they'll notice you've gone.'

'What's Plan B?' asked the Dorysk as Jack looked around the larder.

'You might have to shape-shift into a dragonette. Do you think you can do that?'

'I'll have to keep my glasses on or I won't be able to see where I'm going.'

'That won't be a problem, it's only in case we're seen and need a diversion. If that happens, Camelin and I will transform, that will be the signal to start Plan B. The light will be so bright it will blind the Spriggans for a few seconds. You'll need to make sure they see you. They'll think the dragonettes are loose and will hopefully follow you. If you lead them off in the other direction it'll give us enough time to get out of the door, then, as soon as you can, shape-shift into a moth and get back to us on the ledge. We won't leave without you.'

'We won't!' said Camelin.

'No, we won't,' confirmed Jack as he looked around the room for two heavy objects to put into the marinade, in place of the lanterns. 'Hopefully we'll be out of here before anyone finds you're missing.'

'You'll need to hurry,' said Snook, 'they've been coming in and out all night.'

'They've not had their pudding yet,' said Norris as he nodded towards one of the tables. 'They never go without their pudding, no matter how much they've eaten.'

'Spriggans!' piped Timmery as he flew into the kitchen. 'There are two of them and they're heading right this way.'

THE MONSTER OF SILVER HILL

'Quick! Hide!' whispered Jack.

Timmery and the Dorysk immediately flitted off towards the darkest part of the tunnel. Jack turned to speak to Camelin but he was nowhere to be seen. The voices from the tunnel were getting louder and Jack knew if he didn't find a hiding place soon he'd be discovered. He wished he'd learnt an invisibility spell or could shape-shift like the Dorysk. There weren't many places to hide in the room. None of the tables had cloths so it wouldn't be safe to hide under them. The cupboards looked too small, even for Jack to squeeze into. He had no idea where Camelin had gone or where he could go. Jack could hear footsteps now as well as voices. He was contemplating using his wand to send the two Spriggans rolling back down the tunnel, but if he did, they'd know straight away that someone was in their larder. A hissing sound brought Jack to a halt.

'Psst!'

'Is that you Camelin?'

'Who else would it be?'

Jack spun around.

'Where are you?'

'Inside the chimney, come on in, there's room in here for both of us.'

Jack looked at the hearth, it had been carved out of the rock and above it was a wide flue.

'What you waiting for? Get in or they'll see you,' whispered Camelin.

Jack stepped around the remains of the fire as best he could and put his hand inside the chimney. To his surprise the flue was craggy; it too had been carved from the rock. Although it was dark, Jack managed to find enough handholds to climb part way up. He had just managed to pull his feet up out of sight when the first Spriggan entered the room. Jack wondered how Camelin had climbed up into the flue as there certainly wasn't enough room to fly. His thoughts were interrupted by the sound of the first Spriggan complaining bitterly in its high-pitched voice.

'Carry this, fetch that, why us? I ask you Grabble, why us?'

'Cos we's the cooks Dugmore, that's why.'

'Cooks yes, servants no!'

'Well at least we've got us some help for the banquet tomorrow.'

'And not before time I says. Took six of us to get that sheep barbecued tonight and we's got four of thems to do tomorrow.'

'And two dragonettes don't forget. They'll have to be cooked up here, can't put them into the big barbecue, be nothings left of thems if we did, then we'd be in trouble again.'

'You're right Dugmore. We'd better check on them.'

Jack heard the Spriggans shuffle over to the side of the hearth. He presumed they were roped together.

'I'll do this one, you do the other Grabble.'

Jack held his breath. He'd no idea what the Spriggans were going to do. Should he jump out and surprise them or not? He decided to wait and listen. The longer the Spriggans were unaware of the rescue party the more chance they had of succeeding. He could hear coughing and spluttering and a lot of splashing.

'There you are little 'uns. That's got yous nice and coated, won't be long now. A couple more hours in there and you'lls be the tastiest treat Chief Knuckle's had in a longs time.'

'Come on Grabble we's better gets the puddings. Don't want to keep *Pig Face* waiting.'

Jack heard both Spriggans twittering and chittering loudly. He presumed they were laughing.

'Better not let him hear you call him Pig Face, you knows we's not supposed to mention his nose. It's the *Big One* what worries me, I don't want to get on the bad side of that one.'

'Only having a bit o'fun Dugmore, but you're right and we's better gets this lot downstairs. It's going to take us a few trips.'

After a few more grumblings and a clattering of plates the Spriggans' voices began to grow quieter. Jack could hear the sound of their footsteps receding.

'They've gone,' announced the Dorysk as he flitted into the hearth.

'Thanks,' said Jack. 'We'd better get out of here and get Norris and Snook to safety before they come back.'

'Give us a bit of light in here so I can see what I'm doing,' whispered Camelin.

Jack made the tip of his wand glow dimly. He looked around expecting to see Camelin but he was alone.

'Where are you?'

'Down here, in the side oven.'

As Jack lowered his wand, he could see Camelin's head poking out of an alcove in the rock.

'Thought you'd have crawled in the other one,' he said and nodded towards another opening on the other side. 'It doesn't look very comfortable up there.'

'It isn't. If I'd known about the side ovens I'd have got in.'

'Well you'll know for next time.'

Jack hoped there wouldn't be a *next time* but he did wonder how Camelin knew about them. If they hadn't been in a hurry he'd have asked. A bubbling sound brought his attention back to the cauldron. Jack scrambled down the chimney and dashed over to see both Norris and Snook's lanterns bobbing around. The little dragons were fighting to keep their heads above the marinade. He grabbed both sticks and lifted them up.

'Don't worry, we'll have you out of here in no time.'

Norris and Snook coughed and spluttered.

'What's it taste like?' asked Camelin.

'That's a terrible thing to say,' said Jack crossly.

'No it's not, it's a good question, I need to know how sorry to feel for them. If the mixture's good they shouldn't be making such a fuss.'

'Do something useful and hold Snook's stick for me.'

Camelin shuffled over to Jack and took the stick in his beak. He held the lantern clear of the marinade while Jack untied Norris. It wasn't long before both dragonettes were on the kitchen floor and two large spoons hung in their places inside the cauldron. Jack hadn't realised there'd be a mess on the floor. The Spriggans would see it as soon as they returned. He also needed to put the lanterns inside something until they got clear of the tunnels or they'd leave an easy trail for anyone to follow. Jack found two small flour sacks, tipped the contents into the marinade and brought them over to Norris and Snook.

'I'm afraid I'm going to have to put you in these but it won't be for long.'

Jack lowered them carefully inside and moved them over to the tunnel entrance. 'Now all I need is a cloth to clear up the puddles and we can go.'

'I'll clean it up,' said Camelin.

'We haven't got time.'

Jack could see Camelin's beak was already glistening.

The marinade on the lantern stick must have been to his liking. Jack grabbed a towel, wiped the floor quickly then tossed it into the cauldron before cautiously putting his head out of the larder and looking down the tunnel.

'It's all clear,' said Timmery.

'Nothing's ahead either,' said the Dorysk as he flitted into view.

'We'd better get going. I can carry both lanterns as long as I don't have to transform. Are we all ready?' asked Jack.

'Ready,' everyone replied.

They set off at speed through the tunnels but as they neared the first junction Timmery stopped.

'What is it?' whispered Jack.

'I don't know but it's heading this way.'

Jack looked around but he couldn't see anywhere to hide. The tunnel they were in led straight back to the larder and the loud rumbling sound seemed to be coming from the way they needed to go. To get to the next tunnel they'd have to cross the open space at the junction. Jack didn't know what to do. They still had a long way to go before they reached the door. He listened intently. He'd no idea what it was.

'It's the monster!' gasped Camelin. 'Look!'

The light coming towards them grew brighter as

the thundering and rumbling sounds got even louder. If it came into their tunnel they'd be crushed. Even if it didn't, they'd be discovered if the monster looked in their direction; the light from its eyes shone brightly. Jack could feel his legs trembling. He didn't know enough magic to do anything useful. He desperately tried to think of something, anything that might help.

The loud rumbling increased. If he could only turn the light off they might have a chance, they'd not be seen if the monster went straight past the end of their tunnel. As Jack put his hand over the crystal on the wall it came away in his hand. For an instant it shone brightly in his palm but as soon as his fingers curled around it, the tunnel went dark. Jack held his breath as the noise increased. He felt the air rushing on his face as the monster sped past their tunnel. A terrible smell followed and hung in the air. The noise was deafening. Camelin had somehow managed to get behind Jack. He could feel his wings shaking next to his own trembling legs. For a few seconds it felt as if the whole hillside was shaking as the monster sped by.

'Are we all alright?' asked Jack when the monster had gone.

'Still here,' replied the Dorysk.

'Timmery, are you OK?'

There was no answer from the little bat.

'So much for being brave,' grumbled Camelin. 'He's flown off and left us.'

'Timmery,' Jack called a bit louder.

'Here, I'm here, I went to see what the monster looked like. It's not a monster at all, it's a train and it's full of Hags.'

'Hags!' said Jack and Camelin together.

'Yes and it looks like it's not going to stop till it gets to the bottom.'

Jack wondered what the Spriggans needed a train for, especially one full of Hags. He turned to Timmery.

'That was a very brave thing to do but we really need to get going.'

'Follow me,' called Timmery as he flitted off down the tunnel.

'Follow me,' grumbled Camelin. 'I can't even see him, someone put the light out.'

Jack opened his fist and the soft glowing light lit the tunnel. Jack looked closely at the small object in his hand; it was crystal shaped and warm to the touch. He'd no idea how to reattach it to the wall or where the light came from. He decided to hold on to it for now.

They hurried across the open junction as fast as they could and started up the next tunnel. It wasn't as easy going up and Jack began to feel out of breath. He was just about to give everyone a brief rest when a shriek echoed through the tunnels. Jack couldn't hear what the Spriggans were saying but he thought he could guess.

'I think it's time to put Plan B into action. It sounds as if Norris and Snook have been missed. We'll get as far as we can before we have to transform, agreed?'

'Agreed,' everyone replied.

Timmery led the way. Jack ran as fast as he could after the little bat.

'You do realise they've got really good sniffers don't you?' wheezed Camelin as he tried to keep up with Jack. 'All they'll have to do is follow the smell of the marinade.'

'Faster,' called Jack.

'Plan B,' shouted the Dorysk. 'They're not far behind now.'

'Ready,' said Jack as he pushed his wand and the crystal into Snook's sack.

'Ready,' replied Camelin.

Within seconds Jack had transformed. He picked up Snook's sack in his beak and Camelin took the other with Norris inside. Timmery flitted impatiently above them. Jack turned to see the Dorysk flying back down the tunnel having taken the form of a dragonette.

'Let's hope Plan B works or we might all end up in the marinade,' thought Jack.

They shuffled along after Timmery as fast as they could. Jack heard a loud chittering. He hoped the Spriggans had seen the Dorysk and gone in the opposite direction instead of following their noses but it wasn't long before he could hear footsteps. He knew the Spriggans were right behind them when he heard a high-pitched voice screeching: 'STOP yous two! STOP!'

That was the last thing Jack wanted to do. They'd have to try to outrun them as there wasn't room for the two ravens to fly in the tunnel. Jack didn't need to look back to know the Spriggans were gaining on them. He could hear them sniffing the air. Timmery fluttered around Jack's head.

'Follow me,' he whispered.

Instead of continuing upwards Timmery took the next lefthand tunnel and then the right. They all followed. Suddenly Jack had to stop. He realised he couldn't see Timmery any more. In fact, he couldn't see anything. The tunnel Timmery had directed them into didn't have any crystals on the walls.

'Don't move,' said Timmery. 'I'll go and see what's happening, they won't come down here, they're afraid of the dark.'

Jack was thankful to the little bat. He could hear footsteps but instead of turning off the main tunnel they carried on past. Neither he nor Camelin spoke, he didn't even know where Camelin was, the darkness was total. It felt like a heavy blanket and Jack could understand now why the Spriggans didn't like it. All they could do was wait.

Jack had no idea how long they'd been in the dark. He thought he'd get used to it but after a while he began to feel uncomfortable. Just when he thought he couldn't stay there a moment longer he heard a fluttering of wings.

'It's all clear,' announced Timmery. 'The Dorysk has led them back down the tunnels. We can go now, but don't make a sound, just take two steps forwards.'

Jack was amazed as he shuffled towards Timmery's voice. After a few steps he was able to see again. Jack heard a low mumbling coming from Camelin as he followed but even he must have realised the danger they were in and didn't say anything out loud. They moved swiftly and were soon back in the main tunnel and heading upwards towards the door. Jack wondered what Pyecroft would say when he found his coat lying in one of the tunnels. He'd probably blame one of the Spriggans.

'We're nearly there,' piped Timmery as a small moth joined them.

'Are we safe,' Jack asked the Dorysk.

'Those two won't be coming this way, they're both off chasing a non-existent dragonette into the dark tunnels below the kitchen. And they won't raise the alarm yet either – they're desperate to catch them before anyone important finds out they're missing.'

Even though Jack felt relieved he didn't slow his pace. They still had to get the two dragonettes safely back to Glasruhen.

INSIDE INFORMATION

They moved as quickly as they could through the last tunnel. Jack couldn't hear anything except the fluttering of wings and the shuffling of his and Camelin's feet. He felt very relieved when he saw the doorway up ahead. Once they were airborne they'd be safer than in the tunnels. Jack was just contemplating how to open and shut the door when the Dorysk landed on the floor and took on his usual prickly form.

'Allow me,' he said as he turned the doorknob.

When everyone was safely through the Dorysk closed the door. Camelin dropped his sack on the ledge, launched himself off the edge and circled back. His great strong claws grabbed the sack as he swooped past.

'Be easier to fly home like this,' he called to Jack before he flew off into the darkness.

Jack waited until the Dorysk had transformed into a tiny bat and attached himself securely onto his back. He knew grabbing the sack wouldn't be easy and he didn't want to drop Snook. Jack hesitated before taking off. He circled once and as he neared the ledge, stretched his feet out and opened his claws. It wasn't quite as he'd planned but he managed to grab the sack firmly in one foot. As he flew after Camelin he closed his other claw securely around the top. He hoped the flight home wasn't going to be too difficult.

By the time they flew over the ruins of Salchester, Jack was tiring. He'd tried to keep up with Camelin but the distance between them grew longer with each minute that passed. It was a twenty-minute flight back to Ewell House from here. If he couldn't keep up, at least he knew his way home; the landscape below was very familiar now. He was unbelievably tired and he was worried – he needed to be at his best for tomorrow's dress rehearsal.

Each beat of his wings got harder and harder. His head jerked. For a brief second he'd fallen asleep. He felt the sack slipping and tightened his claws. It was no use, he was going to have to stop and rest. He scanned below to find somewhere to land. A familiar voice made him jump and for the second time he nearly lost his grip on the sack.

'What's wrong?' called Camelin. 'I thought you were right behind me.'

'I'm so tired, I couldn't keep up,' Jack managed to call back.

It was then Jack realised that Camelin didn't have his sack. He was suddenly very wide awake.

'Where's Norris?'

'Safe at Ewell House. I thought I'd better come find you. See that haystack down there? Drop your sack on the top. I'll take it from here and meet you back in your room. I bet I can beat you back.'

Jack didn't doubt Camelin would be there first. He'd no energy left to even contemplate racing. He followed Camelin and flew low over the haystack. When he was directly over it he gently dropped his sack on the top. Moments later Camelin was flying back towards Ewell House with Snook's sack securely in his claws. Jack found it much easier flying without the sack. He felt lighter and was able to fly faster. The welcome sight of Grandad's house and his bedroom window were soon before him. As they approached the end of the forest the Dorysk detached himself from Jack's back.

'I'll be off now, but remember, if I can be of service you only have to ask.'

'I will. Thank you for everything you've done tonight.'

Jack yawned deeply and nearly misjudged his landing.

'What took you so long?' said Camelin as Jack skidded to a halt on the windowsill.

Jack was too tired to reply. Once they'd transformed Jack could feel every muscle in his body aching. He struggled into his pyjamas and fell into bed.

Jack heard his name being called, from what seemed like a long way away. He wasn't awake enough to work out what was being said. When it stopped he could feel himself drifting back to sleep. A loud knock on his door made him sit up with a jolt. 'Come on Jack or you'll be late. I've been calling you for ages, are you up?'

Jack swung his feet out of bed.

'Sorry, I won't be long.'

Jack felt awful. He could hardly focus and he knew that if he closed his eyes, even for a second, he'd fall asleep again. Maybe he could find a *Staying Awake* spell in his Book of Shadows. He reached for his wand but it wasn't there. He looked under the bed, on the table and behind the curtain. Then he remembered – he'd dropped it into the sack. Was that why Camelin had been so helpful last night? He wasn't going to be able to find out until after school. It was going to be a long day.

'How was the rehearsal?' asked Grandad when Jack got home.

'Awful. I think it was the worst I've ever sung.'

'Not to worry, I'm sure it'll be perfect for tomorrow afternoon's performance.'

'But what if I don't sing well tomorrow either?'

'Nonsense you'll be fine, you'll see.'

Jack was grateful his Grandad had faith in his

singing. Maybe after a good night's sleep he'd be fine. He could hardly tell Grandad why he hadn't been able to do his best.

'Can I go to Ewell House and leave a note for Nora? She's going to be back later tonight.'

'That's fine, there's no need to feed the birds, I did it earlier. Dinner's at six.'

Jack didn't even bother to change out of his school clothes. He went straight down to the bottom of the garden and made his way through the tunnel to Nora's. He wasn't sure what he was going to say to Camelin but he needed to get his wand back. There was hardly a sound from the garden. He couldn't hear Gerda or Medric and Camelin wasn't anywhere to be seen. When he peeped into the cave behind the rockery there was no sign of Saige either. It was only as he neared the open patio doors that he heard squeaky voices. Without his wand he'd no idea what was being said. He wondered if Nora was already home.

'Anyone there?' he called.

The voices stopped and Motley came scurrying onto the patio and began squeaking at him.

'Hold on a minute, I've got to find Camelin and get my wand.'

'We're in here, come on in, your wand's on the

table,' Camelin called from inside the kitchen.

Motley followed him in and scurried onto the table where the rest of the Night Guard sat.

Jack picked up his wand and looked Camelin in the eye.

'You tried it didn't you?'

'Oh that's nice after I cleaned it for you, it was covered in marinade. You don't have to worry. It only works for you so you won't have to go telling Nora anything.'

Jack smiled. He wondered if Camelin had spent most of the day trying to get his wand to work. He looked over at Motley who didn't look at all happy.

'What's wrong?'

'Oh Jack, we've been waiting for you to arrive, such terrible, terrible news and we don't know what to do.'

'What kind of news?'

'Not good,' said Camelin.

Jack sat down at the kitchen table. In the middle were the two lanterns each with a dragonette still inside. They looked almost identical to Charkle with their purple wings and green shiny scales. The only difference Jack had noticed the night before was that the tip of Snook's tail had a sharper point but now they were clean he could see Norris was a paler shade of green. They both bowed to Jack. Norris began speaking before Motley could continue.

'How can we ever thank you enough?'

'They'd have eaten us for sure,' added Snook.

Jack looked at the two little dragons. He wished Nora was here, she'd have had them out of their prisons in no time.

'Are you both alright? I thought you might still be covered in marinade.'

Camelin coughed.

'I helped to get them clean.'

Jack gave him a disapproving look.

'Before you say anything, I took the lanterns down to the lake and they had a wash. Waste of a good marinade if you ask me but there was no other way to get it off.'

'Everyone's been so kind,' said Snook. 'And Camelin told us how he rescued Charkle, it was so brave of him.'

Norris nodded.

'It'll be wonderful to see him again. Camelin says he's a bat now so he can fly around without anyone knowing he's a dragonette. Do you think Nora will let us stay? Maybe she could turn us into bats too.'

'Of course she'll let you stay,' said Jack, 'and I know Charkle will be overjoyed to see you both. As soon as they're back you'll be able to have your freedom.'

Motley coughed loudly.

'Aren't you forgetting something Jack? We've had some most distressing news, most distressing. Needs immediate attention, don't you know.'

'I'm sorry, what's wrong?'

Motley walked over to the lanterns.

'These two here have valuable inside information but it's not good news, not good at all.'

Jack looked at the dragonettes then back at Motley and then at the rest of the Night Guard. No one spoke.

'Will someone explain?'

'Too upsetting for any of us to say,' replied Motley and promptly went over to the rest of the rats and sat down next to Raggs.

Jack looked at the dragonettes.

'Camelin asked us about the monster, you know, the train,' began Snook. 'It runs from the top of Stonytop to the bottom of Silver Hill but it doesn't have an engine, it rolls down its own tunnels until it comes to a stop at the terminus.'

'How does it get back up without any power?'

'Bright boy, bright boy,' interrupted Motley.

Norris sighed before continuing.

'The last carriage is a cage and it's full of what the Spriggans call *pullers*. Once all the passengers are off they harness them to the back of the last carriage and they pull the train all the way back to the top of the other hillside.'

Jack tried to visualise the distance between Silver Hill and the crags.

'That's a long way to haul a train. How big are the pullers?'

Snook looked at Motley before answering Jack.

'The *pullers* are rats, the strong ones. All the small or weak ones go for *eaters*.'

Fergus and Berry gasped and the rest of the Night Guard winced.

'That's awful!' said Jack. 'We've got to do something to help them.'

'We're not going back to Silver Hill again tonight are we?' groaned Camelin.

'No, not tonight, but I'm sure when Nora gets back she'll think of a way we can rescue them. As you say Motley, Norris and Snook will have lots of valuable inside information. I'm sure between us we'll be able to help them.'

'Wait till you hear why the train was full of Hags,' chuckled Camelin.

Jack gave him a look. It didn't seem right to be having a laugh when the rats were so upset. Jack looked at the two dragonettes.

'I'd forgotten about the Hags,' said Timmery. 'There were lots in the train we saw.'

'Hags have been coming into Silver Hill over the last two days,' explained Norris. 'The train's been going up and down every hour. There are two passenger carriages and the last one's where the r…'

'Yes, yes, yes, we know what the last carriage is full of,' interrupted Motley.

'So how many come down from the crags at a time?' asked Jack.

'Eight,' croaked Saige as she hopped out from behind Nora's umbrella stand.

'I wish she wouldn't do that,' complained Camelin. 'You never know where or when she's going to turn up.'

Jack did a quick calculation.

'That's a lot of Hags. I didn't think they liked each other's company. Why would they be visiting the Spriggans?'

'It's for the banquet, for the *Candleless Feast*, the one they were going to roast us at,' explained Norris. 'They're celebrating because they don't need candles any more.'

Snook picked something up from the bottom of his lantern and tossed it through the bars towards Jack.

'All the main tunnels have these. It's because of the

new lights that we aren't needed any more, they never go out, not like the candles used to.'

Jack picked up the crystal. It looked familiar but he couldn't think where he'd have seen anything like it before, apart from the tunnels inside Silver Hill.

'And the Hags?'

'They're the choir,' said Norris. 'They're going to sing at the banquet. We've heard them. They make a dreadful noise.'

Jack wondered what the little dragonettes would say if they heard Camelin sing but now wasn't the time to mention it, his own singing hadn't been too good either today.

'If they're having a banquet, why didn't they use you two to help barbecue the food?' asked Jack.

'No need,' replied Snook, 'they've got a barbecue pit in the big cave at the bottom of the mountain. They wouldn't have much use for us two when there's a dragonair down there.'

'You mean the legend's true? There really is a big dragon at the bottom of Silver Hill?' asked Jack excitedly. 'The dragon must be *the big one* the Spriggans were talking about.'

Norris nodded and shook his wings till he was comfortable.

'It used to be known as Howling Hill but that was a very long time ago. When the Spriggans first captured the dragonair it used to roar and stomp around. It used to make the whole mountain shake. I heard one of the Spriggans laughing once and saying it kept the *nosies* away. He meant people.'

'Or Bogies,' suggested Camelin.

Norris and Snook exchanged looks.

'There's a Bogie moved in not so long ago. They wouldn't normally let one in but this one's been getting them things they need in exchange for gold. He's the one who showed them where to get the crystals from,' explained Snook. 'They call him *Pig Face* behind his back.'

'We know who that is, his name's Pyecroft,' said Jack. 'We've had dealings with him before.'

'He's been doing a lot of bossing about recently and there's a lot of Spriggans down there don't like him,' explained Norris.

'I wonder if Peabody knows where his brother's living?' said Jack.

Motley coughed to get everyone's attention.

'Podge, your report please, speak up now lad so we can all hear.'

The roundest rat, with the darkest fur and longest tail stood up. He took a couple of steps towards Jack before speaking.

'I've been watching the area northwest of Ewell House, commonly known as Newton Gill Forest. Nothing suspicious to report; Peabody's been home for weeks and hasn't left the forest. He's not had any visitors either.'

Jack nodded to Podge before speaking to the Night Guard.

'I'm sorry but I'm not going to be able to do anything tonight, I've got to go now. We'll just have to wait until Nora gets back. She'll know what to do but I promise I'll help you rescue the rats in Silver Hill.'

Camelin let out a great sigh.

'I suppose that means I'll be helping too.'

Jack smiled.

'I suppose it does, but that shouldn't be too hard for a brave raven like you.'

For once Camelin didn't reply. Jack got up and stood by the kitchen door, everyone except Camelin waved goodbye to him. Jack walked down to the hedge alone. He wasn't too worried if Camelin was annoyed with him, it meant he'd at least get an undisturbed night's sleep. Jack ran all the way back to Grandad's house.

NEWS FROM ANNWN

Jack woke to sunshine streaming through his open curtains. He'd been so tired he'd forgotten to draw them before falling asleep. He remembered telling Grandad he needed an early night and lying down on the bed but that had been last night and now it was morning. He squinted at his clock. It was nearly six o'clock. Grandad wouldn't be up for at least an hour. Jack took a deep breath and let it out slowly. He'd not had time, over the last couple of days, to stop and think. Everything had happened so quickly. He wondered if Nora and Charkle were back, if they were they'd already know that Norris and Snook were safe. Jack smiled. He wished he could have seen Charkle's face when he saw his brothers again. Jack went over to the window and looked out at the trees surrounding Ewell House. He stood lost in thought for a few moments and was just about to go back to bed when a high-pitched squeak above his head made him look up.

'Timmery?'

Jack grabbed his wand and came back to the window in time to see a long tail with a pointed end unfurl from the upside down bat.

'Charkle! When did you get back? Have you…'

'I come to thank you, to thank you from the bottom of my heart. My brothers send their thanks too.'

'You need to thank Camelin, Timmery and the Dorysk too, without them we'd never have rescued Norris and Snook. Have you had a chance to speak to your brothers yet?'

'Not really, we got back this morning at first light. Nora's released Norris and Snook from the lanterns and they're sleeping now. She didn't want me to disturb them. She said we'd have lots of time later to catch up but I couldn't wait to come and thank you. Nora said it would be alright as long as I didn't wake you, she said you'd probably be exhausted. She knows all about the rescue and how brave you've all been. Everyone's asleep now so I came over to wait until you got up.'

'Was it Camelin's version of the rescue that Nora heard?'

'Partly, but Timmery was there too and so were the Night Guard so Nora knows everything that's happened since she's been away. I couldn't believe my eyes when we got back and saw Norris and Snook on the table. Thank you so much Jack Brenin, you truly are a friend to us all.'

Jack didn't know what to say. He didn't want to change the subject but he desperately wanted news of Elan.

'So what's the news from Annwn?' he said as casually as he could.

'Oh Jack, they've got an awfully big problem, bigger than even Nora, Elan, Gwillam and the whole Blessed Council can solve.'

'What kind of problem?'

'A desperate one. Nora summoned me to try to melt a hole into the ice sheet, the one that seals the front of the Caves of Eternal Rest. Do you remember when we went and looked at the caves when we were in Annwn?'

Jack nodded.

'I don't understand. Why would they need a hole in the ice?'

'Gwillam's been dream messaging with Mortarn, the Gatekeeper of the caves. Most of the Druids want to be woken so they can help the Queen put Annwn to rights. Gwillam arranged for the Blessed Council to meet and perform the wakening ceremony.'

'Wakening ceremony? That's a lot of Druids to waken at once.'

'They use a ritual to awaken the Gatekeeper first. He then goes and turns the big diamond-shaped crystal, it's the key to the caves and melts the ice that seals the entrance. Once the cave is open the Druids can be woken. The ones who wish to leave can, and those who wish to remain sleep again when the cave is resealed. The Gatekeeper can never leave the caves. He has to stay there for eternity.'

'That still doesn't explain why you needed to make a hole in the ice.'

'When the Blessed Council got to the cave entrance it was so dim inside they could hardly see anything. They couldn't wake the Gatekeeper and nothing they did would unseal the entrance. They're all very worried. Something dreadful must have happened for the light to fade.'

'Is that why Nora left for Annwn in such a hurry?'

'It is. Elan tried to help but none of her magic was strong enough. She thought if everyone tried together they'd be able to at least make a hole in the ice and let some air in.'

'But isn't there plenty of air inside the cave?'

'There was when the crystals were working properly. They not only give out light but they also keep the Druids alive. Without the light from the crystals the cave will become a tomb. That's why Nora needed me to try to melt the ice. Even a little hole would have helped but it was impossible. The magic seal is too strong. Unless Mortarn wakes and turns the crystal key all the sleeping Druids inside the caves will die.'

'That's terrible. Do you think if you went back with Norris and Snook you might be able to melt the ice? Three dragons breathing fire together would be better than one.'

'I already suggested that to Nora this morning but she says we're going to need a much bigger dragon.'

'I know where we can find a bigger dragon.'

'I presume you mean the one inside Silver Hill.'

'Yes. Does Nora know about it?'

'She does now. She's waiting till Norris and Snook wake up so she can get as much inside information as possible. Camelin wasn't pleased when Timmery suggested we rescue the dragon but Nora seemed to think it was a good idea.'

'Rescue a dragon,' laughed Jack. 'It used to be the other way round. Knights would fight a dragon to rescue a princess, I've never heard of a dragon being rescued before.'

'Oh yes you have. We dragonettes were rescued and will be forever grateful.'

'Let's hope the big dragon will be grateful too, it isn't going to be easy. I've read Nora's book about Dragon Lore and dragonairs are notoriously bad tempered. They used to roast people first and never bothered to ask any questions. They're very partial to barbecued human.'

'But they wouldn't roast another dragon.'

'How do you know?'

'Dragons can smell another dragon from quite a distance away. I told you I could smell dragon's breath through the doorway in Silver Hill.'

'Dragon's Breath! I helped make a cauldron-full for Nora. She said we'd need all the help we could get if we were going to look for dragons but I thought she meant dragonettes.'

'She did, but it'll work just as well for big dragons.'

Jack felt dizzy; he went and sat on the bed. He'd

read all about dragonairs so he knew what they'd be dealing with. Nora would too. If they were relying on the potion he'd made, to protect them from the dragon in Silver Hill, he hoped he'd made it right. If he hadn't they'd be in trouble. Charkle flitted into Jack's room and fluttered around his head.

'Are you alright? You don't look too good.'

'I'm fine but I've got to get ready now, it's the concert this afternoon. I expect Nora's forgotten. I really wanted her to come but she's got enough to do.'

Before Charkle could answer Grandad's alarm started ringing. Charkle fluttered around Jack's head one last time before heading for the open window.

'We'll see you later Jack.'

'Yes, see you later.'

Jack's head was spinning. He needed to concentrate on the concert, dragons and druids were going to have to wait until later but no matter how he tried he couldn't put them out of his mind. A knock on his bedroom door made him jump.

'Oh good, you're up,' said Grandad as he poked his head round the door. 'Here's your white shirt and bow tie for the concert, now mind you don't get them dirty, come down and have your breakfast first before you get dressed.'

'I'll be down in a minute,' Jack said.

He needed a moment to steady his legs.

Jack could feel his stomach churning as he stepped out of the school hall and led the rest of the choir towards the stage that had been set up underneath the trees at the back of the field. He held his back straight, as his teacher had asked, and walked with confidence even though he felt very nervous. The dress rehearsal had been a disaster and the fear of not being able to sing his best was worrying him badly. When he passed the front row of visitors he saw his Grandad. The smile on his face helped, and the reassuring nod he gave Jack made him feel a lot better, but the seat where Nora should have been sitting was empty. Jack wished she could have come but he understood why she'd not been able to make it. He scanned the trees but there was no sign of Camelin either.

Once the choir was seated the orchestra arrived and positioned themselves in front of the stage. The head teacher stepped out and welcomed everyone and then came the three taps of the teacher's baton on the music stand that was the cue to begin. The orchestra played four pieces. Jack knew they'd only got one more to play before it was his turn. His solo was sung unaccompanied at the beginning of the choir's performance. He began to feel hot under the collar. He wasn't used to wearing a bow tie but he couldn't loosen it, they'd all been told not to fiddle with them. As the audience applauded the orchestra's performance, Jack saw Nora walking around the side of the seating. She sat down next to Grandad and gave Jack the most welcome smile he'd seen in a long time. From the corner of his eye, in the tree by the school gate, he saw Camelin and next to him on either side sat four small birds. As he watched, a fifth bird fluttered down onto the branch and joined them. Now Jack knew he could sing his best because he'd be singing for his friends. He wanted the Gnarles in Newton Gill Forest and the Dryads to hear him too.

As soon as the applause died down and the choir stood, Jack stepped forward. He hit the first note perfectly and the sound of his voice rang, as clear as a bell, towards the forest. He knew the trees were listening, he could see their branches swaying, even though there wasn't any breeze. He sang as well as he could for all his friends and when he reached the very last note a great sense of pride swelled up inside him. For once he'd done something special on his own, without using magic or relying on Nora. The applause was deafening. The teacher had to wait until everyone was quiet before the rest of the concert could proceed. Jack sang like he'd never sung before. It was a wonderful feeling.

The concert finished with the orchestra playing and the choir and the whole school singing together. Most of the audience joined in too. The head teacher thanked everyone for coming and Jack led the choir back to the hall to another round of rapturous applause. He couldn't wait to see Nora. As soon as they were dismissed he ran across the field to Grandad. Nora wasn't there. He glanced up at the tree. Camelin and the other small birds had also disappeared. He felt very disappointed but didn't want Grandad to notice.

'Did you like it?' he asked.

'Like it? I loved it, you sang beautifully. I told you it'd be alright didn't I.'

Jack nodded. His heart was beating fast and he couldn't tell if it was from running or excitement.

'Did Nora enjoy the concert too?'

'Of course she did, she's invited us both for tea. I'll come in for a cuppa but I've got to get back and start watering the plants. You can stay as long as you like and we'll have a bit of supper later if you're hungry.'

'That would be nice,' said Jack.

It was a beautiful afternoon and they walked the short distance to Nora's in silence. Jack was lost in thought. He knew Camelin wouldn't be pleased that he was going to miss out on tea but he couldn't sit at the table with Grandad there. He had so many questions to ask Nora too, but they'd have to wait until they were alone.

'You took your time,' grumbled Camelin once he was allowed back in the kitchen. 'I hoped you'd save me something.'

'There's plenty left,' said Nora. 'Help yourself.'

For an instant Camelin looked shocked.

'You mean I can have what I want, and in any order?'

'You can, just this once, but make sure you mind your manners, I hear you've let them slip a bit while I've been gone.'

Camelin didn't reply. He was too busy sorting out the cheese sandwiches.

Nora turned to Jack.

'You know how grateful we all are, don't you Jack. What you did was very brave.'

Camelin's head shot up.

'I was brave too.'

'So were the Dorysk and Timmery,' added Jack.

Nora smiled and nodded.

'You all were, but you shouldn't have had to do all that on your own. I'm sorry I was gone so long, I think Charkle has told you about our problem in Annwn.'

Nora paused and looked thoughtfully at her teacup.

'I've had a long chat with Norris and Snook. They know the tunnels inside Silver Hill really well. We need a plan to rescue the dragon. A fully grown, fire-breathing dragon will surely be able to melt a hole in the ice sheet.'

'I don't want to have to fly over to Silver Hill again,' grumbled Camelin.

'You won't have to,' replied Nora. 'Next time I'll drive us all there.'

'I think the dragon might be a bit too big to get in the car,' said Jack.

Nora laughed.

'I wasn't thinking of bringing it back here but I believe we have some rats to rescue too. We're going to need all the help we can get.'

'We couldn't have rescued Norris and Snook without the Dorysk and he said he'd help us again any time,' said Jack.

'Help you,' corrected Camelin.

'No,' said a familiar voice from the patio, 'he's going to help us all.'

'Elan,' cried Jack, 'I didn't know you'd come back.'

'I've been gathering some support for our rescue mission at Silver Hill. I've just had a very interesting conversation with the Dorysk. He'll be here later tonight. He's very grateful to you Jack for all your help.'

Jack felt his cheeks reddening.

'It was nothing,' he mumbled.

'You were great this afternoon. I loved your solo,' said Elan.

'But how did you hear it?'

'Didn't you see five little birds sitting with Camelin?'

Jack nodded.

'Nora used a temporary transformation spell, the dragonettes and Timmery were changed into sparrows and the fifth one was me! I wouldn't have missed your solo for the world.'

'I'm really glad you heard it. It's the best I've ever sung.'

'The dryads were impressed too. I've been to see them this afternoon.'

Camelin coughed.

'Don't you think we ought to be sorting out a plan?'

Nora started to clear the table.

'You're right, but thanks to Jack we've got our protection sorted out.'

'Thanks to Jack, thanks to Jack. It's always thanks to Jack. What about all the brave things I've done.'

'From what I hear you refused to help Jack make the potion. If you'd helped I'd be thanking you too,' replied Nora. 'Without Jack we wouldn't have a whole cauldron of Dragon's Breath. It's going to protect us all from being roasted.'

At the mention of the potion Camelin pirouetted and began to cough and choke.

'I'd rather be roasted than drink what's inside the cauldron.'

Nora and Elan started to laugh and Jack joined in too.

'What's so funny, you won't be laughing when you smell it.'

'It's not for drinking! Jack made it into a shampoo, we're going to smear it all over our hair and let it dry. It'll wash off later. Jack can help you get it off your feathers in the bath when you get back.'

Camelin hunched his wings and looked annoyed. Jack presumed he didn't like having a bath.

'Have you any idea why the lights have faded inside the caves?' asked Jack.

'None at all, crystal magic is the most powerful kind of magic, it shouldn't fail. It's almost as if the crystals aren't there any more,' replied Elan.

Jack felt a shiver run down his spine. He suddenly realised why the crystal, he'd taken from the tunnel in Silver Hill, looked so familiar. He stood up quickly and looked around the kitchen. It had to be here somewhere. Everyone was looking at him.

'What's wrong?' asked Nora.

Jack turned to Camelin.

'Where's the light I brought back from Silver Hill?'

'In my loft, where else would it be?'

'What kind of light Jack?' asked Elan.

'It's like a crystal and I think I know where I've seen something like it before.'

'You'd better go and fetch it,' said Nora. 'I think we need to see this light.'

Camelin didn't hurry. He waddled slowly to the door before taking off for his loft. Jack hoped he was wrong but when Camelin returned and dropped the crystal onto the table, a soft light glowed from its centre.

Nora reached over and picked it up.

'Oh my goodness! Look Elan it's the same. How on earth did the Spriggans get hold of this?'

Jack swallowed hard.

'Most of the tunnels inside Silver Hill are lined with them. That's what the Candleless Feast is all about, they don't need candles any more now they've got the crystals.'

Nora looked very carefully at the crystal again before speaking.

'Someone else is behind this. The Spriggans wouldn't have been able to do this on their own.'

Jack remembered the conversation he'd had with Snook.

'The one they call Pig Face has something to do with the lights, he seems to be in charge and he's the one who's organised the feast, it has to be Pyecroft.'

Nora began pacing up and down.

'This is more serious than I thought. How did anyone get in? It can only have been through the Western Portal, the other three gateways haven't been opened yet.'

'Four,' croaked Saige.

Everyone looked at the little frog as she hopped across the kitchen floor. Elan gently picked her up.

'How many portals are there into Annwn?' she asked.

'Five,' croaked Saige.

'She's never wrong,' said Camelin.

'I know,' replied Nora. 'This changes everything.'

Elan looked shocked.

'Why haven't we ever heard of a fifth gate before? We've got to find out where it is and we've got to stop any more crystals from being taken, if we don't, we'll never be able to awaken the Druids. The crystal power keeps them alive. If any more are stolen none of the Druids will ever be able to leave the Caves again.'

'Does that mean we don't have to rescue the Dragon?' asked Camelin.

'Of course it doesn't,' replied Nora. 'We can't leave the poor thing captive and besides we don't have much time. We need to retrieve the crystals and get them back into the Caves of Eternal Rest as soon as possible. The quickest way will be through the ice sheet. We'll still have to find the entrance to the fifth gateway and that isn't going to be easy. Whoever's been taking the crystals obviously knows where it is. Before we do anything else, we need to ask Pyecroft a few questions.'

'He's not going to want to talk to you,' chuckled Camelin.

Nora frowned.

'This isn't a laughing matter. We're going to have to go into Silver Hill and bring him out.'

'Bogienap!' croaked Camelin.

'Precisely,' agreed Nora. 'And it's going to have to be tonight.'

INFILTRATION

'Now let me see,' said Nora as she got out her map and spread it on the kitchen table, 'here's Silver Hill, Winberry Hill, the Westwood Roost and above them is Stonytop Ridge.'

Jack remembered the feeling he'd had the first time he'd seen the crags, and a shiver ran down his spine. Just looking at the map made the hairs on the back of his neck stand on end.

'It's a big place. How are we ever going to find the entrance?'

'You don't need to worry about that Jack, we'll sort this out later tonight,' replied Nora.

'You mean I can't go with you? I want to help. If

we go now I can be back before it's time to go home, Grandad's not expecting me for ages.'

'I'm not sure you'll like what I've got in mind.'

Camelin looked worried.

'Do I have to go?'

Elan frowned at him.

'We'll all go. I agree with Jack, if we go now we can be there before the Candleless Feast begins.'

Jack smiled gratefully at Elan.

'If I go and tell Grandad I might be a bit late, I can get changed and collect my wand at the same time.'

'That's a good idea and by the time you return we'll be ready to go.'

Jack was already on his feet and heading towards the patio door.

'That was quick,' croaked Camelin as Jack stepped through the hedge.

'I ran all the way.'

'You'll wish you hadn't when you find out what they're planning.'

'Whatever it is at least we won't have to fly there and back.'

'We're going to be disguised. As Hags.'

'Hags!'

'I knew you'd be pleased. Nora says that when we find the way in we can pretend we're late for the choir and whoever's in charge at the platform won't worry about four Hags. They'll let us get on the train, and the good thing is, if we all go no one else will be able to get into the same carriage.'

'That's brilliant.'

'It is?'

'Yes, no one will suspect anything.'

'Aren't you forgetting something? We not only have to look like Hags, we have to smell like them too.'

'We do?'

'We do.'

'I hadn't thought of that.'

'Come on, we might as well get on with it.'

Jack followed Camelin back to the house. He could hear the sound of squeaky voices as they neared the kitchen. The Night Guard were sitting at the table talking excitedly to each other. The room went quiet as Jack entered.

'Good,' said Nora, 'let's begin. Norris and Snook

have told me all they know about the Candleless Feast. It's to be held in the great hall, which is roughly in the middle of the hill. The Bogie's room is on the next level down. We need to find Pyecroft and get him into the train before he goes to the feast.'

'But won't the train driver be suspicious if we get back on the train before the feast's started?' asked Jack.

'There isn't a driver,' explained Nora. 'When the train reaches the bottom the rats are harnessed to the rear of the train and they pull it all the way back to the top so it's ready for the next journey down.'

'You mean there won't be a train to catch back,' moaned Camelin. 'We're not going to have to walk all the way to the top, are we?'

'Don't worry, it's all been taken care of,' said Elan.

Motley coughed and stood to attention.

'May I brief the Night Guard?'

Nora nodded. Jack smiled as the rest of the rats stood to attention. Motley walked up and down in front of them a couple of times before he spoke.

'As you know, Nora and I have had a very important meeting. Very important. Tonight we're going on a vital mission. Vital. We're going to infiltrate the ranks of the poor creatures who have been captured.'

Fergus and Berry exchanged looks.

'Are we going too?' asked Berry.

Motley smiled but Fergus and Berry didn't look too happy.

'All the Night Guard are required. Nora will make sure the cage can't be locked again and while the train is in motion, we, the Night Guard, will change places with eight of the captives.'

'You mean we're going to have to pull the train all the way back up the hill and then stay?' squeaked Fergus.

Nora smiled.

'Don't worry. I think we might use a little bit of magic to get the train back to the top. The only pulling you'll have to do will be to the platform on the next level up. Wait for us there, we'll meet you there with Pyecroft. Once we get back to Ewell House we can see what he's got to say for himself. When we know what's going on we'll go back and rescue the rats and dragon.'

'Are you ready?' Elan asked Jack. 'We're going to have to put a temporary transformation spell on both of you before we go. Nora and I can transform when we get there.'

Nora put her hand on her Book of Shadows. The Book opened immediately and the pages flicked rapidly until they found the right spell. Nora read through it once before picking up her wand.

'Ready?'

'Ready,' Jack and Camelin replied.

'*Coverto... diminutus... vetula,*' Nora commanded as she pointed her wand at Jack.

He immediately doubled over and his body began to shrink rapidly. Once he'd reached the same height as Camelin, his nose began to grow. He watched in fascination as his hands changed. He was soon looking at long bony fingers with long claw like nails. Black and purple hair flowed over his shoulders down to the floor. Nora turned and pointed her wand at Camelin.

'*Converto... vetula.*'

Camelin didn't shrink. His beak stayed the same length but changed into a nose. His feathers disappeared as a mass of purple and black hair covered his body.

'Where are my arms?' croaked Camelin as he flapped his wings.

'I'm afraid you're going to have to keep to the shadows, it's only a temporary disguising spell, I can't magic you arms,' explained Nora.

Camelin looked disappointed.

'I've got feet, you'd have thought I'd at least have had some arms.'

'I can give you a wart,' said Jack as he looked at

Nora. 'If I'm allowed?'

'Been memorising spells have you?'

'I had a lot of time when I had chickenpox.'

'What kind of a wart?' asked Camelin.

'It's alright, go ahead, the more authentic we look the better,' said Nora.

Jack picked up his wand and thought about a big wart with a hair growing out of the middle. He visualised it on his nose and repeated the word he'd memorised. The wart appeared from nowhere.

'Oh wow!' said Camelin excitedly, 'I'll have one of them but I want three hairs in mine.'

Jack pointed his wand at Camelin's nose and out popped a wart. Three long hairs stuck out at different angles from the middle.

Camelin shuffled over to the mirror.

'A three hair wart! Thanks Jack.'

'Very convincing,' said Nora. 'Now, I think we'd better get a move on if everyone's ready?'

Motley ushered the Night Guard out of the kitchen and started them marching towards the garage behind Nora and Camelin. Elan picked up some sacks before she and Jack followed the rest.

'What about the Hag smell?' asked Jack.

Elan laughed.

'We'll add that at the last minute when Nora and I transform, it'll be better than having to drive all the way there with it in the car.'

Jack thought that was a good idea. From what he remembered, Hags smelt revolting, but not as bad as the potion he'd made.

Nora parked the car as close to the crags as she could. Jack looked up at Stonytop Ridge, it didn't seem as forbidding as it had the first time he'd seen it.

'Ready everyone?' asked Nora.

'Ready,' they all replied.

The rats scampered on ahead and soon Jack couldn't see them anymore. The ascent wasn't too steep but the sharp fragments of rock that littered the path hurt his feet. Jack remembered the rhyme Timmery had told him. Were these pieces of shattered stone from exploded rocks? Were they being watched? Jack shuddered at the thought and looked around. This part of the hillside was covered in heather and small bushes. Jack recognised the winberries and could see Camelin looking longingly at them.

The landscape changed as they climbed higher. Rocky outcrops jutted from the hillside. Their strange shapes reminded Jack of Finnola Fitch and he was glad Nora and Elan were with them. It wasn't long before they reached the top. Bare craggy rocks, of all shapes and sizes, stretched to the end of the ridge. The last of the day's sun caught the rocks and made them sparkle. Jack turned slowly in a circle, he could see for miles in every direction. He recognized Silver Hill, Winberry Hill and the Westwood Roost, and in the distance, on the horizon, was another familiar sight.

'Is that Glasruhen Hill over there,' he asked Nora.

'It is, but we don't have time to stop and admire the view tonight, we've got an entrance to find.'

Elan gave a long low whistle and the rats came bounding over to her.

'Have you seen anything that looks like an entrance?' she asked.

'Nothing to report,' announced Motley.

'We're going to be hours if we've got to search this lot,' grumbled Camelin.

'What exactly are we looking for?' asked Jack.

'Now that's a good question,' said Nora. 'We don't

really know. Something not too big but not too small; a secret way into the hillside, maybe a hidden door, a concealed tunnel or even a special rock that opens to a touch. We'd better spread out. The sooner we find the entrance the better.'

Jack and the Night Guard started searching on the left hand side, Nora and Elan on the right. When Jack looked up Camelin didn't seem to be searching at all. It looked as if he was heading for a rock that was shaped like a chair.

It was hard work searching with so much hair because it kept getting in the way. He looked over at the rocks where he'd last seen Camelin but he'd disappeared. Maybe he was round the other side? Jack felt a prickling sensation run up and down his spine, something didn't feel right. He made his way over to the strange looking rock and called Camelin's name but he was nowhere to be seen. Jack spun around, he felt nervous and apprehensive.

'Camelin's gone!' he shouted to Nora and Elan. 'He was over here but I can't see him any more.'

Nora and Elan ran over to Jack and the rats scampered after them. They stood and looked at the rock.

'They call this the Devil's Chair, it's mentioned in an old rhyme,' mused Nora.

Sit upon the Devil's Chair,
Sit upon it if you dare,
But if you do you must beware,
For you might vanish into thin air.

'I wonder,' said Elan. 'Maybe it isn't just a silly rhyme.'

'Shall I try it?' asked Jack.

'You'd better let me,' said Nora.

They all held their breath as Nora sat on the rock. Nothing happened except a chilly breeze appeared from nowhere and made Jack's long hair flap around his face. It died down as quickly as it had arrived and everything went quiet apart from a strange sound. It wasn't the wind. It seemed to be coming from beneath Jack's feet.

'Can you hear that?'

A muffled rumbling was definitely coming from below the ground.

'Camelin,' Jack shouted. 'Where are you?'

'I smell brimstone,' said Nora as she sniffed the air around the rock.

She took her wand and pointed it at the chair.

'*Cardea*,' she commanded.

Jack expected the rock to open and reveal an entrance but again, nothing happened.

'Allow us,' said Motley as he ushered the Night Guard onto the seat. 'If there's anything to be found we'll find it.'

The rats scampered onto the chair bottom and began exploring the bumps and cracks in the rock with their front paws and noses. As soon as Motley joined them the rock tilted.

'Watch out!' shouted Nora as the Devil's Chair tipped the rats into the ground.

It happened quickly. One minute they were there, the next they were gone. Jack jumped as the rock swung back into position with a resounding thud.

'Well I never,' said Nora. 'I think we've found our way in.'

'But why didn't it work when you sat on it?' asked Jack.

'I think you'll find it works perfectly well for anyone of Hag size and shape. When Motley joined the rest the added weight probably tipped the balance. I suspect if your feet touch the floor it won't work. Time to transform I think.'

Nora and Elan held their hands up above their heads and began to spiral downwards. When they stopped two grotesque Hags stood next to Jack.

'Now for the finishing touch,' cackled Nora as she

passed a small bottle to Jack. 'Dab some of this behind your ears.'

As soon as Jack opened the top, the smell of rotten eggs and dirty dustbins filled the air. He swallowed hard and put his finger over the top of the bottle, tipped it up and dabbed the foul smelling liquid behind his ears. Nora and Elan did the same.

'We'll do Camelin once we get inside,' said Elan. 'I image he'll complain bitterly. At least he doesn't have to pretend to be bad tempered. He makes a very convincing Hag! I'll go first, just in case there's a problem.'

Elan shuffled over to the rocks and climbed up onto the seat. As soon as she was in the middle the rock tipped.

'Your turn,' said Nora.

Jack braced himself for the fall but as the rock tilted he slid down a short chute.

'You took your time,' grumbled Camelin, and then added, 'eugh! You stink!'

Nora slid to a halt at his feet. Camelin didn't have time to say anything else. In a flash Nora had the bottle out and was dabbing a generous amount of liquid under his chin.

Camelin scowled at her.

'Now, which way?' said Nora as she looked at the two openings in the rock.

Motley pointed to the one on the right.

'The platform's at the end of the tunnel. We've already done a bit of exploring.'

'Well that's saved us time.'

Elan gave Nora a sack.

'Are you ready,' she asked as she opened it.

'Ready,' replied Motley.

Jack watched as four of the Night Guard jumped into the sack Nora held open and four scampered into Elan's. As soon as the rats were safely inside Nora and Elan lifted the sacks carefully over their shoulders.

'Hold tight,' said Nora.

The tunnel wasn't very long. At the end a small platform had been carved out of the rock. Next to the platform stood a small train with three carriages. The first two had seats and the last one held a large cage full of rats. Jack could see how sad they looked. He wondered how long they'd been held captive. He wanted to go over and tell them that everything was going to be alright but he knew it wasn't something a Hag would do. His thoughts were interrupted by a high squeaky voice.

'What yous lot doing? Yous supposed to be down in the hall.'

Jack could see an old Spriggan tethered to an iron ring on the wall. He wondered if he was a prisoner too until he remembered that all Spriggans needed to be secured or they grew to gigantic proportions. Nora started grumbling at the Spriggan in a screechy voice.

'Couldn't make it last night, had to take it really easy, it's daylight out there, didn't want to be seen, had to wait 'til the coast was clear. We're here now so hurry up and let us get on board.'

The old Spriggan shook his head and chittered to himself before opening the first carriage door.

'That won't do, won't do at all,' grumbled Elan. 'I get sick if I sit at the front, open the other door.'

There was more chittering and grumbling as the Spriggan banged the first door shut and opened the second. They pushed and shoved each other to get inside the carriage first. It crossed Jack's mind that Camelin might not be acting. Once they were seated, the Spriggan guard hesitated before closing the door.

'What's yous got in the sacks?'

'Presents for Chief Knuckle,' said Elan.

'Off yous go then,' he squeaked as he went round to the front of the train and started pulling on a rope.

The old Spriggan must have been incredibly strong. He managed to move the large rock that had been acting as a brake in front of the front wheel of the train. Once the rock was gone the train began to move. The movement was slight at first as they slowly rolled forwards. A sudden drop made Jack's stomach lurch. His head hit the back of the seat and he grabbed for the handhold. The train thundered down the tunnels. It swerved round corners and sped over bumps gaining momentum all the time. Jack felt queasy as they were thrown from one side to the other. Tunnel entrances whizzed by. They passed several platforms but the train never stopped, it just hurtled downwards towards its destination.

'Whee!' shouted Camelin. 'This is great!'

Jack felt too ill to answer. He couldn't wait for it to stop so he could put his feet on the ground again.

'We must be nearly there,' shouted Elan.

She wasn't wrong. The tunnel began to level out and as they travelled along a long straight stretch the train began to slow down. Jack was expecting it to roll gently to a halt so he was totally unprepared for the sudden jolt as the train's front bumpers bashed into a solid wall. Two Spriggans, who were roped together, hurried over to the carriage.

'Wasn't expecting any more of yous.'

'Late,' grumbled Nora as she leapt out of the carriage. 'Need to hurry.'

Jack, Camelin and Elan followed. The two Spriggans didn't pay any more attention to them as they busied themselves harnessing the rats to the back of the train.

Jack hoped the Bogienap wasn't going to take too long. It was hot inside the hillside, very hot, and he still felt a bit sick. They made their way up the only tunnel. Nora tutted when she saw the crystals lighting the walls. The soft glow made it easy to see where they were going. Elan opened the sack she was carrying. Jack expected to see the rats jump out but it was empty.

'We might as well collect these as we go,' she said. 'If you can knock them off Camelin, we'll pick them up.

Camelin fluttered up and poked each crystal they passed. They fell onto the soft earth of the tunnel floor and Jack and Elan took it in turns to pick them up. When they reached the end of the tunnel Elan twisted the top of the sack and slung it over her shoulder.

'Come on,' said Nora, 'it can't be too far. I can see some rooms with doors from here. Let's go and find ourselves a Bogie!'

UNINVITED GUESTS

Jack found it difficult to tiptoe down the tunnel. He kept tripping over his long hair. Camelin was having problems too. At least Jack had arms to push the hair away from his face, poor Camelin only had wings and could hardly see where he was going. Jack wondered how they were going to find the Bogie. He watched as Nora put her ear to each door in turn before using her long, Hag-shaped nose to sniff the keyholes. None of the doors were very big but they were all different. When they were halfway down the tunnel Nora stopped outside a faded brown door and pointed to the sign that hung on the doorknob.

'This is it,' she whispered. 'Look!'

A message had been written in untidy capital letters on a tatty piece of cardboard: *DO NOT DISTURB*.

Elan put her ear to the door.

'Someone's inside, I can hear them moving around.'

Nora turned to Jack and Camelin.

'Go back down to the end of the tunnel and keep a lookout. Elan and I will get the Bogie inside the sack and then we'll be on our way out of here.'

Neither Jack nor Camelin spoke as they shuffled back down the tunnel. When they got to the end they stood back-to-back and peered into the gloom. Jack could hear the slow progress of the train being pulled up one of the other tunnels. It would soon be on their level. Everything was going to plan until suddenly a door opened behind them. They didn't have time to turn round. A hand grabbed Jack by the scruff of his neck. He could see Camelin was being held too but he couldn't see who was holding them.

'Skulking or sulking?' a rasping voice asked.

Neither Jack nor Camelin said a word.

'So, sulking it is. There's many won't be pleased if we don't start on time. Up to the great hall with you. The rehearsal's about to begin.'

Jack swallowed hard. The last thing he'd expected was to be singing in another choir quite so soon, especially not a Hag choir. There'd been no time to warn Elan or Nora. They were going to wonder where they were. He hoped that maybe after a couple of songs they'd be free to go, but then he began to worry again as they were pushed along several tunnels. How would they ever find their way back to the platform?

Jack managed to catch a glimpse of their captor. It wasn't a Hag or a Spriggan. It wasn't like any creature Jack had ever seen before. Although it had arms and legs, the creature's face was covered in silvery grey feathers, its beak-like nose and fiery red eyes made it look owl-like and ferocious. Jack and Camelin were suddenly thrust into a huge chamber. A long table ran down the middle with stools, chairs and benches arranged around it. Stag's antlers swung on chains from the ceiling. Each one was covered in candles and as they swayed gently to and fro, the soft candlelight sent shadows around the cavern.

'Over there,' hissed the creature. 'Go and join the rest so we can get started.'

As Jack turned he saw an amazing sight. In the shadows a group of Hags, of all shapes and sizes, were assembled. Many were jostling to try to get to the front but none of them shouted, they all spoke in whispers. Jack nodded towards the owl-man.

'What is it?' he whispered to Camelin.

'A Draygull. Don't tell me you don't know what a Draygull is.'

'No, I don't. Whatever it is, it doesn't look very friendly.'

'It isn't.'

'We need to get out of here.'

'I know but I think we're stuck for a bit, we're not going to be able to just walk out.'

The Draygull produced a long stick and began tapping it noisily on the side of a metal stand. The whole room went quiet.

'You'd better sing your best. This is our last rehearsal...'

The Draygull suddenly stopped and tapped his stick again.

'Enough!' he screeched towards the back row where a scuffle had broken out.

He waited with his stick poised in the air until the Hags were still.

'That's better. Now let us begin. Our first song will be *Creatures of the Deep*.'

'Do you know it?' Jack asked Camelin.

'No, don't you?'

Jack didn't get chance to answer. The most awful sound he'd ever heard filled the hall and echoed around the room. It went on and on for what seemed like an age. Both Jack and Camelin opened and shut their mouths in what Jack hoped were the right places. The baton tapping the metal stand brought the singing to an end. The smell of barbecued food drifted into the great chamber.

'Oooh!' crooned the Draygull, 'won't Chief Knuckle be pleased when he hears that. Music to the ears, you may congratulate yourselves. You'll be singing throughout the feast, which will begin shortly, so go and help yourselves to some food now. You'll find yours on the tables at the back. Don't wander off when you've eaten, and try to keep yourselves looking tidy, no hair pulling or pushing one another around. We want to look our best for Chief Knuckle, don't we?'

Jack wanted to laugh. Not one of the Hags, including himself or Camelin looked neat or tidy. There was a great rush for the back of the room. Camelin began to follow. Jack frowned and pulled him back. This wasn't the time to hang around.

'We've got to go now. We need to get out before the feast begins.'

'But he said we could eat.'

'If you go and eat you'll be trapped in here, besides you haven't got any hands to pick anything up with, remember. I don't know how good our disguise will be when the feast starts, look over there.'

Jack nodded towards the far end of the great hall. Candles had been placed in every available space. Two groups of Spriggans had begun to work their way around the room lighting them. Eventually the great hall would be ablaze with light. Jack watched as they went back and forth to the fireplace with tapers. At least it would take them a while to get round them all.

'We've got to go. Can you remember which way we came in?'

Jack turned around. They'd come through one of the tunnels opposite to where the choir had been standing, but which one?

'Psst!' said a tiny voice in Jack's ear. 'Follow me.'

A small moth, wearing a pair of spectacles fluttered around Jack's head.

'Camelin, look! It's the Dorysk!'

'What's he doing here?'

'Rescuing you two. Come on we haven't got much time.'

The little moth kept to the shadows. Jack and Camelin did their best not to be seen as they followed the Dorysk. He eventually stopped and fluttered around one of the entrances.

'This way.'

Jack and Camelin found it hard to keep up with the little moth on their short legs. He led them through a maze of tunnels. A short darkened tunnel led them to a lighted platform alongside which stood the train. The door of the second carriage was open. Jack could see Elan and Nora in the first and a lumpy sack, tied up with a rope, on the seat opposite them. They leapt into the carriage. As soon as Jack closed the door the train lurched forward. They sped up the tunnels. Jack knew the rats were being assisted by Nora's magic.

'How did you find us amongst all those Hags?' Jack asked the Dorysk who'd already changed into his usual prickly self.

'Easy! I spotted Camelin's three hair wart straight away. The polite Hag with him had to be you!'

Camelin grumbled something Jack couldn't hear.

'We're very grateful to you. We could have been down there forever trying to find our way out.'

A small brown rat scampered onto the seat opposite Jack.

'Please, let me introduce myself, Whortle at your service.'

The little rat bowed low to Jack.

'Pleased to meet you.'

'I'm a *puller* or I was until one of your Night Guard changed places with me. There's more hiding in the sacks. I've got a message for you from Nora. She wants you to carry one of the sacks when we get off the train. It's not far now.'

'But we're nowhere near the top.'

'We're not going to the top. There are platforms all the way along where Spriggans can get off, we're being dropped off at one of them. I'll get back in the sack now, we're nearly there.'

As soon as Whortle was back inside Jack carefully picked it up. He could feel the movement from within as he placed it on the seat opposite. The train began to slow down and soon stopped altogether. They all piled out and shuffled towards a doorway at the end of the platform. The train pulled away and continued its journey to the station at the top. Jack could see Fergus and Berry. They didn't look too happy. He didn't think they'd complain in future about being left out of the important jobs. Nora pulled her wand out before swinging the sack she was carrying onto her shoulder. She waited until the train had gone.

'Everyone alright? Good. Let's not waste any time, we don't know how long it will be until they discover their Bogie is missing. This way.'

As they approached the door Nora took out her wand and sent a single bolt of light into the keyhole. The door swung open.

'Bogie doors are the easiest thing in the world to open,' she said as she shuffled out into the light.

When they'd all gone through the door Nora pointed her wand at the keyhole.

'*Obfirmo*,' she commanded.

The door slammed shut.

'That'll slow anyone down who tries to follow us,' explained Elan. 'They'll need an axe to open it. No key will ever work in that lock again.'

Jack looked up. He was surprised but relieved to see they were at the bottom of Stonytop Ridge. Tall bushes hid them from sight. He could see Nora's car through a gap in the leaves. Nora and Elan put down their sacks and raised their arms in the air. They spiralled upwards and soon shape-shifted back to normal.

'I suppose we have to wait 'til we get home to get rid of all this lot,' grumbled Camelin.

'You will,' agreed Nora. 'Your spell won't wear off for a while but we can at least get rid of the smell.'

Elan passed a small bottle to Jack.

'A couple of dabs behind your ears should help.'

Jack was amazed. Within seconds the revolting Hag smell had disappeared. Elan did her own ears and gave Camelin a good rub under his chin before passing the bottle to Nora.

'Shall we go? I've got a lot of questions to ask our visitor before bedtime.'

There was a muffled protest from the sack that lay on the grass and a lot of wriggling. Nora ignored the complaints as she stood Pyecroft up on his feet and led him to the car.

'So what exactly were you doing here?' Camelin asked the Dorysk.

'An important job for Nora,' he replied before following Elan.

Camelin shuffled ahead. Jack wondered if he was going to try to get more information from the Dorysk but he wasn't sure he'd learn much. Jack and Elan walked back to the car together.

'We were worried about you,' said Elan.

'*I* was worried about us! I didn't like the look of the Draygull, he frightened me.'

'It's a good job we used the Hag smell, Draygulls have an amazing sense of smell and they don't like humans.'

'They can't have very good hearing. You should have heard the Hag choir! I've never heard such a dreadful sound.'

'I'm sure Chief Knuckle will enjoy it, but it might spoil his fun if he finds out they've had uninvited guests tonight.'

'There's something I don't understand; when we were in the great hall the whole cavern was filled with candles. Everyone's been calling it the *Candleless Feast*. It doesn't make sense.'

'Norris and Snook told us all about that. Tonight, the Spriggans are celebrating their new light source. They're burning every candle they have. The feast won't end until the last flame goes out.'

'I see; they'll be *candleless* once they've all gone.'

Nora took the sack from Jack and opened it so the rats could jump out.

'Ready everyone?' she asked.

It wasn't long before the car was on its way back to Glasruhen.

Nora turned into the garage as the last light from the sinking sun disappeared below Glasruhen Hill.

'We'd better transform you so you can get off home,' said Nora.

'Me first,' croaked Camelin as he pushed in front of Jack.

'It's alright,' said Jack, 'do Camelin first.'

'I can't, he's got a temporary disguise spell, which is different to yours. It'll wear off soon enough.'

Camelin humphed loudly before shuffling off, with his shoulders hunched, towards the house.

'He'll be fine in the morning,' said Elan. 'We'll see you tomorrow after school and hopefully by then we'll know exactly what's been going on. I'll take Pyecroft in while Nora transforms you.'

Jack watched as Elan marched Pyecroft into the kitchen. Eight rats scurried around Nora's feet. Jack recognised Whortle as he stood on his hind legs.

'How can we ever thank you? We are very grateful.' Nora smiled.

'When Motley gets back he'll sort you all out. If you've got families to go back to we'll get you there, if not, you're welcome to live here.'

Whortle wiped a tear from his eye.

'I thought we'd end our days in those tunnels, many have before us.'

'You're safe now, make yourselves at home,' Nora

told the rats before turning to Jack.

'Ready?'

'Ready.'

Although he was prepared, the jolt to his body made him jump. He began to stretch and grow while his nose shrank back to normal. He watched as the long claw-like fingers and long nails receded. Finally his spine straightened and he was back to his own body shape again.

'I'm not sure I ever want to be a Hag again.'

'I don't think any of us do. Now, remove your wart and then you can be off, it's getting late. If there's any news I'll send you a message.'

Jack had to squint to see the long hair sticking out from the end of his nose.

'Why didn't it disappear in the transformation?' he asked Nora.

'It was your spell so you need to remove it,' she explained.

Jack took his wand and closed his eyes. He thought hard about the wart no longer being on the end of his nose. A small popping sound told him it was gone.

'Well done,' said Nora. 'Soon you won't need a wand for that kind of magic.'

Jack didn't really understand, he thought he

needed his wand for every kind of magic. He wanted to ask Nora what she meant but it was getting late and he really ought to go home.

Jack ran all the way back to Grandad's. It felt good to be a boy again. He wished he could have stayed to listen to the information the Bogie had about the Caves of Eternal Rest and the stolen crystals but he knew he'd have to wait. He was happy Nora and Elan were back, even if it was only for a short time. He knew they'd have to go back to Annwn to save the Druids. He was glad he wasn't going to have to go back to Silver Hill again in a hurry. As Jack reached the bottom of Grandad's garden he stopped in his tracks. There'd been so much going on he'd forgotten all about the other dragon in Silver Hill, *the big one*, and the Night Guard were inside there now. If he wanted to help rescue them he'd have to go back again, and soon.

THE DAY OF BAD OMENS

Jack's last day at school seemed to last an eternity. His teacher had promised they'd have some fun and although he'd enjoyed the games and quizzes he couldn't wait for the day to be over. His mind was preoccupied with thoughts of the strange owl-like man that Camelin had called a Draygull. The big dragon they had to rescue was worrying him too. He knew it wasn't going to be easy but it was vital if they were to help the Druids.

After lunch he began to wonder about the important job the Dorysk had been doing for Nora and no matter how hard he tried he couldn't stop thinking about the three dragonettes. He'd spoken to them all briefly after the rescue but since then he'd not seen them at all. Jack suddenly realised that all the things he'd been thinking about started with the letter D. It must be an omen. He'd even spread damson jam on his toast while Grandad had been telling him about his double dahlias. He wondered what Camelin would have to say when he told him.

It was a relief when the end of the day finally arrived. He'd be at the secondary school after the holidays, which he really wasn't looking forward to. He wanted to get home as quickly as possible but he had too much to carry to run. He was really happy when he saw Grandad waiting by the school gate.

'Pass me some of your things. I thought you might need a hand.'

'Thanks,' replied Jack as he began to work out the best way to ask Grandad if he could go to Ewell House.

'I had a visitor today, your young friend Elan came to see me.'

'Is she alright?'

'Oh yes, everyone at Ewell House has been invited to a barbecue tonight and they wondered if you'd like to go with them.'

'Could I?'

'You can, but as I explained to Elan, it's the County

Flower Show on Sunday and tomorrow morning I've got to be up nice and early to help with the marquee. Would you mind staying the night? Then it won't matter what time you get back.'

'I'd love to,' replied Jack as he tried to contain his excitement.

'The barbecue isn't 'til later so I've got some doughnuts we can have with a cuppa before you go.'

'Doughnuts!'

'Don't you like doughnuts?'

'I love them, you just surprised me.'

'See you tomorrow night,' Jack called as he set off.

'I'll come along as soon as we've finished but it won't be 'til late, have a good time,' Grandad called back.

Jack turned and waved when he reached the gap in the hedge. He could feel his spine tingling. The leaves brushed against his legs and almost pulled him into the hedge as if they were eager for him to be on his way. As he made his way to Ewell House, Jack tested his memory trying to recall everything he'd read in Nora's

Dragon Lore book. She wouldn't have lent it to him if it hadn't been important. He couldn't wait to hear what they'd got planned. The rescue had to be tonight, the barbecue must be an excuse so he could stay over.

Jack felt slightly disappointed when he stepped into Nora's garden. He'd expected Camelin to be there to meet him but the garden was deserted. The herborium and kitchen were empty too.

'Hello, anyone there?' he called from the patio.

'We're in the library,' Elan shouted, 'come through. Leave your bag, you can take it up later, we've got far more important things to sort out first.'

Jack found his wand and made his way to the library. The first thing he saw as he entered the room was Pyecroft sitting on a chair by the open window. He didn't look at all pleased. His legs were bound to the chair with ivy, which trailed into the room through the window. It was wound around his waist and both arms too. The table was spread with a large sheet of paper and Nora was busy writing. A pile of books stood next to several rolls of paper and the Dragon Lore book was open on top.

'We have a problem,' explained Nora. 'Our friend here has been very helpful but I'm afraid it isn't good news.'

Pyecroft began to struggle at the use of the word *friend*. Another tendril of ivy crept in through the window and wound itself around his chest. Nora looked over at the Bogie and sighed.

'The more you struggle the worse it will be and after what you've told us I can't believe you'd be in any kind of a hurry to return to Silver Hill.'

The Bogie stopped struggling and glowered at Nora but didn't say a word.

'What kind of bad news?' asked Jack.

Nora gestured for him to sit on the chair next to Elan.

'It seems Pyecroft isn't in charge after all, the *Big One* is.'

'That doesn't make sense. How can a big dragon be in charge when it's a prisoner?' asked Jack.

'The Big One isn't the dragon, in fact the Big One has deceived them all into believing he can shape-shift into a wasp whenever he wants and sting them any time he chooses.'

Jack gasped.

'You mean Velindur's inside Silver Hill?'

'He is. It's no wonder there wasn't any news of him. It seems he entered the hill through a keyhole in one of the doors. Once the transformation spell wore off he soon made his presence felt. Pyecroft here had a nice little trade going with the Spriggans in return for a place to live, until Velindur arrived. Now, it seems, he's been turned into Velindur's servant.'

Jack looked over at Pyecroft. He could see his legs shaking beneath the ivy. Velindur must have frightened the Bogie badly.

'Is that how Pyecroft found out about the crystals? Did Velindur tell him?'

Elan nodded and sighed deeply before speaking.

'If only I could have been back in Annwn sooner none of this would have happened. I'm afraid Velindur must have taken advantage of his position when he set himself up as King. In the palace library are many ancient books, which contain all the secrets of Annwn. Knowledge is a powerful thing, especially when you don't possess magic. I suspect Velindur learnt all he could over the years and now he's in a better position than we are. I don't think he made his way to Silver Hill by accident. I think he was looking for it.'

'But why?' asked Jack.

Nora began tapping the table with her wand.

'Do you remember the story about Howling Hill?'

'I do. Timmery thought it might be more than a legend.'

'We think Velindur must have come to the same conclusion. He's probably known for a long time that the dragon inside Silver Hill was real. In the story the dragon guards a priceless treasure, those who've tried to find it have never returned. It looks like the dragons set up their home in front of the tunnel which leads to the fifth gateway. They couldn't have known they were guarding a secret entry into Annwn as well as their own horde of treasure. Velindur knew about the fifth gateway but he couldn't have known about the other inhabitants of Silver Hill. We can only presume that once he'd found the only surviving Dragon tethered, and the gateway open, he set about using the Bogie and Spriggans to further his own ends.'

'Which were?' asked Jack.

Elan sighed again and walked over to the window before answering.

'He wants to destroy the Druids completely. He knows they can't survive inside the Caves of Eternal Rest without the life-giving magic the crystals provide. He knows where the fifth gateway into Annwn is located. He's known all the time. When he swore he'd have his revenge it wasn't a hollow promise, he knew exactly what he was going to do. He must have been overjoyed to find the Spriggans inside Silver Hill and a willing fool to do his bidding. Pyecroft's been paid handsomely for his part in all this with Spriggan gold. They think he found the crystal cave especially for them. It seems they don't like the Bogie but they're grateful to him for the new lights. I doubt even they know they've been part of a bigger plan. Thanks to Pyecroft and the Spriggans, Velindur hasn't had to lift a finger to get his revenge and if we don't act soon he'll succeed.'

Jack didn't know what to say. Nora had been right – the news wasn't good.

'What are we going to do?' he asked.

Nora pointed at the map.

'Tonight, we rescue the dragon. Once we have it outside the hill, Elan and I will take it through the Western Gateway into Annwn. We'll see if its fiery breath can melt the ice sheet. If we could make even the smallest hole we'd be able to save the Druids.'

Elan nodded in agreement.

'Once we've opened the caves, with Cora and Gwen's help, I can put the crystals back. The magic will be replaced and we'll be able to awaken the Druids who wish to return to Annwn. Those who choose to stay inside the caves will once more have an eternal resting place.'

'It's not going to be easy to collect all the crystals,' said Jack, 'they're everywhere inside the tunnels.'

'On the contrary,' replied Nora, 'we've got nearly

all the crystals back already.'

'How!'

'Last night while we were Bogie-napping, Charkle, Norris and Snook, along with the Dorysk, were crystal collecting,' explained Elan. 'The dragonettes are incredibly strong for their size and were able to fly back here with the sacks they'd filled. When the candles finally burn down in the great hall, the whole of Silver Hill will be in darkness.'

Jack smiled.

'That's brilliant. The Spriggans are really frightened of the dark. It'll make it easier to travel along the tunnels when we go in to rescue the dragon. How can Camelin and I help?' Jack looked around. 'Where is Camelin? I haven't seen him yet.'

Nora laughed.

'He's in his loft. He's not been down, not even for his meals. Today is known as the Day of Bad Omens and he seems to think he's been cursed.'

Jack wondered what terrible thing could have happened to make Camelin stay in his loft all day. There was only one way to find out.

'Is it alright if I go and see him now?'

'Of course it is,' said Nora. 'When you've sorted him out come back down and we'll tell you all about our plans for tonight.'

'Hello,' Jack called as he got to the bottom of the ladder that led up to Camelin's loft.

'You can come up but you've got to promise not to laugh.'

'Laugh at what?'

'I've been cursed. I knew when I woke up it wasn't going to be a good day but I didn't think it would be this bad.'

'Nora says it's the Day of Bad Omens,' replied Jack as he poked his head through the hole into the loft. 'Wow! Fergus and Berry really did do a good job!'

There wasn't anything on the floor except the two soft cat baskets that Camelin insisted were *raven baskets* and Jack's beanbag. Camelin was nowhere to be seen.

'Shh! Nora thinks I did it.'

Jack looked in the direction Camelin's voice had come from and could just make out a black shape in the far corner.

'Did you get your wand back?'

'No.'

'Why are you hiding?'

'Hasn't anything strange happened to you at all today?'

'I suppose it did earlier, everything I thought about started with the letter D.'

'Like doom, disaster and destruction?'

Jack laughed.

'You promised you wouldn't do that. Besides what's so funny?'

'I meant Druids, dragons, Draygulls, Dorysks, dragonettes, damson jam, dahlias and doughnuts!'

'Oh!' said Camelin. 'I bet you haven't still got your wart on your nose, have you?'

As Camelin stepped out from the shadows Jack could see why he was so upset. There on the end of his beak was the three-hair wart. Jack had to suck his cheeks in tight to stop himself from laughing.

'It's a punishment, I know it is,' wailed Camelin. 'I've had so many bad omens I shouldn't have been surprised when I saw it.'

'What kind of bad omens?' Jack managed to ask.

'Well, walking under a ladder without realising it.'

'Where did you find a ladder to walk under?'

'I was hungry last night and when the Hag spell wore off I went out for a snack, I didn't know I had this on my beak, no wonder they shooed me off.'

'That's not a bad omen; they only say that to stop people from getting hurt. If you walk under a ladder something could drop on your head.'

'I swallowed a cherry stone too, that's a bad omen; you never know what might happen when you swallow a cherry stone.'

Jack sat down and clutched his sides. Tears ran down his cheeks, he knew if he didn't laugh soon he'd burst.

'You're laughing aren't you? Well it's not funny. How would you like it? How am I ever going to get an extra snack again looking like this?'

Jack swallowed hard and wiped away his tears.

'I can remove it if you like.'

'Can you? Really? Do you mean it Jack? Go and get your wand, but don't tell Nora.'

'No need for the wand,' said Jack as he concentrated hard and imagined Camelin's beak without the three-hair wart. A slight popping sound told him he'd been successful.

'There you are, all gone.'

Camelin shuffled over to his mirror. He examined his beak from both sides then moved his head up and down.

'Run your hand over it Jack, just to make sure it's really gone.'

Camelin hurried back to Jack and let him rub his hand up and down his beak.

'It's gone.'

'Aw Jack, you're a real pal. How did you do that without a wand?'

'It might be because I gave it to you in the first place.'

'But without a wand, that's real magic.'

'I'm sorry, it was my fault.'

'Not to worry, you didn't ask to get all those D-words. I told you it's the Day of Bad Omens, things never go right on those kinds of days.'

Jack hoped it wasn't true. They were going to need all the luck they could get if they were going to rescue the dragon tonight without being barbecued. Jack suddenly realised the *barbecue* had been Nora's way of letting him know they were going to try to rescue the dragon tonight. Jack swallowed hard. Talking and reading about dragons was one thing but knowing he was going to come face to face with a real live one was a scary thought.

'Nora wants us in the library if you're ready,' Jack told Camelin.

'Never felt better. I thought I was stuck with that wart for life.'

Camelin shuffled over to the window.

'See you downstairs,' he cawed as he took off.

When everyone, including the Dorysk and dragonettes, was assembled in the library Nora tapped her wand to gain their attention.

'Tonight we are going into the depths of Silver Hill. Our mission will be dangerous. We're going to attempt to rescue one of the most deadly creatures ever born. If it breathes on any of us with its dreadful flames we'll be barbecued.'

Camelin cocked his head on one side and looked at Jack.

'That's three more *D* words, dangerous, deadly and dreadful, none of them good!'

Nora frowned at Camelin before continuing.

'Luckily Jack has prepared a potion for us. If the dragon smells another dragon it will be curious. It should buy us some time so we can talk to it and hopefully gain its trust. The first thing we need to do is to shampoo our hair with the potion. Charkle, Norris and Snook obviously won't have to.'

'That's not fair,' grumbled Camelin.

'They won't need to,' explained Jack. 'A dragon can tell another dragon by its breath. It can tell what kind of dragon it is too so when it smells Charkle, Norris or Snook it will know they're dragonettes and no threat.'

'How do you know?'

'I read the Dragon Lore book, remember? I did tell you all about it.'

'Is that true?' Camelin asked Nora.

'It is.'

'What kind of dragon are we going to smell like?'

'We're all going to smell like dragonettes. Charkle gave me one of his own scales to go into the potion.'

Camelin leant over and sniffed the little dragonettes and then pulled a face.

Nora ignored him and carried on speaking.

'This is the plan: Motley and the rest of the Night Guard will be there to help us from the inside. We'll all go back to Stonytop Ridge in the car, including Pyecroft.'

'What we taking him for?' grumbled Camelin.

'He's going to instruct the guard to release the train so we can get down to the bottom of Silver Hill without being seen by anyone.'

'And he's just going to stand there and do that for us?'

'Release the train,' said Pyecroft grumpily.

Everyone looked at the Bogie who began to wriggle again.

'What do you think?' asked the Dorysk. 'Think it will fool the old Spriggan?'

Camelin's beak fell open.

Nora smiled.

'Our friend, the Dorysk, has many talents. He can mimic anyone's voice.'

'That's not fair,' said the Dorysk in Camelin's grumbling tone.

'That's not fair,' Camelin mumbled back.

'When you've quite finished,' said Nora. 'I've put a silencing spell on Pyecroft. It will be dark in the caves and I don't think the old Spriggan will be able to see if his lips aren't moving. Once we get to the bottom of Silver Hill, we'll need to get out on the other side, opposite the platform. I'll use a sleeping spell on the two Spriggans at the bottom. The last few crystals we

235

need to collect are on the walls by the platform and we mustn't forget the ones from the front of the train. Motley and the Night Guard should see to that. We'll find the dragon in the barbecue pit. It's not far from the platform.'

'Barbecue pit!' said Camelin excitedly.

Norris flitted over to Camelin.

'The Spriggans have long metal rods. They put the food on the end and hold it out for the dragon to breathe fire over it.'

'Why would it do that?' asked Camelin.

'Because three more Spriggans go round to the other end and give it a good prod. The dragon gets angry and out come the flames.'

Camelin must have been satisfied by the answer because he didn't ask anything else.

Nora looked at everyone in turn.

'No one is making you go tonight. If you don't want to you don't have to.'

No one spoke, not even Camelin.

'Good. Our plan, once we get into the barbecue pit, is for Norris, Snook and Charkle to try to communicate with the dragon and persuade it we're there to help it. We need to find out how it's tethered and if it knows a way out. I'll use my wand to release it and then we'll make our getaway. The dragonettes and Timmery, Camelin and Jack can all fly after the dragon. Elan and I will transform so we can fly too. The Dorysk and rats will need to climb onto the dragon's tail. It will be able to carry them all to safety. Let's hope it's willing to help us. Once we get out we'll head for Glasruhen Gate. Is everyone clear what we've got to do?'

Everyone nodded.

'Let's go and use the shampoo. Rub it all on but don't rinse it off,' explained Elan as she gave Jack and the Dorysk a small bottle each. 'It will be dry by the time we get back inside Silver Hill.'

Elan held out her arm for Camelin.

'Do you want to go first,' she asked.

He hopped onto Elan's arm without answering but once he was there he hunched his wings and scowled.

'I'll do yours Timmery,' said Nora.

Before they left the library Elan smiled at everyone in turn.

'Thank you, Annwn and the Druids will be eternally grateful.'

DRAGON'S BREATH

Jack collected his bag and went up to his room. He could hear Camelin grumbling from the kitchen as Elan applied the shampoo to his feathers. Jack held the bottle up to the light and examined the contents before taking the stopper out. It didn't smell as bad as it had before but it was still green. The potion didn't run out of the bottle when he tipped it, so he shook it hard. Thick green goo splattered into his cupped hand. It felt cold as he began rubbing it into his hair. It had a smoky tinge to it and reminded him of fireworks and bonfires. When he looked in the mirror he laughed. His hair was green all over and stood up in spikes. It reminded Jack of an unripe conker shell. Streaks of the green goo had run down his face.

He was going to wash it off when he had a better idea. He rubbed his gooey hands all over his face and spread the potion up his arms too. This was like camouflage, or maybe dragonflage would be more accurate.

'Eurgh! What have you done?' croaked Camelin as he walked into the library.

Jack looked at Camelin. He obviously hadn't seen himself in the mirror. His beautifully groomed glossy black feathers were covered in green goo. Nora and Elan looked strange too. Everyone laughed except Camelin and Pyecroft.

'I think we ought to get going,' said Nora. 'Let's hope nobody sees us!'

Camelin was about to take off when Nora stepped in front of him.

'I'm afraid you're going to have to walk to the garage, no flying until the potion's dry, I don't want you flapping it off, that includes you too Timmery. It's for your own good.'

Camelin hunched his wings and shuffled towards the door.

'Now,' continued Nora, 'Norris, Charkle and Snook have gone on ahead. Jack, can help Elan with Pyecroft, Timmery will have to go with the Dorysk and I'll drive.'

'Where is the Dorysk?' asked Jack.

A large green frog, too big to be Saige, hopped into view.

'Ready when you are,' said the Dorysk. 'I thought the green skin would blend in with the potion, and besides, the shampoo wouldn't stick to my spikes.'

Timmery climbed onto the frog's back.

'Ready?' asked Nora.

'Ready,' they all replied.

No one spoke as Nora drove along the winding roads towards Stonytop Ridge. Jack's heart was pounding in his chest and he wondered if any of the others felt as nervous as he did. He'd read Nora's book and had every reason to feel apprehensive. Dragons could be dangerous, even dragonettes if they were threatened, and the one they were trying to rescue had been a prisoner for a very long time. Jack didn't think it would be very friendly and it had no reason to trust any of them. Nora hadn't said anything about what would happen to the dragon after they'd got it back to

Annwn. What if the dragon let them release it and then it refused to go with Nora and Elan? They wouldn't be able to force it to go anywhere it didn't want to. Jack hoped it would be grateful for being rescued and be willing to help. Unfortunately there hadn't been anything in Nora's book about kind-hearted dragons. Most of the big ones seemed to be bad tempered or vicious, or both. The one thing he remembered above all, and something the book had left him in no doubt about, was that all big dragons were ferocious.

When Stonytop came into view, Pyecroft began to struggle.

'I wouldn't do that,' Elan told him. 'You don't want to be bound again do you?'

Pyecroft made a strange grunting noise.

Nora pulled off the road and stopped the car. Before she got out she turned round and looked directly at Pyecroft.

'I expect you to behave or I will never forgive you. When you're sorry for everything you've done, come and find me and I'll restore your voice. Until then you can keep the grunt, it goes with your nose.'

Pyecroft glowered at Nora.

'What will happen when Velindur finds him?' asked Jack.

'I'm hoping he thinks he's transforming slowly into a pig. At least he won't be able to tell Velindur anything.'

'He could write it down,' said Jack.

'Hmmm! Let me see,' said Nora as she aimed her wand at Pyecroft's hands. There was a crackle and a flash as the Bogie's hands transformed into two pig's trotters. 'That should solve that little problem. Shall we begin? I do believe we have some help waiting for us.'

They made their way to the top of the ridge with Pyecroft walking obediently in front of Nora. Every so often he turned and looked suspiciously at her wand. Jack was in no doubt that Pyecroft would take on more and more of the attributes of a pig if he didn't do as he'd been told.

Jack found it easier walking on the small shards of rock this time because he was wearing his trainers. A thought hit him like a thunderbolt. Trainers! What was going to happen to them and his clothes when he transformed? The last thing he wanted to do was to come back for them. It was then that he also realised that they were going to have to fly all the way back to Glasruhen. Again.

'Elan,' he whispered so Nora wouldn't hear, 'how are we going to get our things back home. Like my clothes and trainers?'

'Don't worry, we've thought of that. The last of the crystals are going into a sack. Anything else that needs to go back can go in there with them. One of the dragonettes can carry it back to Glasruhen. We'll leave your clothes by the standing stones. Once you transform you'll have to walk back to Ewell House. We won't have time to wait for you at the Western Gateway – Nora and I have to return to Annwn as quickly as we can.'

Jack felt relieved. It wasn't long before he could see the Devil's Chair up ahead.

'Time to transform,' said Nora.

Jack and Camelin touched foreheads. The blinding flash brought the Bogie to his knees. He shook his head several times. While he was temporarily blinded Nora put Jack's clothes and trainers into the sack before she and Elan raised their arms above their heads and began to spiral downwards. Jack was eager to see what they were going to change into. He was very surprised when two more ravens appeared once the spiralling had stopped. They all looked the same as Camelin. The dragon's breath potion had set and made their green feathers stick up in a strange way. Timmery flitted over and attached himself to Nora's back.

'Now you,' Nora said to the Dorysk.

Jack watched as the Dorysk closed his eyes and squeezed them shut. A loud *pop* followed and the Dorysk transformed into a beautiful green moth.

'Are you ready?' Nora asked Pyecroft.

The Bogie grunted.

One by one they sat on the Devil's Chair and disappeared into the hillside. Nora was the last to slide down the chute.

'Let's go and rescue ourselves a dragon,' said Nora before grabbing the end of her wand in her beak and pulling it out from under her wing. 'We'll just make this look a bit more convincing.'

From nowhere a rope twirled around Camelin's neck, then Jack's, Elan's and finally Nora's. The end came to rest in the Bogie's hand. She hid her wand again and they shuffled down to the end of the platform.

The old Spriggan was asleep and woke with a jolt.

'What's yous doing here? Aren't yous supposed to be at the feast?'

'More food for the barbecue,' the Dorysk replied for Pyecroft. 'I was sent out to find something special for Chief Knuckle.'

'They looks a bit off to me. Never seen green birds that big before.'

'Something special they asked for so something special they got. Been basted already, just need to get them down to the pit for barbecuing,' replied the Dorysk.

Pyecroft added a grunt and a bit of a moan on the end but the old Spriggan didn't seem to notice. He'd already opened the first carriage door.

'Squash up yous lot.'

'Release the train,' the Dorysk shouted.

The large rock scraped as the Spriggan pulled it from under the wheel. The train began to roll and they were on their way. Jack braced himself for the sudden lurch. It wasn't as bad when you knew it was going to happen. He could see Camelin was enjoying the ride again. The four of them were tightly packed onto one seat so they didn't get bumped around too much. Pyecroft wasn't so lucky; he sat opposite on his own and was thrown from one end of the seat to the other as the train sped along the tunnels. When it began to slow down Jack knew they'd almost reached the end. He braced himself for the sudden thump as the train's bumpers, once more, hit the solid rock. Pyecroft was unprepared for the jolt and was thrown onto the floor of the carriage. He looked crossly at the Spriggan who came over and opened the door.

'What's all this then? Them green birds don't looks too good to me.'

'Barbecue food,' replied the Dorysk.

'Other side then, yous going to have to open your own door,' the Spriggan told Pyecroft.

Once the Spriggan had turned away Nora pulled out her wand.

'*Somnus*,' she whispered.

The Spriggan staggered and then collapsed onto the platform. Before he landed he was snoring. The other Spriggan he was roped to felt the jolt and spun around quickly. Nora pointed her wand again. The second Spriggan pirouetted then landed with his head on the other Spriggan's chest and he too began snoring loudly.

As soon as Nora stepped out of the train she put her wings above her head and Elan did the same. They spiralled upwards and transformed into their usual form.

'Now you Jack,' said Nora, 'it will be easier if you've got hands.'

Elan opened the sack and removed Jack's things.

'Would you turn around please?' Jack asked them.

Nora and Elan turned and let Jack transform.

'I'm ready now,' he announced.

'Good,' said Nora as she turned to Pyecroft, 'this is where we part company. Remember what I said, if you want me to restore you back to your former self, you're going to have to be sorry and change your ways.'

Pyecroft grunted and leapt out of the train. As he reached the platform Nora pointed her wand at his back. He slumped to the floor and joined the sleeping Spriggans.

'They won't wake up for hours, by which time we'll be long gone,' said Nora as she opened the cage and let the rats out.

Motley was first to land and took up his position at the head of the Night Guard. The other rats formed ranks behind them.

'All present and correct, fully briefed and ready for action,' he announced.

Jack looked over at Fergus and Berry. They didn't look at all ready for action.

'You must all stay away from the dragon's head,' said Elan. 'Do you understand?'

All the rats nodded.

'When it's time to go, climb onto the dragon's tail and don't let go. It might be a bumpy flight. This dragon hasn't flown for years.'

'Have you seen the dragonettes?' Nora asked Motley.

Before he could answer Charkle, Norris and

Snook flitted out of the tunnel. There was a loud *pop* in mid-air as the Dorysk changed from a green moth into another dragonette.

'Follow us,' said Charkle. 'We've found the barbecue pit and the dragon's asleep.'

The smell of roast lamb hung heavy in the air, as they got closer to the pit. The soft glow of crystal light was coming from the end of the tunnel. Jack was expecting the barbecue pit to be similar in size to the great hall. He was surprised when he stepped out of the tunnel and found himself in the biggest cavern he'd ever seen, in the middle of which was a sight that took Jack's breath away. An enormous sleeping dragon lay curled up next to a small lake. It was covered in red scales from the tip of its long twisted horn to the end of its pointed barbed tail. Its wings were folded and its four legs were tucked tightly under its body. Thin plumes of smoke trailed out of its nostrils as it slept. Two long ears were draped over the back of its head. Jack jumped when they twitched. The dragon's skin was identical to the one Nora had used to bind her Dragon Lore book. Jack's legs began shaking. They felt like jelly and refused to go any further. If he felt like this now, what would he be like when the dragon was awake? He'd never seen anything as big as this before. The single horn, in the middle of the dragon's forehead, looked dangerous. It was twisted to a point and glinted in the light from the crystals.

Nora held her finger to her lips and signalled for everyone to stay where they were.

'I think it's time you three introduced yourselves,' Nora whispered to the little dragonettes who were hovering near the cave entrance.

'Do you want me to go too?' asked the Dorysk.

'Maybe you should stay here with us, I'm not sure we have time to explain why a dragonette is wearing glasses,' replied Nora.

Charkle, Norris and Snook flew around the cave in a wide arc. They circled around the dragon's head, taking care to keep away from its long snout. Jack could see the dragon's nostrils flare slightly. The plume of smoke stopped. Jack held his breath. Everyone must have done the same because the only thing Jack could hear, apart from his own heart beating, was the flapping of tiny wings. The dragon seemed to hold its breath too and become motionless. Without warning the great beast threw back its head and roared loudly. The cavern echoed with the dreadful sound. As the dragon lowered its head its eyelids opened. A great yellow eye looked straight at Jack. He was so frightened he couldn't move. Charkle darted in front of the dragon's glaring eye. If it hadn't seen the little dragonette before it had now. There was a loud crash as the dragon snapped its teeth and lunged at Charkle. Again a mighty roar filled the chamber as the dragon lifted its head. Jack shook all over as a mighty flame leapt from the dragon's open mouth. The dragonettes flitted around the top of the dragon's head until its fiery breath finally turned to smoke and it lowered its head again.

'Find out its name,' Elan shouted.

The dragon immediately turned in her direction and roared again.

'No,' shouted Nora, as Snook landed on the dragon's snout. 'Don't put yourself in danger.'

Snook ignored Nora's pleas and bowed low to the dragon. Norris and Charkle landed next to each of the dragon's ears. Jack couldn't hear what they were saying but the great beast had at least stopped roaring. Without warning it lifted its forearm. Jack gasped when he saw the size of the dragon's sharp talons.

'Watch out,' cried Elan as the dragon swiped at Snook.

The little dragonette was too quick and darted out of the way as another flame gushed from the dragon's mouth. Snook flew high above the flame and looped-the-loop breathing his own trail of flame as he spiralled around.

'She doesn't believe us,' Charkle called to Nora. 'And she won't tell us her name.'

'How does he know it's a *she*?' Camelin whispered to Jack.

'Shhh!' said Nora, 'I need to think. Tell her we're here to set her free, tell her we can take her to another land where she'll be safe and can have a whole mountain to herself, tell her...' Nora stopped. She didn't seem to know what else to say.

'TELL HER WHAT?' roared the dragon.

Nora swallowed hard and stepped out from the safety of the tunnel. She looked directly at the dragon and shouted as loudly as she could.

'We're sorry for what's happened to you but not all creatures are cruel, some are kind and care for others. We are here to help if you'll let us.'

The dragon lowered its head and sniffed the air around Nora.

'And what creatures, who smell like dragonettes but aren't, would care about me?'

Nora bowed low.

'Eleanor Druid, Seanchai, Keeper of Secrets and Ancient Rituals and Guardian of the Sacred Grove.'

Elan stepped forward and also bowed low and introduced herself.

'Elan, Queen of the Fair Folk and Guardian of the Gateways of Annwn.'

Both Nora and Elan looked at Jack. He bowed but didn't know what to say. Nora smiled and Elan spoke to the dragon.

'Jack Brenin, Friend to All and rightful King of Annwn.'

The dragon roared again but this time it didn't sound as threatening.

'You'll never be able to free me so you might as well go away and leave me be.'

'At least let us try,' said Nora. 'If we can, will you help us?'

'In return for my freedom I'll help you but you'll have to open the padlocks that chain me first.'

As the dragon stood, Jack could see great manacles, secured by padlocks, around her hind legs. The manacles were attached to a huge chain, which was threaded through a metal ring that had been sunk into the rock. Nora stood in front of one padlock and breathed deeply before aiming her wand at the keyhole. Red, green and yellow sparks flew from the tip of her wand and disappeared into the hole. She stood back and waited but the lock remained closed. She aimed at the metal ring on the floor but the sparks hit it and bounced off.

'I don't understand,' said Nora. 'Perhaps if we all try together.'

'It's useless,' the dragon told her. 'I've tried melting the metal and my breath is as fiery as they come. Unless you have the right key you'll never open it.

Nora went over to the padlock and examined it.

'Come and help me,' she shouted to Jack and Elan.

No one else moved out of the entrance of the tunnel but they all craned their necks to try to see what was happening. Jack and Elan moved slowly around the dragon towards Nora. Jack's heart was racing, at any minute the dragon might lose its temper and strike out at them.

'Concentrate and imagine the lock opening,' she told them.

All three pointed their wands and the light from the sparks lit the chamber but the lock remained closed.

'I told you it was useless. The padlocks won't open without the key.'

'Key!' said Jack. 'I'm so sorry Nora, I forgot to tell you, so much has happened and I didn't mean to keep it but I've found your special key. You know, the magical one, the one that opens any lock.'

Nora laughed.

'There isn't a special key, that's something Camelin thinks I've got, it's not real.'

'But it is. Look!'

Jack pulled out the silver chain. A tiny key, next to the heart-shaped locket, dangled from the middle. An ear splitting sound filled the chamber and Jack realised the dragon was laughing.

'Look at the size of the key, you don't really think it's going to open great padlocks like these do you?'

'I do,' said Jack.

Nora and Elan also looked at him in disbelief.

'It will change shape to fit any lock. It's done it before so I don't see why it won't do it again. It's magic, watch.'

Jack took off the chain and pointed the key towards the great padlock. He concentrated hard and with each step he took nearer to the keyhole, the small key grew. He could feel it tingling in his fingers. The metal sparked and it began to change shape rapidly. When he reached the padlock the tiny key had grown bigger than his hand. Everyone was silent as he slipped the key into the lock. A loud click echoed around the chamber as the lock sprang open; the dragon shook her hind leg and freed it from the chain. Jack moved swiftly to the other padlock and released her other leg.

'Well that was a surprise,' said Nora. 'We'll talk about it later, but now we need to find a way to escape.'

'That won't be a problem if you can find my tail shield,' the dragon informed them as she shook her legs and brought her tail around for them to see.

'Tail shield!' said Nora. 'You mean they exist? They're not a myth?'

'What's a tail shield?' asked Camelin.

Charkle flew over to the tunnel.

'Don't you know anything? A tail shield gives dragonairs invisibility. How do you think they survived for so long without people seeing them?'

'I told you about them,' said Jack. 'There was a whole chapter in the Dragon Lore book, a dragonair is given one at birth, it has its name inscribed on it. Only dragon's breath can reveal the name on the shield. Once it's in place, on the tip of its tail, the dragon becomes invisible.'

'Do you have your tail shield?' asked Elan.

The dragon sighed and the force of her breath sent the rats rolling backwards down the tunnel. She slumped down in a heap on the floor and started to explain.

'Dragon's have always lived inside Silver Hill. This cavern was home to my family. A long time ago we were free and happy and of course, with our tail shields, invisible to the outside world. I'm the only one left now. I never expected creatures to invade the hill. They captured me, tethered me with those cruel chains and stole my hoard. It took my family hundreds of years to collect all the silver, gold and jewels. It was easy to protect when there were lots of us. I got careless when my family had all gone and I used to fly around the caverns inside the hillside. One day, when I returned to my lair, the hoard was gone. The Spriggans had taken it down one of their tiny tunnels where I couldn't follow. My tail shield was in the hoard along with every tail shield that ever belonged to my family. Find the hoard and I'll be able to escape. Without my tail shield I can never leave this place. They might have melted the shields down by now and made them into something else. Even if you could find the tail shields you'd need to find the right one. I can't get into the tunnels and it takes dragon's breath to reveal the name.'

The dragon sighed again and its eyelids drooped.

Jack saw movement from the tunnel entrance. Motley stepped out and bowed to the dragon.

'We are at your service. If there's something needs finding, rest assured, my Night Guard will find it.'

Snook flew over to Nora.

'I know where the Spriggans keep their gold, we only need to know the right name, I'm sure we can find it. We won't have to bring them all out. If the rats can find them we can breathe on them and reveal the names.'

A great tear fell from the dragon's eye and splashed onto the floor.

'You really mean it? You're all going to help me?'

'We are,' said Nora. 'Once we're out of here we can take you into the Otherworld, you'll be free and can have your own mountain but we really could do with your help once we get to Annwn.'

'Free me and I'll help you in any way I can.'

Motley coughed.

'Your name?'

'Ember Silver Horn the Magnificent,' the dragon replied.

'Right men,' commanded Motley, 'let the search begin.'

ESCAPE

Motley began organising them into three groups, each led by a dragonette.

'Jack, you can go with Fergus, Berry and Raggs. Camelin join Morris, Lester and Podge. Midge, Timmery and the Dorysk can come with me.'

The other rats fell in behind the Night Guard. Before Jack joined his group he pointed the huge key he was holding at the small keyhole on his locket. The key shrank immediately and once the chain was safely round his neck again he followed the rest. The dragonettes swooped down and each collected one of the big crystals to light the way. Snook flew over to the head of Motley's group, Norris joined Camelin, and

Charkle circled in front of Jack.

'Follow me,' shouted Snook as he set off at speed down one of the smaller tunnels.

The rats were able to scamper quickly after the little dragonette but it wasn't long before Jack and Camelin were struggling to keep up. The further behind they got, the darker the tunnel became. Soon it would be pitch black.

'Any idea why we had to come?' asked Camelin.

'To help,' panted Jack even though he couldn't see what use they were going to be.

'You might have brought a crystal with you,' Camelin grumbled. 'That would have been helpful.'

Jack lifted his wand and made the tip glow. There wasn't much light but there was enough to see that the small tunnel was about to branch in three different directions.

'Oh great!' said Jack. 'I've no idea which way to go now.'

'But I do,' a tiny voice said from above.

Jack looked up and saw Charkle flitting around overhead.

'Motley sent me back to look for you. I'm supposed to tell you how important it is to keep up with the rest.'

'It's easy if you've got four legs or the tunnel's wide enough for you to fly through,' complained Camelin.

'It's not that far, this way.'

They followed Charkle into the middle tunnel and soon Jack could hear lots of scampering feet and Motley giving commands. The tunnel ended in a small cave. Even in the dim light, the contents sparkled and twinkled. The cave was filled with gold, silver and jewels. The pile was so high it almost reached the top of the cave.

'It's vast, it's going to take ages to search through all this,' groaned Camelin.

'It's going to be noisy rummaging around. What if someone hears?' said Jack.

'Camelin, keep watch,' Motley ordered.

'Do this, do that,' mumbled Camelin as he shuffled back to the opening.

Jack couldn't begin to estimate how much the contents of the cave would be worth. He sank knee deep in a pile of silver coins as he tried to make his way over to the middle.

'What we're looking for is huge,' Jack told them as he tried to describe what he'd seen in Nora's Dragon Lore book. 'It's a triangular piece of gold, one that will fit over the tip of Ember's tail. It shouldn't be too hard to find something that big.'

They began to try to dig down through the coins but it was impossible to make a space. The mound slid and moved each time they moved an object. Jack could see coins of all shapes and sizes, jewellery, plates, cups and strange objects, but nothing like the size and shape they needed. The rats frantically tried to burrow into the hoard but their tiny paws weren't big enough to move the heavy objects. It occurred to Jack that he might not be able to lift the tail shield even if they could find it.

'This is useless,' panted Fergus, 'the pile's too big. It'll take us weeks to get down to the bottom.'

Jack knew the little rat was right. He'd come to the same conclusion himself. The only place the great tail shields could be was on the bottom. He was about to go and tell Motley they needed Nora's help when a sudden thought struck him. He'd been faced with an almost impossible task before, when he'd looked inside the key drawer in the herborium. He'd asked for the right key and it had come to the top of the pile. Maybe he could try to do the same again. It was worth a try.

'Motley,' he called, 'I've got an idea.'

Jack made his way over to the left-hand side where Motley's group were busy searching. All the rats looked tired. Jack held up his wand.

'Can I try something?'

'Step aside men,' Motley ordered.

By the time Jack reached the mouth of the cave everyone was behind him.

'Is it time to go?' asked Camelin.

'No not yet,' replied Jack, 'I want to try something and if this doesn't work Timmery will have to go and fetch Nora.'

Jack concentrated hard. He visualised the size and shape of the triangular shields and directed all his energy into the tip of his wand.

'Where are the tail shields?' he commanded.

A bright light from the end of his wand lit the chamber and when the light faded the precious hoard began to erupt. Gold coins rose into the air like a fountain. Jack watched in amazement as the pile began to ripple until the tips of gigantic triangular objects appeared. The little dragonettes flew around the cave.

'Look!' cried Norris, 'over here.'

'And here,' called Snook.

'They're everywhere,' said Charkle, 'we just need to find the right one.'

Jack hoped Ember's was going to be there. He concentrated again but he couldn't get the tail shields to rise any higher out of the heap.

'That's the best I can do,' he told them.

'Not to worry, not to worry, said Motley as he leapt into action. 'One at a time men, one at a time, help to pull them out.'

The rats surrounded the nearest golden object. Some began digging down while the others pulled. Jack went over to help. With a lot of effort they managed to free the triangular piece of gold. Jack stood back to get his breath and looked at the tail shield. It was beautiful. It wasn't two flat pieces joined together as he'd expected. The side he was looking at had been beautifully worked into a curved shape and engraved with circles. Near the top was a plain solid area but no name was visible.

Charkle swooped down low.

'Allow me,' he said as he breathed onto the metal.

Strange writing began to appear but too faint to read and it soon disappeared again.

'I think you're all going to have to breathe on it at once,' called Jack.

The three little dragonettes hovered above the tail shield and blew a strong steady breath over it.

'Here it comes,' said Jack excitedly as he watched the strange writing appear. He'd never seen anything like it before. The letters were all capitals, some had more lines than usual but all of them were straight. They looked as if they'd been etched into the gold with a sharp object. Jack wondered if the claw of some dragon had scratched the words on long ago. The words weren't too hard to decipher, the letters were different from those Jack was used to but not impossible to work out.

'*BRYNOG LONG TAIL THE INVINCIBLE,*' Jack read as the letters became clearer.

'Try another one,' ordered Motley.

They pulled the next tail shield free and Jack waited for the dragon's breath to reveal the name.

'*WYGRYM SHARP CLAW THE FEARLESS*, this isn't it either,' called Jack, but he remembered the name. It was this dragon's shed skin that Nora had used to bind her book.

The next shield revealed the name *ZACYRY JAGGED TOOTH THE MIGHTY* and the next *PETRYN LONG BEARD THE BRAVE*. Jack began to worry that the one they were looking for no longer existed. It was hard work and there were still lots of tail shields to pull out. He could see the rats were tiring.

'What's this one say?' asked Motley as he nudged Jack.

'*EMBER SILVER HORN THE MAGNIFICENT,*' read Jack. 'This is it! We've found it.'

A great cheer filled the cave. Motley at once took charge and started giving orders. He directed groups of rats to stand along each side of the shield. He waited until everyone was in position.

'Heave!' he ordered.

Jack held the tip and lifted with all his might. The tail shield was heavy but between them they managed to get it off the top of the pile. It was easier once they reached the tunnel and had a flat surface to walk on. Norris and Snook flew at the front with the crystal lights while Charkle and the Dorysk flew behind. Timmery flitted around Jack's head.

'I can see without the lights, I'll go on ahead and tell them the good news.'

Jack felt pleased. They'd found the tail shield and everything was going to be alright. The rats were chattering happily together too as they progressed along the tunnel. Jack hadn't expected Timmery to return.

'Shhh!' Timmery cried as loudly as he could. 'We've got to be quiet. The Draygull's found Pyecroft and the sleeping Spriggans. Nora's worried we might be discovered. Not a sound and don't go into the barbecue pit until we know it's safe.'

In all the excitement they'd not even thought about the noise they'd been making. Jack began to worry. He hoped the Draygull's hearing wasn't as good as a dragon's. If it was they were in trouble.

Jack could see light coming from the great cavern not far ahead. He stopped and signalled for the rats to put the tail shield on the ground and then tiptoed to the entrance of the tunnel. He knew if he stayed in the shadow he wouldn't be seen. Ember was slumped in the centre of the pit. No smoke came out of her nostrils so Jack presumed she was pretending to be asleep. The rest of the cavern was empty. Jack looked at each tunnel entrance in turn to see if he could locate where Nora and Elan were hiding. Everywhere was quiet. Jack began to feel better. Maybe the Draygull was just cross when he found the sleeping Bogie and Spriggans. He might not be suspicious at all.

An ear-piercing screech came from the tunnel leading to the platform. It filled the cavern and bounced off the rock, the echo lasted long after the screeching stopped.

Jack's heart began pounding. The sound had been terrible. All the hair on the back of his neck stood on end.

The silence that followed was broken by the sound of running feet. If the Spriggans swarmed into the cavern and searched the tunnels they'd all be discovered. To Jack's surprise the footsteps stopped and were replaced by loud shouts. Something must have happened to stop the Spriggans getting any closer. The screeching began again and the sound filled the cavern. This time, when the screeching finally died down, there were no pounding footsteps. Jack thought he knew why. The Spriggans must have discovered that all the tunnels were dark. It was pitch black from the great hall to the platform. It wouldn't matter to the owl-like man, who could probably see in the dark, but it would be a big problem for the Spriggans.

Jack knew they'd have to make their escape soon. A slight movement from one of the tunnels caught Jack's attention. He expected to see Nora or Elan step out but instead the strange looking owl man entered the cavern. Jack held his breath as the Draygull sniffed the air. He walked slowly round the cavern, keeping to the rock and carefully avoiding Ember. He sniffed each entrance in turn. When he got to their tunnel Jack's heart thumped so hard his chest began to hurt. If the Draygull could see in the dark he'd already have been seen. He tried to inch backwards but his legs wouldn't move. The Draygull lunged forwards and made a grab at Jack.

'Charge!' shouted Motley before the Draygull's hand could close around Jack's arm.

A mass of furry bodies, with lashing tails and many legs bounded past Jack and hit the Draygull in the chest. He was knocked off his feet and lay winded on the floor. If Jack didn't do something immediately, the Draygull would start screeching again. The whole hillside would know where to find him. Jack could see he was trying to struggle to his feet. He pointed his wand at the Draygull and repeated the word Nora had used on Pyecroft and the Spriggans.

'*Somnus.*'

In an instant the Draygull's body went limp. A strange whistling sound told Jack he'd been successful as the owl man began to snore.

'Well,' said Nora, 'it looks like we're too late. We were just coming to help!'

'I think it's time to leave,' said Elan. 'It won't be long before the Spriggans find some torches and there are enough of them to search all the tunnels. That was a warning the Draygull sent them, they'll know by now that something's wrong and so will Velindur.'

Jack watched as Nora pointed her wand at the Draygull again. He rose from the floor and Nora sent his sleeping body over to the other side of the lake. She lowered it onto the shingle.

'That should keep him out of our way. When he wakes up he'll have a problem. Draygulls can't swim. Now, let's get out of here.'

Elan signalled to the rats to bring the tail shield in. They stopped in front of Ember and stepped back as she breathed gently over the golden shield. Tears ran down her face when she saw her name appear.

'To the tail,' ordered Motley.

The rats leapt into action and scurried back to take their places around the tail shield. They moved as fast as they could towards the tip of Ember's tail. She carefully brought it round to meet them. Nora signalled to the rats to put the shield down.

'Once this is in place Ember will be invisible. She's agreed to transport you all back to Glasruhen. You all know what to do?'

Nora waited until everyone had nodded back before turning to Ember.

'Are you ready?'

'Most certainly,' Ember replied as she began to unfold her wings.

'If you lead us out of the hillside, the dragonettes will show you the way to Glasruhen Hill and we'll be with you as soon as we can.'

'I think it's time to go,' said Elan as she nodded towards one of the tunnels where a dim light flickered in the distance.

Jack could hear the high-pitched chittering getting louder and louder as the Spriggans made their way towards the barbecue pit.

'Climb on men,' Motley ordered, 'and hold tight.'

The rats scampered onto the dragon's tail. Nora, Jack and Elan struggled to lift the tail shield and held it off the ground so Ember could slot the barbed tip inside it. Jack heard a loud click as the tail and shield locked together. Although he could still feel its weight, the shield in his hand was no longer visible. Ember had also disappeared from sight.

Off you go!' said Nora.

The noise was deafening as Ember flapped her huge wings. The draft they created sent those who were left staggering backwards. As Ember rose, great gusts of air swept them down the nearest tunnel. Jack managed to brace himself against the rock until it stopped.

'We'd better hurry,' said Elan.

'Do you know which way to go?' Nora asked the

dragonettes.

'Easy,' replied Charkle, 'follow me.'

Jack quickly knelt and touched Camelin's forehead. Nora helped him out of his clothes and stuffed them, along with his trainers, into the sack with the last of the crystals. The only light in the cavern now came from the open sack.

Nora and Elan raised their arms and spiralled downwards. Jack was expecting to see two ravens but they both shape-shifted into owls. One was snowy white and the other a magnificent eagle owl. The white owl, screeched loudly as two Spriggans entered the cavern, the first one carried a rush torch which it dropped on the floor as Elan opened her wings, put her head down and also began screeching loudly.

'Let's go,' Snook shouted to Jack and Camelin.

Once he was airborne, Jack looked down at the cavern floor. It was empty apart from the abandoned torch. Nora and Elan joined them as they flew upwards through a wide natural chimney towards the top of the cavern. The three dragonettes took it in turns to breathe fire to light the way for Jack and Camelin whilst Nora and Elan flew on ahead. Now Jack knew why they'd chosen to be owls, they wouldn't need any help seeing in the dark.

They didn't fly out of the top of the cavern, as

Jack had expected, instead they turned into an opening in the rock face. Jack could see a glimpse of a light in the distance. He didn't know how long they'd been inside Silver Hill but it wasn't yet dark outside. They flew swiftly along the tunnel, no longer needing the dragonettes' flames to guide them.

'Make for the standing stones,' Nora hooted when they were nearly at the entrance.

Jack could see that Elan had the sack safely in her strong talons. As they flew out into daylight Jack heard a rushing sound. He didn't have time to see what it was. A torrent of water nearly knocked him sideways. He pulled hard on his wings and struggled to fly through the wall of water before it swept him downwards. When he looked back he could see he'd flown through a waterfall, which completely hid the entrance to the dragon's lair. Camelin emerged coughing and spluttering.

'Ugh! No one told us about that.'

Jack laughed.

'At least you won't need a bath when we get back. It's washed all the Dragon's Breath goo off! Come on, we've got a long flight ahead of us. I just hope my clothes and trainers dry out before we get back to Glasruhen.'

AN UNEXPECTED PROBLEM

'Going down!' croaked Camelin when the standing stones came into sight.

Jack followed. He scanned the ground below for any sign of the others. The circle of stones looked deserted and Jack couldn't see his clothes.

'Do you think they got back alright?' he asked Camelin when he landed.

'They did,' replied a voice from one of the tangled bushes that surrounded the stones. A tall willowy Dryad with long chestnut hair stepped out and bowed.

'Cory?' asked Jack.

'You remembered! Nora said you would. She also said to give you these.'

Jack was relieved to see that Cory was carrying his clothes and trainers. His wand was on top of the neat pile.

'Were there any messages?'

'No, they were in a bit of a hurry.'

Jack looked around the clearing. It was big enough for Ember to land in without any difficulty.

'What's happened to the gate?' asked Jack.

'She's hidden it hasn't she,' grumbled Camelin as he looked around. 'They didn't want us following them into Annwn. Well they needn't have worried, I'm too tired to do anything else tonight.'

Cory didn't reply but Jack knew Camelin was right. He'd been told the last time they'd visited the stone circle that it was a place of deep magic. It wouldn't be difficult for Nora to hide the gateway from sight. If she'd wanted them to go they'd have been invited.

'Could you put my clothes by the big stone?' Jack asked Cory. 'Please excuse us a moment while I change.'

It didn't take Jack long to transform and dress. Although he liked being a raven it felt good to be himself again.

'Are you going to come to see us soon?' Cory asked Jack as he reappeared from behind the central stone, 'We heard your wonderful voice. It reached the very top of Glasruhen, you're welcome to come and sing with us anytime you like.'

Camelin humphed.

'We'll come back as soon as the Druids have been rescued.'

'We!' he grumbled.

'I'll come back,' said Jack and gave Camelin a look before turning back to Cory. 'But we ought to be going now.'

'I'm off to bed, see you later,' Camelin called as he took off in the direction of Ewell House.

Jack walked with Cory to the edge of the bushes that surrounded the clearing. When she touched one of the leaves, the tangled branches parted.

'Thank you,' he said before the bushes closed and Cory disappeared from sight.

Jack wasn't in a hurry to get back to Ewell House. After all the excitement it felt good to be alone. As he made his way through the tunnel his mind was racing. He went over the events of the last week. No one would ever believe he'd been face to face with an enormous fire-breathing dragon. He wondered how things were going in Annwn. Had Ember managed to melt the ice sheet? Were the Druids awake? He was going to have to wait until Nora returned for the answers.

As Jack walked through the yew tree tunnel he caught glimpses of Dryads flitting from tree to tree. He felt so lucky – this really was a magical place.

When he got back to the house he went into the library. The map was still on the table. They'd all been in such a hurry he'd not had a chance to look at it properly. He recognised the outlines of the hills and Stonytop Ridge. Written around the sides, in Nora's neat handwriting, was the information she'd been given by Norris, Snook and Pyecroft. A lot of tunnels, platforms and doorways had also been filled in. He followed the journey the train had taken from the platform underneath the Devil's Chair to the bottom of Silver Hill. Their exit from the Barbecue Pit wasn't marked. That would be something Nora could add when she returned. Jack would have liked to have seen where all the tunnels from the barbecue pit led. Their entrances were all different shapes and sizes. Two led to train platforms, another wound its way up to the great hall but the tallest tunnel of all didn't go up or down. It travelled in a straight line to a door. Nora had drawn an arched doorway, just like Glasruhen Gate and next to it had written The Fifth Gateway. Jack blew out a long slow breath. This was the other portal into Annwn, which led straight into the Caves of Eternal Rest. It wasn't like the other portals. It didn't have two Hamadryad oak trees on either side to mark its position. Jack wondered why there was a gateway here at all. Even if you got into the caves, there was no way out into Annwn unless the gatekeeper awoke and opened the ice sheet. The other four gateways were able to move but this one obviously didn't, it had its own tunnel. Jack wondered how it opened. It couldn't be difficult if the Spriggans had been able to walk straight in and take the crystals. A sudden thought struck Jack. Instead of trying to melt the ice sheet, Nora and Elan could have entered the caves through the fifth gate. They could have returned the crystals, woken the Gatekeeper and the Druids who wanted to leave the caves and then left through the cave entrance. What could be simpler? Why hadn't Nora or Elan thought of it?

There was a lot to think about but Jack was tired. He'd talk to Nora when she got back. He went to his room and checked his Book of Shadows for messages but none had come through. The whole house was quiet. He called Camelin but got no reply, maybe he'd taken a slight detour and wasn't home yet. Jack decided to go up to the loft; if Camelin wasn't there Jack would wait until he returned, he wanted to tell him the news about the fifth gateway.

The first thing Jack saw when he got to the ladder was the big *KEEP OUT* sign. Jack moved it to one side and pulled himself up into the loft. He smiled when he saw Camelin lying on his back in his raven basket. Jack flopped down on his beanbag.

'We haven't had any messages.'

'Didn't you see the sign?'

Jack decided to ignore the question.

'How long do you think they'll be?'

'Hours, with any luck. I want to get some sleep. If you're going to stay you're going to have to be quiet. It's my loft.'

Jack was about to tell Camelin about the map when Timmery flitted in through the open window.

'Noooo!' groaned Camelin.

'Oh Jack, I'm so glad you're here!'

Camelin turned noisily until his back faced Jack and Timmery.

'Is everything alright?' asked Jack.

'No it's not. Motley sent me, he wants to know if he can climb up the ivy and come in, it's urgent and he needs to see you right away.'

'Of course he can.'

'May I remind you whose loft this is? Some of us are trying to get some sleep.'

Timmery was gone before Camelin could say anything else. It wasn't long before Motley appeared on the window ledge. He paced up and down a few times before speaking.

'Don't know how to tell you this, we've searched everywhere and he's nowhere to be found.'

'Who isn't?' asked Jack.

'Raggs. You haven't seen him have you?'

'He was next to me when we carried the tail shield in.'

'That's what Podge said but nobody's seen him since. What if he's still in there? Everything happened so fast. I was concerned about the new recruits, I expected the Night Guard to be able to look after themselves, didn't get a chance to check they were all aboard the tail before we took off. You'd have seen him if he'd been left though, wouldn't you?'

'We all got blown down one of the tunnels when Ember beat her wings,' said Jack slowly as he recalled the sequence of events. 'But it was dark in the tunnel. If Raggs was blown in there too we wouldn't have seen him and he'd probably have ended up further down than we did.'

'What do we do?' groaned Motley.

'You say you've searched everywhere?' asked Jack.

'Everywhere,' confirmed Timmery. 'We've searched every inch of ground between here and the Standing Stones.'

'Maybe he fell off,' said Camelin. 'He'll have a long walk but he should be back by morning. I told you it was the Day of Bad Omens. Bad things can happen to anyone.'

'I don't think he got on the dragon's tail,' sighed Motley. 'I've questioned all the rats, no one saw him.'

'We'll have to go back,' said Jack.

'Noooo!' wailed Camelin. 'I'm not flying all the way back tonight.'

'You know you don't mean that,' said Jack. 'If you were in trouble everyone would help you.'

Jack looked over to the window. The light was beginning to fade. Everyone waited expectantly for Jack to speak. Motley slumped down on the window ledge.

'What if he's caught and they want to eat him?'

'If he's been caught they'll more likely want to question him to find out what's been going on. They'll know by now that something's wrong. At the very least they'll want to know where their rats and dragons have gone, not to mention their lights.'

Motley stood to attention.

'Raggs would never talk, he'd never betray us.'

'I'm sure you're right but that makes his rescue even more urgent. Hopefully he'll have managed to hide somewhere. Do you think we'll be able to find him before the Spriggans do?' Jack asked Motley.

'It's not the Spriggans I'm worried about, it's the Draygull. He can see in the dark and has a very powerful sense of smell. He found your hiding place and made a grab for you, didn't he?'

Jack felt a cold shiver run down his spine.

'They'll know it was us, won't they?'

'Course they won't. We were ravens, remember?' said Camelin.

'I wasn't, we'd transformed, remember? Motley's right, he definitely saw me.'

'He'd only have seen your shape, not your face. He probably thought you were an overgrown Hag or a Bogie.'

'Let's hope so because I can't go back inside as a raven, we'll have to transform outside like we did before and I'm going to need my wand.'

We're going to need a light too,' said Motley. 'It's going to be dark inside the tunnels.'

'We!' croaked Camelin. 'What d'you mean, *we*?'

'I'm definitely going, he's my responsibility,' added Motley. 'I can't leave a man in enemy territory.'

'Count me in too,' said a tiny voice from Motley's fur.

'Oh no! Not the Dorysk as well!' grumbled Camelin.

Motley looked embarrassed.

'He won't take up much room. I don't mind him travelling around in my fur.'

'You don't?'

'He helped us search and he's really useful in a tight corner, a brilliant impersonator and master of disguise too. I'm thinking of recruiting him into the Night Guard.'

'Well I'm not leaving my comfortable basket, if you want my help you're going to have to make it fly over there.'

'I wish I could,' said Jack.

'You made the boat go over the lake so why can't you make my basket fly?'

'That was different.'

'Why?'

Everyone looked at Jack.

'I don't know. It might be dangerous. What if it

282

worked for a bit then stopped? What would Nora say?'

Motley leapt off the windowsill and bounded over to Jack.

'If you can make the raven basket fly we'll all be able to go.'

'All!' said Camelin.

'I want to help too,' said Timmery. 'The others have gone off into Annwn without me so I don't see why I can't come with you.'

Jack concentrated hard and pointed his wand at Camelin's raven basket. It rose off the floor and hovered.

'Fly,' Jack commanded and made a sweep with his wand around the loft.

'Whoa!' cried Camelin as the raven basket sped around the loft in a wide circle. Jack had to duck as it rushed passed his ear.

'Oh Jack Brenin, you're the best,' Timmery called as he flew after the basket.

'Well, that was a surprise,' said Jack. 'I really didn't think I'd be able to do it but the basket isn't going to be big enough for all of us.'

'If you go and get my wand I can *big* it,' croaked Camelin.

'You could tell me the *bigging* spell and I could do it,' replied Jack.

'My spell, my basket.'

Again everyone looked at Jack.

'Alright, we'll try. I'll go and get your wand.'

Jack rushed down to the herborium. He pushed the stool under the cupboard so he could reach the door and took off the silver chain. He pointed the key at the cupboard on the wall. It grew immediately to the size of the keyhole. The wand was propped up inside with a lot of other things so Jack relocked the cupboard before shrinking the key back down. He was halfway up the stairs when he remembered the map. It would be invaluable if they knew where they were going. He didn't want to take Nora's map so he decided to magic a copy. Part of the wart spell he'd used contained the word to *create*, if he used the word on its own and concentrated all his attention at the map it might work.

'*Creo*,' he commanded.

Nothing happened at first then a sheet flew off the top of the map and landed at his feet. It was an exact replica of Nora's map. Jack picked it up and was about to leave the library when another map rose from the table, and another, and another.

'STOP!' yelled Jack and breathed a great sigh of relief when the map stopped duplicating itself. He wished his knowledge of magic were better. He was really going to have to be careful when he gave the basket directions, he didn't want any accidents. With the map safely rolled up under his arm, Jack ran up the stairs. He was out of breath when he reached the loft. Camelin was waiting expectantly and looked really excited when Jack handed him his wand.

'Here you are, please be careful.'

'Stand back,' Camelin ordered as he pointed it at the basket.

The tip of the wand glowed with a soft yellow light that travelled rapidly towards the raven basket. The sides grew as the bottom expanded. Jack was impressed, Camelin was not only doing the spell carefully but it was working really well.

'It's still not big enough,' said Motley.

'Leave me alone,' grumbled Camelin, 'I'm doing my best.'

He pointed his wand for a second time but instead of the soft yellow light, orange sparks flew out of the tip. The basket rapidly doubled in size before exploding with a bang. Oversized round polystyrene balls filled the loft as the bottom of the raven basket erupted.

'Oops!' said Camelin. 'That's what happened to the cake on the third *bigging*.'

'Try it again on my basket,' said Jack.

Camelin looked surprised, and said, 'That was your basket.'

'It doesn't matter. If you want to fly to Silver Hill keep the light from the tip of your wand yellow and hold the spell until the basket's big enough for all of us.'

Camelin followed Jack's instructions. The raven basket grew slowly as the soft yellow light engulfed it. When it was three times its original size, Camelin stopped.

'How's that?'

'Brilliant,' replied Jack, 'but how do we get out of the window?'

Camelin turned quickly and pointed his wand at the round glass. In an instant, the soft yellow light spread over the surface and surrounded the frame.

'Oh my!' exclaimed Timmery as the window doubled in size.

'That's enough!' shouted Jack. 'We'll get through it now.'

Camelin looked pleased with himself as he climbed inside the basket. Jack waited until everyone was aboard before climbing in himself. Now all he had to do was get everyone there safely. He knew it was important to use the right command. He'd nearly crashed the rowing boat by being careless. Jack spread the map out and examined the different entrances into Silver Hill. They didn't want to go back in through the waterfall. Maybe halfway down would be a good place to start. The great hall would be easy to reach and the tunnel with all the doors.

'Where to?' asked Camelin.

'Here,' replied Jack and touched the map to show Camelin the route he'd chosen.

The basket lurched, rose from the floor and hovered in front of the window for an instant before setting off at speed towards Silver Hill.

THE DWINDLING DOOR

'This is great,' Camelin called as the basket quickly left Glasruhen Hill behind.

Jack wasn't so sure. As a raven he had no fear of flying but now, as a boy, it was different. He held on tight to the sides of the basket but it swayed alarmingly as they sped through the air. Every time he looked down his stomach lurched and he felt queasy. The others seemed to be enjoying the flight but Jack couldn't wait for it to end. He was grateful the darkness had reduced the landscape to black outlines. He tried shutting his eyes but it made him feel worse.

'We're nearly there, look!' said Camelin as he nodded towards the three mounds.

'You'd better hold on tight,' Jack called. 'I don't know how well this thing is going to land.'

The basket didn't falter or slow down. Jack could see even Camelin looking worried as they headed straight for the side of Silver Hill.

'We're going to crash,' Jack yelled as he saw the closed door the basket was speeding towards.

'Can't you open it?' cried Motley.

Jack pointed his wand at the hillside. He didn't have time to think of the right words to say. 'Open,' he commanded.

To his surprise the door sprung open and the basket flew in before bumping along the floor of the tunnel. It wobbled violently from side to side and each time it hit the ground they were nearly thrown out. As the end of the tunnel came into view the basket finally slowed and with one last bump, came to a halt.

'Not brilliant, but it got us here, and in double quick time,' said Camelin as he hopped out.

Jack made the tip of his wand glow, spread out the map and tried to work out where they were. The basket had taken them to the exact place he'd touched. The tunnel with all the doors wasn't far away.

'We've got to be quiet,' Jack told them. 'We need to find Raggs and get out of here before anyone notices us.'

The Dorysk sprang out of Motley's fur and changed in mid-air into a tiny bat.

'Timmery and I will go on ahead and have a look around.'

'Stay close,' Jack told Motley.

It seemed very quiet inside Silver Hill. Jack hoped the inhabitants were all asleep. They stopped at the end of the tunnel with all the doors. Jack peered into the darkness and could just see Timmery flitting around one of the doors. The Dorysk was nowhere to be seen. Jack signalled to everyone to follow as he tiptoed down the tunnel. Timmery moved on, from door to door, and by the time they reached him they'd come to the largest door. A tiny beetle crawled out of the keyhole.

'Your rat's inside, in a cage suspended from the ceiling and there's no one else in the room,' the Dorysk told Jack as it transformed back into a bat and joined Timmery again.

Jack nodded his thanks and tried the handle but the door was locked. Before taking off his chain he looked back down the tunnel to make sure they hadn't been seen; it was still deserted. The key quivered between Jack's fingers. Sparks danced over the metal as it changed shape. There was a loud click as Jack turned it in the keyhole. He pulled the handle down and pushed the door open a fraction. Everything inside the room was man-sized. The table, desk and chair were far too big for any Bogie or Spriggan, either the Draygull or Velindur lived here. Suspended over the desk was a small iron cage and inside it was Raggs. He sat up when he saw them enter the room. Jack closed the door quietly before making the light from the tip of his wand brighter. Motley darted up the chair onto the table and stood on his hind legs to try to reach the bottom of the cage.

'Have you out of there in no time,' he assured Raggs.

'Are you alright?' asked Jack.

'Fine, apart from a bump on the head. It was my own fault I got left. I wasn't quick enough and hadn't got a good grip on the tail when the dragon took off. I fell and the draught from the dragon's wings sent me rolling down one of the tunnels. Went down with such a force I banged my head on the rock and knocked myself out. Next thing I know that Draygull's standing over me. I thought he was going to eat me when he grabbed me but instead he brought me here, for questioning. The Big One locked me in the cage. They spoke together and then left, no one's been back since. I thought it was them coming back when I heard the key in the door. How did you ever find me?'

'Team work,' said Jack. 'Did you hear what they were saying? It might help if we knew what they're doing.'

Raggs sat up on his hind legs and began talking rapidly.

'They went to help the Spriggans look for two owls, some green birds and an ugly goblin.'

Camelin hunched his wings and chuckled to himself.

'An ugly goblin. That'll be you Jack, told you they wouldn't know you were a boy.'

Jack ignored the comment and used his key to unlock the cage. He held out his arm so Raggs could scamper out onto his shoulder. Camelin shrugged his wings and began looking around the room.

'Did you find out anything else?' Jack asked Raggs.

'All the Hags have been questioned. They've been locked inside the great hall and they're not happy. Pyecroft and the two sleeping Spriggans have been put in there too. The Draygull thinks the two Hags he found sulking in the corridor were probably skulking after all and the Spriggans are really mad their lights have gone out, especially since they haven't got any candles left. The Draygull said he'd organised the

Spriggans to make rush torches, they're going to light them from the fire in the great hall. I think that's where the Draygull and Big One were off to. The last thing I heard, before the door shut, was the Big One vowing he'd get to the bottom of all this. He said he'd find out what happened to the dragons too.'

'We'd better go,' said Jack. 'We don't want them coming back and finding us here.'

Jack looked around for Camelin. He could see his tail feathers sticking out of a cupboard.

'Are you ready?' Jack asked him.

'Come and have a look at this. There's another one of those light crystals here, a big one. Do you think we ought to take it with us?' Camelin replied as he emerged from the cupboard.

Jack went over and picked up the large crystal. It was a lot bigger and heavier than the others, and it wasn't glowing, it sparkled in the light from his wand.

'This is different, it's not a light,' said Jack as he held it up for everyone to see.

'It looks like the diamond-shaped key that opens the Caves of Eternal Rest,' said Timmery. 'Do you remember, we saw it when we went to look at the caves.'

'If it is, what's it doing here?' replied Jack. 'Maybe we should go and find the fifth gate and see if the diamond's missing. We've got nothing to lose. If Ember can't melt the ice and it is the key we'll be able to let everyone in.'

'Maybe we could just go home,' grumbled Camelin.

Jack ignored Camelin and looked at the others.

'Worth a try,' said Motley. 'Let's have a look and see how to get there.'

Jack unrolled the map and spread it out on the table and traced the route, being careful not to touch the map after what happened last time.

'We're here and need to get down to the bottom where Ember was tethered. The tallest tunnel is the one that leads to the fifth gateway. It shouldn't be too hard to find.'

'Ready men?' said Motley.

'No,' said Camelin. 'We came to rescue Raggs. Why don't we take the diamond back and let Nora sort it out? I've had enough excitement for one night.'

'We should vote,' piped Timmery as he flitted around Jack's head.

'Good idea,' said Motley. 'Those in favour of finding the fifth gateway say *aye*.'

'Aye,' said Jack, Timmery, the Dorysk, Motley and Raggs.

'Outnumbered,' Motley told Camelin. 'Chin up, we'll be out of here and heading for home in no time, it's only a small detour.'

Jack opened the door a fraction and peeked out. The tunnel was still empty. They hurried back to the basket and once they were inside it Jack opened the map and put his finger on the arched doorway Nora had drawn.

'We need to go here,' he commanded.

The basket rocked gently and hovered for a moment before setting off at speed down the tunnels. Jack could see Raggs wasn't enjoying the ride.

'Don't close your eyes,' he whispered in Raggs' ear, 'it makes it worse.'

As they approached the entrance to the great hall the double doors swung open. Jack caught a glimpse of a large group of Spriggans each holding a burning torch. As they whizzed by the torches flared making billows of smoke swirl around. Everyone coughed. Jack could see the Draygull at the head of the Spriggan band. His head whipped to the side as they passed. Jack caught a glimpse of the look in his fiery red eyes.

'Intruders!' he yelled before letting out an ear-piercing screech.

The sound of pounding feet echoed through the hill. Jack could see the flickering lights not far behind as the Draygull and Spriggans chased after them. Each time the Draygull caught sight of the basket it screeched loudly and the terrible sound bounced off the walls.

'They're gaining on us,' cried the Dorysk.

Jack's mind went blank, the giddy motion from the swaying basket made it hard to concentrate. Nora would know what to do but Nora wasn't here. Jack saw a bright orange flash streak towards the Draygull as Camelin pointed his wand down the tunnel. It hit the Draygull right in the middle of his chest. It didn't slow him down but Jack could see he'd grown considerably. Jack turned to Camelin and watched as he steadied his wand in his claw. There was a second flash of light before the bigging spell went hurtling once more towards the owl-man.

'That's enough,' shouted Jack, 'that's enough! Look, he's too big to move.'

A great cheer went up from everyone in the basket as the Draygull struggled to free himself. His enlarged body was now wedged fast in the tunnel and none of the Spriggans could pass him. Jack patted Camelin on the back.

'I didn't know you'd brought your wand but I'm glad you did, you saved us and it looks like your bigging spell's come in useful again.'

Camelin puffed out his chest feathers.

'Do you think Nora will let me have it back now, for good?'

'I'm sure she will, but we've got to get out of here first.'

The basket lurched suddenly and Jack nearly fell out as it veered around the next corner into the barbecue pit. The great chain and open padlock still lay where Ember has shaken them off her legs. The basket made another sharp swerve to the left through the tallest entrance that led off from the pit.

'This is it,' said Jack, 'the fifth gateway's at the end of this tunnel.'

Jack made the tip of his wand grow brighter. They were in a high walled passageway. There were strange carvings on both sides of the rock walls. Jack could see tight spirals, circles, loops and interlocking shapes. He knew they were in the right tunnel; Spriggans had not made these carvings, Jack had seen the same patterns on buildings in Annwn. The basket slowed to a halt and settled onto the soft earth of the tunnel floor. Jack pointed his torch towards the end of the tunnel expecting to see two arched doorways but it was a dead end. He stared at the rock face but there wasn't any sign of a door.

'We've come the wrong way,' grumbled Camelin.

'This is the tunnel,' replied Jack. 'Didn't you see the carvings?'

Jack went over to the rock and ran his hands over it. There was no gap or crack.

'Try your magic,' suggested Timmery. 'You opened the other door.'

Jack pointed his wand at the rock: 'Open,' he commanded.

Nothing happened.

'It's a dwindling door,' the Dorysk announced excitedly, 'We're in the right place. This door was made by Druids.'

'What door?' asked Camelin. 'I can't see a door.'

'It's disappeared down to almost nothing,' explained the Dorysk. 'It should be here but the

Spriggans have been in and out of it collecting the crystals. Each time they've gone in it's got smaller, that's what dwindling doors do, so now it's that small there's almost nothing left of it at all.'

'That's stupid,' grumbled Camelin.

'It was done on purpose,' the Dorysk continued, 'so the Druids would know if anyone had been through the door since they used it last. They would never have expected it to be used by Spriggans though. They're lucky they got in and out, if a human entered without permission the door dwindled down instantly cutting off their only way out.'

'That's all very interesting,' said Camelin, 'but it doesn't help us get in.'

'Well at least we tried,' said Jack as he climbed back into the basket.

Motley began sniffing the wall.

'What's this?' he asked the Dorysk.

'Well I never! It's a keyhole. Come and look Jack, it's tiny.'

Jack had to lie on the floor to see the tiny black speck Motley had found.

'It's too small for a keyhole. It must be a dent in the rock face.'

There was a popping sound as the Dorysk

disappeared. Jack screwed up his eyes and could just see a minute pair of spectacles on the tiniest fly he'd ever seen. He watched as it landed on the rock and made its way to the hole. No one spoke after the Dorysk disappeared from sight. When the tiny fly reappeared again it changed in mid-air into a bat and started speaking rapidly. Jack could see the Dorysk was really excited.

'Use your key Jack, it is a keyhole, I've been right through, it is a dwindling door. There's a big cave on the other side.'

Jack took off his chain and pointed the tiny key towards the even tinier hole. It made his fingers tingle as it shrank down to the size of a small pin. As he turned it in the lock two little bats flew excitedly around his head.

'Look Jack! Look at the doors!' cried Timmery.

Jack stepped back and watched in amazement as an arched doorway began to form. It was almost identical to the gateway on Glasruhen Hill. The rock rippled and faded as carved wooden doors appeared. Once they were solid they parted in the middle and slowly opened. The cave looked dark and empty. It felt cold inside. Jack shone his wand towards the darkest end. Carved ledges and niches came into view and there, in each hollow lay the still body of an ancient Druid.

'We've done it,' said Jack excitedly. 'We've opened the fifth gateway. We're inside the Caves of Eternal Rest.'

'Are they dead?' whispered Motley.

'I hope not,' said Jack, 'but it's cold in here.'

As they walked through the cave Jack shivered. The only sound he could hear was their footsteps on the cavern floor. Timmery and the Dorysk flew around the huge cave and soon disappeared into the darkness. Jack was beginning to lose heart when Timmery began squeaking noisily.

'Hurry Jack, come and see.'

Jack's heart leapt as he ran towards Timmery's voice. At the far end of the cave, between two columns was a smaller cave. Light streamed onto the floor through a great sheet of ice that covered the entrance. Beside it was an empty space where they'd seen the diamond key before.

'Look!' cried Jack. 'Timmery was right, this is the key.'

A movement on the other side of the ice sheet caught Jack's attention. He ran over quickly. Nora, Gwillam and Elan were making their way back down the path. He banged on the ice and shouted but he couldn't make them hear.

'Turn around,' Jack shouted and concentrated hard on the three figures.

Nora suddenly stopped and turned. Jack smiled when he saw how surprised she looked. He held up the huge diamond for them to see.

'Look what we found,' he called as loudly as he could.

'Thank you,' said a voice from behind him, as Jack's wand and the diamond were both ripped from his hands. 'I'll take charge of these.'

Jack spun around.

'Velindur!' he cried.

CRYSTAL MAGIC

Time seemed to stand still as Jack's joy turned to dread. He knew he was powerless and at Velindur's mercy, there was nowhere to run. Velindur laughed. The hairs on the back of Jack's neck stood on end as the mocking voice echoed around the cavern.

'Once more we meet,' snarled Velindur. 'A raven and a useless boy.'

Jack looked around desperately. The cave was cold and lifeless. Velindur made a sweeping gesture with his arm.

'There's no help here. If these Druids aren't dead already, they soon will be.'

'Camelin, do your spell,' yelled Jack.

303

'I don't think your friend can hear you.'

Jack's heart sank as Velindur produced Camelin's wand and tossed it away.

'He's not going to be much help now,' he sneered as he nodded towards the rock face.

Jack peered into the darkness. Camelin's body lay slumped on the floor. Jack summoned up all his courage and took two steps in Camelin's direction. Velindur started chuckling to himself.

'I told them I'd be back. They underestimated me. I'll make them sorry they turned me out of Annwn.'

Jack took two more steps towards Camelin but stopped abruptly as a loud squeaking came from the doorway. Motley and Raggs charged towards Velindur's legs as Timmery and the Dorysk attacked his head.

'No!' shouted Jack as Velindur kicked out at the rats and swiped the two little bats with the back of his hand. 'No!' Jack sobbed again as he watched his friends fall.

Velindur brushed past Jack and stood before the ice sheet. He sneered and laughed loudly as he held up the diamond key so that everyone on the other side could see it. Jack's heart sank.

'Now I'll have my revenge,' he bellowed before hurling the diamond, with all his might, against the rock. It shattered into thousands of fragments. Jack ducked as the shards rained down on them. He wanted to cry when he saw the damage Velindur had done. The diamond key was broken beyond repair.

Velindur held his arms out wide.

'Vengeance is mine,' he yelled as he lunged at Jack. 'None of you will leave here alive.'

Jack leapt aside, ducked under his arm and ran over to Camelin.

'Wake up,' he shouted as he shook Camelin's limp body.

Camelin didn't stir. Velindur's evil laugh sent a shudder down Jack's spine. He stood and turned slowly to face him. Concern for Camelin and his friends replaced Jack's fear. He could see Nora, Gwillam and Elan on the other side of the ice sheet. From the looks on their faces Jack knew they were powerless to help. He instinctively clutched his golden acorn and wished with all his heart that Velindur would disappear.

A sudden gust of wind pushed Jack from behind. He staggered as a more powerful shock wave knocked him over and sent him tumbling towards the wall. An invisible force pinned him there. He watched in fascination as Velindur was swept off his feet and began to rise slowly into the air.

'NO! STOP!' Velindur screamed as he began to spin round.

Jack held his breath as Velindur whirled faster and faster until his body became a blur.

'What's happening?' Camelin called to Jack, as he stirred. 'What did you do?'

'I don't know. I don't know if it was me. I wished he wasn't here and the whirlwind came. Maybe it was Nora or Elan. Are you alright?'

Jack didn't hear Camelin's reply as the noise from the spiralling whirlwind got louder and louder until it filled the whole chamber. Velindur's screams made Jack shudder. He tried to cover his ears but he was unable to move. Then there was a great cloud of smoke as the spinning column unexpectedly evaporated. Jack's body suddenly went limp. He slid down the wall and landed on top of Camelin. When he looked up Velindur was gone and Jack's wand lay on the floor next to Camelin's.

'Where did he go?' Jack asked.

'I don't know and I don't care, he stole my wand, Now can you get off me?'

'He took mine too, but he didn't take them with him, they're over there, on the floor.'

Jack carefully tried to avoid stepping on any of the crystal shards as he went over to pick up the wands.

'What's all that on the floor?' asked Camelin.

'It's the diamond key. Velindur destroyed it before he disappeared. We've failed. The Druid's will never be woken now.'

Jack heard a low whimpering sound.

'What's that?'

They turned to where it was coming from and then Jack ran over to Raggs, who lay hunched on the floor.

'What's wrong?' said Jack.

Jack knelt down and supported Raggs' head. Timmery and the Dorysk fluttered overhead and Raggs moaned loudly as Motley scampered to his side, followed by Camelin.

'Done for I am, done for, at the end of my days. I've been run through.'

Jack could see a pool of blood underneath Raggs.

'Stand back,' said Motley. 'Let me look.'

Jack moved back.

'We've got to do something.'

Raggs moaned as Motley searched his fur.

'Nothing broken, you've got a shard from that crystal in your backside, once we get it out you'll mend. Come and help me Jack.'

Raggs moaned again. He was obviously in pain. Jack looked at the entrance to the cave. He could see

Nora, Elan and Gwillam's faces pressed against the ice sheet as they tried to see what was going on.

'*Somnus,*' Jack said as he pointed his wand at Raggs.

The spell worked immediately, the old ship's rat slumped heavily and fell fast asleep. Motley and Jack carefully pulled the shard from the top of his leg. Jack held it up to the light. He was about to throw it aside when there was a tinkling sound. The other shards began to rise from the ground. The sliver Jack held was whipped out of his hand and joined the rest as they rose into the air. They spun round and round until every shard was airborne. Jack watched in amazement as the pieces formed themselves into a spinning sphere, getting smaller and smaller until a great flash of light filled the cavern. When Jack could see again, the crystal key was whole and lay on the ground.

'Was that you?' asked Camelin.

'No, I didn't do anything, it happened on its own. I've no idea what's going on.'

'But I have,' said a voice from the shadows.

Jack braced himself, expecting Velindur to step towards him. He reached for the crystal key and shielded it against his chest before turning to point his wand towards the voice.

'That won't be necessary.'

Jack didn't recognize the old man who stepped out into the light.

'Let me introduce myself. My name is Mortarn, Gatekeeper of the Caves of Eternal Rest and Guardian of the Crystal Key.'

The old man bowed low and then held out his hand to Jack.

'If you'd be so kind, I can now put this back in its rightful place and let the others in.'

'I thought you were all asleep and couldn't be wakened,' said Jack.

'The others sleep on. My awakening is due to the return of the crystal key. I would have helped you sooner if I'd been able to. I felt the crystal's presence as soon as you came through the fifth gateway but it took time for my strength to return.'

Jack handed Mortarn the diamond-shaped crystal and watched as he went over to the entrance. He placed it carefully into the empty socket and turned it slowly three times then held his hands above it and began chanting. When Mortarn stopped he bowed to Jack.

'It won't be long now, the entrance will open shortly.'

They all watched as the ice rapidly thawed. Nora, Elan and Gwillam ran into the cave.

'We were so worried,' said Nora. 'What happened?'

'We found the crystal key in Velindur's room and came in through the fifth gate,' explained Jack.

'It's a Druid's dwindling door,' said the Dorysk, 'but Jack's key opened it.'

'The same key?' asked Nora. 'The magic key?'

Jack nodded.

'What happened to Velindur,' Elan asked.

'I don't know,' replied Jack. 'I held my acorn and wished he'd disappear, and he did.'

Mortarn walked over to Jack and placed his hands on his shoulders.

'I think you'll find crystal magic was responsible for Velindur's disappearance. It's the most powerful magic of all. It has a life of its own and can't be controlled by anyone. I've spent my life in these caves as their Guardian and I still don't understand how it works. It chooses its own path. The crystals have always given rest and refuge to any who came to the caves. Now the crystals are gone, I fear those who have chosen to rest here will never awaken. It is I, not you, who has failed.'

Mortarn sat on a ledge and put his head in his hands.

'It wasn't your fault,' said Elan. 'Velindur must

somehow have found out about the gateway.'

'He's had a Bogie and Spriggans stealing the crystals,' said Jack. 'I don't think they even know they've been into Annwn.'

'They'd never have taken them if they did,' agreed Nora. 'I suspect Velindur convinced them they were free for the taking.'

'What are we going to do now?' Mortarn asked Gwillam.

'Don't worry, all is not lost.'

The sound of beating wings made everyone turn and look at the cave's entrance. Three dragonettes flew into the cave, each grasping a bulging sack which they carefully lowered at Mortarn's feet.

'Look inside old friend,' said Gwillam.

Mortarn opened one of the sacks. A ray of warm light burst from within.

'The crystals! But how?' he cried.

'It's a long story but thanks to an old legend about a place called Howling Hill, some lost dragonettes and some very brave deeds, the crystals have been saved,' replied Nora.

'I think it's time we got them back to where they belong, don't you?' said Gwillam.

Nora opened the other two sacks and stood back.

'Can we help?' asked Jack.

Gwillam laughed.

'No, but thank you for asking, this won't take long, stand back everyone.'

He pointed his staff at the sacks. A shaft of white light illuminated the cave. The crystals rose and hovered in mid-air before dispersing themselves over the walls. Soon the whole cave was transformed. Every inch glowed with a warm light.

'Magnificent,' said Motley as he looked around.

'Truly amazing,' added the Dorysk as he flitted around the cave.

'I think it's time we left Mortarn to sort things out here,' said Nora.

'Shall we go back to the palace?' asked Elan.

'Palace!' said Raggs sleepily. 'Where am I?'

'Raggs!' cried Jack and ran over to the little rat. 'Are you alright?'

'My leg hurts.'

Nora went over and examined him.

'I need to put something on this leg of yours to stop the pain and help it heal.'

She gently lifted Raggs and cradled him in her arms.

While everyone made a fuss of Raggs Jack went over to Mortarn.

'What do you think the crystal magic did to Velindur?'

'Crystal magic never destroys it only ever protects or gives life.'

'You mean Velindur isn't dead?' croaked Camelin as he waddled over from the doorway to join Jack.

'Oh no, he won't be dead but the magic could have taken him anywhere.'

This wasn't the news Jack wanted to hear. He'd thought Velindur had been destroyed. He hoped the crystal magic had transported him a long way away. He didn't ever want to see him again.

'Time to go,' said Elan turning to Camelin and the dragonettes. 'Fly on ahead and let everyone know we're on our way.'

'I'll come too,' piped Timmery.

As soon as he crossed the entrance he changed into a beautiful hummingbird.

'Wait for me,' said the Dorysk as he transformed into a hummingbird too, identical to Timmery except for the glasses.

Elan bent down and let Motley scamper up her arm. He sat proudly on her shoulder as they said their goodbyes to Mortarn. As Nora passed Jack she held out her hand and said, 'I think I'll take charge of Camelin's wand for now.'

Jack handed her the wand. He watched as she and Gwillam set off for the palace. As Elan joined him at the entrance, Jack turned and took one last look at the cave. They waved to Mortarn before following Nora and Gwillam down the path.

'Ember wasn't able to melt the ice then?' he asked.

'No, she tried her best but as you've seen, crystal magic is very powerful.'

Jack yawned.

'It's been quite a night, I'm glad I don't have to get up for school in the morning.'

'We'll celebrate before you return.'

'You mean you're not coming with us?'

'I'll be back soon, really soon, I promise. Winver and Hesta will be pleased to see you both.'

Jack didn't answer. At least he was a boy this time. With any luck they'd be more interested in Camelin.

'Do you think Nora will be cross with me for giving Camelin his wand back? Only, without his help we wouldn't have rescued Raggs or found the crystal key.'

'I'm sure she'll be fine once you've explained. From what I hear Camelin's only learnt one spell.'

'He has, but it came in very useful tonight.'

Jack could see the tips of the four glass turrets

coming into view as they wound their way down the mountain.

'Is the glass palace crystal magic too?'

'I don't know,' replied Elan. 'It might be made from the same crystals. I don't ever remember a time when it wasn't there. You can look it up in the palace library. Everything that's ever been written about Annwn is in there.'

'Maybe another time, I'm a bit tired now.'

'Nearly there, after you've rested we'll celebrate.'

Jack smiled. He hadn't anticipated being back in Annwn so soon.

When they reached the Druid's village Gwillam was waiting for them. He was leaning on his staff, by the open door of his house.

'You look tired out Jack, why don't you sleep here for a while, I'll wake you when it's time to go.'

Jack looked at Elan.

'It's alright, I'll see you later. I'll tell Nora where you are.'

As Gwillam stood aside Jack entered the house and crossed the circular kitchen to the room he'd shared with Camelin when they'd stayed here before. As he opened the door he heard snoring. There on the straw pallet, lay Camelin, with his feet in the air. He didn't wake as Jack flopped down beside him. As soon as his head hit the pillow he fell fast asleep.

Jack heard someone calling. He struggled to open his eyes and was just drifting back to sleep when the door opened: 'Wake up sleepy head. Everyone's waiting for us at the clearing.'

Jack squinted at Gwillam as sunlight streamed in through the window.

'Where's Camelin?'

'Winver and Hesta came for him. Nora wanted to see him, something about his wand I think.'

'That was my fault, I ought to go and explain.'

'Not until you've had a wash and made yourself look respectable.'

'How's Raggs?'

'Nora's dressed his wound, he'll be fine but she thinks he might have a limp for the rest of his life. He didn't seem too pleased when she said he ought to retire from the Night Guard, and Motley made it worse when he asked if the Dorysk could join them. Nora's asked Raggs to take on sole responsibility for guarding the herborium, she said he could have a hammock in there with a feather mattress if he liked. I'm sure he'll enjoy not having to patrol the forests and he certainly seemed to like the feather bed he slept in last night. Now come on, get a move on.'

Jack washed quickly, tried to make his hair lie flat and then hurried through the circular rooms to the kitchen.

'That's much better,' said Gwillam as he walked around Jack. 'Are you hungry?'

Jack's stomach growled loudly.

'I think I must be!'

'That's good. If we hurry we'll see the barbecue being lit.'

Jack and Gwillam chatted as they made their way to the clearing. Tables and chairs had been dotted around the Monolith and a great crowd of people stood talking near the great stone. Jack didn't recognise any of the tall, cloaked men who bowed their heads slowly as they passed.

'You should be proud of yourself Jack,' said Gwillam. 'Without your help they wouldn't have survived.'

'Are they Druids from the Caves of Eternal Rest?'

'They are, at least they're the ones who've chosen to awaken and help the Queen. There are a lot of things that need doing before our land is restored to the happy place it once was.'

'Where's Camelin and the others?' asked Jack, as he looked around the crowd.

'They won't be long. Have you seen who's up there?'

Gwillam nodded towards the three great hills that formed the back of the amphitheatre. Ember was at the top of the middle hill. Her great twisted, silver horn glinted in the sunlight and her red scales flashed like burnished leather. As she raised her front claw, Jack could see her long talons had been polished. She really did look magnificent now.

'Do you think she's happy?' asked Jack.

'I'm sure she is. She'll be safe here and there are lots of caves in the mountains where she can make a new home. We'll make sure she's alright.'

Jack smiled and waved but Ember's head was turned towards the palace.

'The Queen!' someone in the crowd shouted.

Jack stood on tiptoe but he couldn't see much until the crowd parted. Everyone bowed as the procession from the palace approached the Monolith. Leading it was Coragwenelan, wearing the silver crown with the three moons that Jack had seen her wearing before. Her long forest green dress swept the floor. Her wand was tucked into a silver girdle and her embroidered white cloak billowed in the breeze, the silver knotwork designs sparkling in the sunshine. Winver and Hesta sat proudly on her shoulders. The crowd bowed as she passed and Jack bowed too. Twelve hooded figures followed behind. The first two stopped when they reached Gwillam and he stepped out in front of them.

'Come on Jack, you need to walk with me before the Blessed Council.'

Jack joined Gwillam and they walked behind the Queen towards a long table. Nora was waiting for them with the two rats on her shoulders. When Coragwenelan was seated in a beautiful carved chair at the head of the table, a dazzling array of colours burst before their eyes as two hummingbirds and three dragonettes darted about. Their iridescent scales and feathers changed colour as they caught the light. Everyone clapped and the Queen signalled for the crowd to be seated.

'Let the entertainment begin,' announced the Queen.

A storyteller walked amongst the tables and retold the legend of Howling Hill. When he got to the end of his tale Raggs stood up with the aid of a stick, and told the story of the adventure they'd had inside Silver Hill. When he reached the part Ember Silver Horn had played he directed the crowd's attention to the magnificent dragon perched on top of the hillside. Everyone clapped and cheered. A mighty roar from the hilltop silenced everyone. Ember Silver Horn the Magnificent opened her wings and swooped towards them. She breathed out a great flame and aimed it towards the barbecue. The charcoal instantly glowed brightly. Jack had never seen such an amazing sight. He'd felt Ember take off from the pit, inside Silver Hill, but it had been dark and he hadn't seen her in flight. Her great wingspan cast a shadow over the whole clearing. The crowd held on to cups and plates so the draught from her wings wouldn't blow them away. Ember circled the crowd once before flying off towards the mountains. There was silence as everyone watched until she disappeared completely from sight.

'My turn now,' said Camelin as he took off.

He performed the most complicated routines he knew, diving, spinning, looping-the-loop and flying on his back. The three dragonettes joined in and blew circles of fire for Camelin to fly through. The crowd clapped loudly in appreciation. When he returned to his perch, Winver made her way over to him and shuffled up close. Camelin looked pleadingly at Jack who grinned back. He stopped smiling moments later when Hesta swooped down and landed on his shoulder.

After everyone had eaten their fill and chatted about their adventures Nora stood and announced that it was time to go.

'Aw, can't we stay a bit longer?' said Camelin.

'I'm afraid not, Jack's Grandad will wonder where he is if he's not back at Ewell House when he comes to collect him. And there's the little matter of a loft inspection too.'

Camelin looked at Jack.

'We had an accident with one of the raven baskets and didn't have time to clear it up,' explained Jack. 'We were in a bit of a hurry last night.'

Nora didn't reply but Jack could see she and Coragwenelan were smiling.

'I believe this is yours?' said Gwillam as he pulled Camelin's raven basket out from under the table.

'Aw great, now we won't have to fly back, we can use the basket.'

'I don't think so,' said Nora as she pointed her wand at it. There was a sudden pop as it shrank to the size of a small plate. 'It'll be easier to carry home like this.'

Camelin pulled a face but didn't complain.

Jack suddenly remembered Nora's key. He took the chain off and offered it to her.

'This isn't my key Jack, it's yours.'

'But it was in the drawer in the herborium,' he replied.

Camelin scowled at Jack.

'You had it all the time?'

'He did,' said Nora. 'And he was right not to use it for the wrong reasons.'

'I don't understand,' said Jack. 'It's a magic key, it shrinks and grows to fit any lock.'

'It's not the key,' said Nora. 'You're the one making it change shape, the magic is coming from inside you.'

'Oh my!' said Timmery. 'Jack can do real magic.'

Camelin humphed.

'How?' asked Jack.

'The power of Annwn is within you,' explained Gwillam. 'Each time you come here it grows stronger. A time will come when you won't need your wand any more.'

Jack was amazed. He didn't know what to say. He would have liked to ask Gwillam more but he didn't get a chance. Gwillam went over to a group of hooded figures waiting by the path that would lead them to the Western Portal. Coragwenelan thanked them all for what they'd done and Jack had a lump in his throat as he said his goodbyes. He wished his visit to Annwn could have been longer.

'We'll be in touch soon,' Gwillam whispered to Jack. 'It won't be long before Elan is back in Glasruhen.'

Everyone waved as they started out along the path towards the Western Gate.

'We'll be home in no time,' said Nora.

'We'd have been there in half the time if you hadn't shrunk my flying basket,' grumbled Camelin.

When they got back to Ewell House Nora went straight to the herborium to make Raggs comfortable.

'Don't disappear,' she called to Camelin. 'Remember, you have a loft inspection.'

Camelin flew around the corner of the house and Nora and Jack climbed the stairs. When they looked inside the loft, Jack's mouth fell open. The floor was spotless. There wasn't a single oversized polystyrene ball anywhere to be seen. Camelin sat on the window ledge with his beak open too.

'How did this get so tidy?' asked Nora.

'We helped,' squeaked Fergus, as he and Berry appeared beside Camelin.

'It was the least we could do since you'd gone to rescue Raggs,' added Berry.

Jack smiled. This time Camelin could find something nice to give the little rats as payment. He owed them.

'What happened to the window?' asked Nora.

Camelin shuffled from one foot to the other, 'If I hadn't bigged it we wouldn't have been able to fly through it.'

Nora pointed her wand at the frame and shrank it back to its original size.

'That's better, everything's back to normal now.'

'I'd better get my things together,' said Jack. 'Grandad will be here soon.'

'We all owe you a great deal,' said Nora. 'We couldn't have saved the Druids without you both.'

Camelin coughed and looked pointedly at the wand sticking out of Nora's pocket.

'Yes, you can have it back now, but if I hear that you've misused it, you know where it's going.'

Camelin jumped onto the floor, and hopped,

skipped and jumped over to Nora. 'I'll be good,' he promised as he carefully took his wand back.

Nora smiled.

'No more bigging. Unless it's an emergency! I think you and Jack ought to have some wand practice tomorrow. One of you has a lot of catching up to do.'

Before Jack went down to the kitchen he went back to the loft to say goodbye to Camelin. He was surprised to find him on his back with his legs in the air, on a raven-sized beanbag.

'Where did that come from?'

'Do you like it? I didn't think you'd mind me shrinking your beanbag, only I wanted something a bit more comfortable than a raven basket.'

'Does Nora know?'

'She said no bigging, she didn't say anything about shrinking.'

'I thought you only knew one spell.'

'Aw, shrinking's easy. You just say the bigging spell backwards.'

Jack smiled. He didn't think Nora would mind too much as long as he didn't start flying around the loft in it.

'See you tomorrow then?'

'Yeah, it's been a brilliant weekend hasn't it?'

Jack struggled to find the right answer.

'Different,' he said in the end before making his way back down the ladder to wait for Grandad in the kitchen.

It felt as if he'd been gone a whole week instead of a couple of days. There were still questions he needed to ask and he wanted to find out all he could about crystal magic. He had things he needed to discover about himself too, especially if Gwillam was right and the magic of Annwn was within him. His hand closed around the small key that hung from the silver chain. Nora had said he'd made the key special. His power had made it change shape. He had six weeks before he went back to school and he wanted to spend them finding out as much as possible about his own powers and what he could do with them. He couldn't wait to begin.

WHO'S WHO, WHAT'S WHAT
and
WHERE IS IT?

Now I can read and write, Nora's asked me to make a list of everyone and everything in Glasruhen and Annwn. She thinks I've done this all on my own so please don't tell her that Catherine Cooper's been helping me. In fact, Catherine's been helping me write my memoirs, the first three books are finished and you can read all about my adventures in, The Golden Acorn, Glasruhen Gate *and* Silver Hill.

Of course, the most important bird in the whole of Glasruhen is me, Camelin. I'm the trusted companion of Nora (Eleanor Ewell) and friend of Elan. I'm also the wise and learned teacher of Jack Brenin who, it appears, is The Chosen One we've all been waiting for. He wasn't much good at first but he's getting better. I am known as: an ace stunt flyer, brilliant Dorysk hunter, food critic, inventor of the raven owl call and operations co-ordinator for the Night Guard (you'll soon find out about all of those things). I've added some comments of my own in brackets.

WHO'S WHO?

Addergoole Peabody – A **Bogie**, one of the **Not So Fair Folk,** who works mainly for **Jennet.** He gathers information for her, especially about the other **Water Nymphs**. The family name is **Addergoole** and **Pyecroft** is his older brother. *(Don't ever tell Peabody anything, he's a snitch.)*

Addergoole Pyecroft – A **Bogie**, one of the **Not So Fair Folk**. He works alone and will trade or sell information to anyone. The family name is **Addergoole** and **Peabody** is his younger brother. *(Pyecroft's an even bigger snitch than Peabody.)*

Agye – One of the two **Gargoyles** that guard **Uriel's Well.** *(Read about how I defeated Agye in* Glasruhen Gate.*)*

Allana – Is now a **Gnori**, she used to be the **Hamadryad** of **Newton Gill Forest** when she was known as:

Allana, the Beautiful, Guardian of the Grove, Most Kind and Wise.

Arrana – The last **Hamadryad** left on earth. Her full title is: Arrana, The Wise, Protector and Most Sacred of All. When Arrana transforms from an oak tree into her **Hamadryad** form she is as tall as the tree. She contains all the magic of **Annwn** within her branches and protects all the trees in **Glasruhen Forest**.

Berry – One of the youngest rats in the **Night Guard**. Berry has smooth fur, which he keeps well groomed. He's not as big as the older members of the guard and can always be found with **Fergus**. *(I can usually get Berry and Fergus to do odd jobs for me.)*

Camelin – The most important raven in the world. *(Read all the Jack Brenin books to find out how special I am.)*

Catherine Cooper – Chronicler of **Jack Brenin**'s adventures. *(I thought the books should have been called the* Adventures of **Camelin** *but I was outvoted.)*

Charkle – A **dragonette** from the **Westwood Roost**. As a baby he was captured by **Spriggans** and imprisoned in a cage. His brothers are **Norris** and **Snook**. *(Charkle's a bit of a show-off sometimes, especially when he tries to copy my stunt flying and blows fire as he circles.)*

Chief Knuckle – Leader of a band of **Spriggans** living underground close to **Ewell House**. He is the Chief because he has the biggest and best *sniffer* of all the Spriggans (that means he's got a big nose). He's brilliant at finding veins of gold, silver and precious stones. There are thirteen Spriggans in Chief Knuckle's band. Their names are Slinger, Swiper, Scratch, Grunt, **Grub**, Grabber, Whiff, Wheezer, Wrecker, Pinch, Pepper and Punch. It was Slinger, Wheezer and Scratch who tunnelled up into **Grandad**'s greenhouse and kitchen. Whiff, Pinch and **Grub** were the ones who captured **Orin**.

Coragwenelan – The **Queen of Annwn**.

Coriss – A **Water Nymph** living in the **Mere Pool**, not far from **Beconbury**. She's an expert on swords and daggers and has a large collection of both. She does not like visitors unless they have a special and unusual gift for her. *(I thought **Jennet** was bad tempered until I met Coriss.)*

Cory – A **Dryad** who knows where the **cauldron plates** have been hidden for safe keeping on **Glasruhen Hill**.

Dorysk – A small creature with the ability to shape-shift. In its natural form it looks a bit like a hedgehog and can only change into something of equal or smaller size. There is usually only one Dorysk living in an area. Dorysks are very hard to catch. If you see a small creature wearing a pair of glasses it will be a Dorysk, without them they can hardly see at all. Dorysks like to gather information. (*I'm the best Dorysk catcher in the whole of Glasruhen.*)

Draygull – A strange looking creature the size of a man with an owl-like, feathered face. One lives in **Silver Hill** and conducts the **Hag** choir. Draygulls have a very good sense of smell and can identify and locate creatures by sniffing. A long time ago Draygulls were **Dragon Screechers**. They would screech strange music that soothed **Dragons** and hypnotised them into a deep sleep. (*Draygulls must be tone deaf if they think Hags can sing.*)

Dugmore – One of the **Spriggan** cooks inside **Silver Hill**.

Elan – One of the **Fair Folk** of **Annwn,** she was trapped on Earth for hundreds of years. Jack sees Elan as she really is when he visits Annwn. She is skilled in magic.

Fergus – One of the youngest rats in the **Night Guard**. Fergus has tousled fur, which he finds difficult to groom. He's not as big as the older members of the guard and can always be found with **Berry**. *(I can usually get Fergus and Berry to do odd jobs for me.)*

Fernella and **Fernilla** – Two **Dryads** who attend the **Mother Oak** in **Annwn**.

Finnola Fytche – A **Hag** living in a cave at the base of **Westwood**. *(If you ever visit a Hag's cave, take a clothes peg for your nose.)*

Gavin – A former **Acolyte** of **Gwillam**, now a boatman in **Annwn**. *(Gavin's great, he bought **Saige** for me from the fair in Annwn.)*

Gerda – A large white goose who guards and keeps watch over the grounds of **Ewell House** for **Nora**. Her mate is called **Medric**.

Gnori of Newton Gill – A Gnori is a dead tree and was once a **Hamadryad**. The other trees refer to it as a hollow tree because the Hamadryad has died and is no longer inside. The Gnori in **Newton Gill Forest** was once a **Hamadryad** called **Allana**, the Beautiful, Guardian of the Grove, Most Kind and Wise.

Grabble – One of the **Spriggan** cooks inside **Silver Hill**.

Grandad – Samuel Brenin, known to everyone as Sam, is Jack's Grandad. The Brenin family have lived in **Brenin House** for generations. It's next door to **Ewell House**. Grandad loves cricket and he looks after the ground at **Glasruhen Cricket Club**. He is also a very keen gardener and is the vice chairman of the local gardening club. He has a very large vegetable garden and greenhouse. Grandad's house is on the **back lane** just past the playing field and close to the cricket club. *(Jack's Grandad doesn't know about me so I have to be very quiet when I visit Jack in his bedroom. I think Jack should tell his Grandad that ravens don't eat birdseed.)*

Grol – One of the two **Gargoyles** that guard **Uriel's Well**. *(You can read about how I outwitted Grol in Glasruhen Gate.)*

Grub – A **Spriggan** in **Chief Knuckle**'s band who gets loose and turns into a giant. *(Giants snore loudly and eat vast amounts of food.)*

Gwillam – Gwillam no longer lives on Earth. He is a Druid and used to be the guardian of the **Oak Well**, which was in the heart of Glasruhen, close to where Newton Gill is today. Gwillam was killed by the Romans in AD 61 and since then has lived on in Annwn, the **Otherworld**. Like all ancient Druids, Gwillam has a magical staff and knows a lot of magic. He is also Nora's twin brother. He is now the leader of **The Blessed Council** in Annwn. *(I miss Gwillam and wish we could go back to the time before the Romans came.)*

Hesta – one of the two white ravens belonging to the **Queen of Annwn**. *(She pesters me and giggles too much – I call her Hesta Pester, but don't tell the Queen.)*

Jack Brenin – He's not much to look at, a bit on the small size with very untidy hair, but he's **The One** we've all been waiting for. He had to help me rescue Nora's lost cauldron plates but to do that he had to become a **Raven Boy**, like me, and I had to teach him to fly. He is very polite, always keeps his promises and tries his best. He likes football and cricket and he was born on October 31st, which is the day we celebrate **Samhain**. He lives at **Brenin House**, with his **Grandad** now, before that he lived in Greece with his mum and dad. Sadly Jack's mum died and his dad is still in Greece, working as an archaeologist. Jack has a special wand, given to him by **Arrana**, the oldest **Hamadryad** in **Glasruhen Forest**. He also has a **golden acorn**, made for him by the master craftsman of **Annwn**, **Lloyd the Goldsmith**. *(He's my best friend and it's great when we go flying together.)*

Jed – One of the guards of the **Western Portal** in **Annwn**.

Jennet – A **Water Nymph** living in the spring by **The Hawthorn Well** on **Glasruhen Hill**. She doesn't like being disturbed and can be very bad tempered at times *(Actually, she's bad tempered all the time.)*

Lloyd the Goldsmith – All the **Druid's Golden Acorns** were made in **Annwn** by Lloyd, the master craftsman and goldsmith.

Medric – **Nora**'s watch-goose and **Gerda**'s mate.

Mortarn – Gatekeeper of the **Caves of Eternal Rest** and Guardian of the **Crystal Key**.

Motley – Leader of the **Night Guard**. *(Of course Motley reports directly to me because I'm the only one who can do the warning call of the raven owl.)*

Myryl – A **Water Nymph** living in the spring by **The Mound**, not far from **Beconbury**. She's an expert on cauldrons and has a large collection. She loves visitors and can talk for hours. *(Be prepared for a long visit if you go to see her, Myryl talks more than Timmery.)*

Nora – Nora's full name is Eleanor Ewell. She's a **Druid** who was trapped on Earth after some of her cauldron plates were lost. Her full title is: The **Seanchai**, Keeper of Secrets and Ancient Rituals, Guardian of the **Sacred Grove**, Healer, **Shape-Shifter** and Wise Woman. Nora is skilled in magic, knows all about herbs and healing, is very wise and can shape-shift into lots of different forms. Nora has her own library, it's full of books she's written and bound herself. Her favourite place is her **herborium** where she makes all her potions and preparations. *(I live with Nora at Ewell House, which is at the bottom of **Glasruhen Hill**. She's nice, but she doesn't always appreciate what it's like to be a raven.)*

Norris – A **dragonette** from the **Westwood Roost**. He was captured by the **Spriggans** of **Silver Hill** and imprisoned in a cage. His brothers are **Charkle** and **Snook**.

Orin – **Motley**'s sister. She is pure white and would be a great prize if caught by a **Spriggan**. She is not allowed to be a member of the **Night Guard** because it would be too dangerous for her.

Raggs – A member of the **Night Guard**. He used to be a ship's rat but when he got too old for a life at sea he made his way to **Glasruhen** and joined the Night Guard. He has long whiskers, grey fur and a very twitchy nose. *(Raggs tells really great stories; he's been around the world several times and has seen some amazing things.)*

Saige – An **Oracular Frog** from **Annwn**. Saige is able to accurately predict the answers to mathematical questions. *(Saige is my frog but I'm not allowed to keep her in my loft. Nora gave her my secret cave to live in.)*

Sam Brenin – See **Grandad**.

Snook – A **dragonette** from the **Westwood Roost**. He was captured by the **Spriggans** of **Silver Hill** and imprisoned in a cage. His brothers are **Charkle** and **Norris**.

Sylvana – The **Mother Oak** in **Annwn**. Her full title is: Sylvana, Mother of all **Hamadryads**, Guardian of the Oaks and Bearer of the Sacred Mistletoe.

Teg – One of the guards of the **Western Portal** in **Annwn**.

Timmery – A very small pipistrelle bat who loves to talk, is full of enthusiasm and enjoys visitors. He roosts in the belfry of All Hallows Church next to Glasruhen Cricket Ground. He's very brave and has a really good sense of direction. *(I like Timmery best when he's asleep in his belfry, as far away from me as possible.)*

Uriel – A **Water Nymph** living in a well on the south side of **Glasruhen Hill**. She does not welcome visitors and is feared by everyone. Her well is difficult to find and is guarded by two **Gargoyles**. *(The Gargoyles were no match for me.)*

Velindur – The self-appointed **King of Annwn**, Velindur has no magical powers. He seeks revenge on all **Druids** because **The Blessed Council** banished him from Annwn. *(He doesn't like ravens either.)*

Winver – One of the two white ravens belonging to the **Queen of Annwn**. *(Just as giggly as Hester but not as much of a pest.)*

WHAT'S WHAT ?

Acolyte – The training for an acolyte is long and hard. You have to learn and be able to recite the histories, sing the songs and tell stories. You have to know all about plants, potions and spells, and eventually learn how to read and write. Acolytes were allowed a **lath** (a twig with magical properties which can be used as a wand) when they'd reached a certain point in their training and were then taught how to use it. **Gwillam** always had several acolytes, all at different stages in their training. *(Gavin was one of his acolytes; he was always kind to me.)*

Bogies – Small, bad tempered little men who snoop and then trade the information they've acquired. They are particularly proud of their noses. The longer a Bogie's nose the more important he is. They are slightly bigger than **Spriggans** and usually live alone. **Addergoole Peabody** and **Addergoole Pyecroft** are brothers. They always like to have a feather in their cap and don't think twice about pulling one out of a bird's tail. Don't ever tell a Bogie anything. *(Peabody's tried to pull out one of my tail feathers more than once.)*

Book of Shadows – This is a magical book, a bit like an encyclopaedia. There is a special way to access the book, known only to its owner. Should anyone else open the book its pages will look blank. The first page can be used to write messages to anyone else who also has a Book of Shadows. *(I've got my own Book of Shadows now.)*

Book of Sorrows – A book kept by **Mortarn**, the gatekeeper for the **Caves of Eternal Rest**. Before **Druids** can enter the caves they have to empty their sorrows into this book, only then will they be able to find rest and sleep peacefully.

Book of Dragon Lore – A book, compiled and hand-made by **Nora,** that contains all the known information about dragons. It was bound with **dragon skin**. *(Jack's read the whole book and told me all about it.)*

Cauldron of Life – One of the **Four Treasures of Annwn**, this is a cauldron made from thirteen bronze plates that can be laced together. Each plate has a different tree symbol on it. The cauldron was too precious to be kept in one piece so all the separate parts were kept in the sacred groves or wells and guarded by **Druids** or **Water Nymphs**. When the cauldron was needed for the ritual opening of the **Western Gate**, the plates would be collected and **Nora** would lace them together. Once the cauldron was re-made the portal into **Annwn** could be opened. The thirteen trees on the cauldron plates are beech, pine, holly, hazel, apple, elm, rowan, ash, birch, yew, hawthorn, oak and willow. *(It was my fault the hawthorn, oak and willow plates went missing.)*

Cauldron Plates – Three of the plates (those bearing the hawthorn, oak and willow tree emblems) were lost in the past, which is why **Nora** was trapped on earth. Without these three plates Nora was unable to remake the cauldron which was needed to open the **Western Portal**. An ancient **Prophecy** foretold the coming of one who would find the missing **cauldron plates** and save everyone.

Crochan Tree – The leaves from this tree are extraordinary. An elixir can be made by brewing the leaves, when this is drunk by the Druids it makes them immortal.

Crystal Key – This is a huge diamond shaped crystal and is the key which opens the **Caves of Eternal Rest**. The caves are sealed with an ice sheet. When the key is in position the gatekeeper can turn it three times to melt the ice sheet and unseal the entrance. **Mortarn** is the keeper of the crystal key and gatekeeper to the caves.

Crystal Magic – The most powerful kind of magic. It can't be controlled by anyone and has a life of its own.

Donar – The coinage introduced into **Annwn** by **Velindur**.

Doors – There are many kinds of doorways. Some lead into hillsides, some into **Fairy Mounds** and some into the **Otherworld**. **Bogie** doors are never well looked after and usually have a sign on them telling the caller to GO AWAY. Fairy doors are always well kept and usually have shiny doorknobs that can speak to the caller. A **dwindling door** is a special kind of magical **Druid**'s door. **Portals** are the doors between Earth and **Annwn**.

Dragons – Long ago there were many dragons but now only a few survive. The bigger the dragon, the longer its name. There were three types of dragon: **dragonairs**, **dragonors** and **dragonettes**.

Dragonairs – Very large with red scales and usually bad tempered. Dragonairs can fly and both males and females can breathe fire. Famous dragonairs include Brynog Long Tail the Invincible, Zacyry Jagged Tooth the Mighty, Ember Silver Horn the Magnificent, Wygrym Sharp Claw the Fearless and Petryn Long Beard the Brave.

Dragonors – These dragons usually had blue scales and were medium sized. They didn't breathe fire but had the sharpest teeth. They were always getting into fights, especially with knights and they are now extinct. The names of the dragonors have been lost and only the slayers' names are remembered, for example, Sir Berwick the Dragon Slayer.

Dragonettes – Very small dragons with shiny green scales and tiny purple wings. Only the males breathe fire. They were highly prized by **Spriggans** who would capture them when they could. **Charkle** was captured by Spriggans and imprisoned in a cage. The Spriggans would pull his tail if their candles went out so he'd breathe fire and light the wicks again.

Dragon Screecher – The profession of a **Draygull** who could screech a song that would hypnotise any dragon into a deep sleep.

Dragon Skin – A dragon sheds its skin every hundred years. The skins are highly prized because they are very strong and fireproof. The **Book of Dragon Lore** was bound with the skin shed by Wygrym Sharp Claw the Fearless.

Druids – Were trained to recite stories, poems and sing songs; they learnt the whole history of the Earth and Annwn this way. They needed to know about herbs and remedies and how to heal people. Anyone chosen to be a Druid would train from an early age, for up to thirty years and while training was known as an **acolyte**. Once a Druid's training was complete they could choose how to use their skills, some would become bards, others healers and some teachers. (*I used to be Gwillam's acolyte but I wasn't able to finish my training.*) Druids each have a ceremonial hooded robe, a staff, which would once have been a branch from a sacred tree, and a golden acorn.

The staff and acorn give them the ability to perform magic. They can live forever if they drink an elixir, a kind of tea, brewed from the leaves of the **crochan tree** which can only be found in Annwn in the Druid's Village.

Dryads – A special type of **Nymph**. Dryads inhabit trees. They can move around from tree to tree and tend all the trees in a forest or wood. If their tree should die they can find another to live in. A special kind of Dryad is called a **Hamadryad**.

Dwindling Door – Any door that is used by a **Druid** can be turned, with a little bit of magic, into a dwindling door. If any if the **Fair Folk** or **Not So Fair Folk** go through the door uninvited it gets smaller. The Druid can then tell if anyone has been where they shouldn't. However, if a human goes through a dwindling door it will disappear altogether and trap the human inside the room, where they must await their fate.

Fair Folk – These are the little people of this world, including fairy folk, **Nymphs**, Brownies, **Dorysks,** and the larger people of **Annwn**. Some can fly, some have magic, some can shape shift and all are immortal. They can sometimes be mischievous but they don't mean any harm. Unless you have special sight you'd find it hard to see any of the small fair folk that inhabit the earth.

Fairy Mound – Any mound found on ground between an oak, ash and thorn tree will be a fairy mound. Sometimes fairies live there all the time; other mounds are just used for feasts and celebrations. All fairy doors have a shiny doorknob. When anyone knocks on the door the doorknob transforms into a face and can speak with the visitor.

Four Portals of Annwn – These are the four ancient and secret **Gateways of Annwn**. They are the boundaries between Annwn and Earth.

Four Treasures of Annwn – These are the **Cauldron of Life**, the **Spear of Justice**, the **Sword of Power** and the **Stone of Destiny**. Each one opens one of the **Four Portals**.

Gargoyles – A creature of stone with a grotesque face. It has a wide gaping mouth and a forked tongue. Never look a female gargoyle in the eye or she will terrify and transfix you. This is how gargoyles catch their prey. *(They didn't get us!)*

Gateways of Annwn - These are the four ancient and secret doorways or portals into **Annwn**. They are the boundaries between Annwn and Earth.

Golden Acorn – All the **Druid**'s golden acorns were made in **Annwn** by the master craftsman, **Lloyd the Goldsmith**. A Druid needs their golden acorn and wand to be able to perform rituals and magic. *(Jack's got his own golden acorn.)*

Gnarles – Are dying trees, no longer under the protection of a **Hamadryad**. They still have some life in them but the **Dryads**, who once tended and looked after them have left the forest and the Gnarles are left to slowly turn into dead wood. *(They don't seem to appreciate my singing.)*

Hags – Small disgusting smelly creatures about the same size as a raven. They live in caves and aren't very hygienic. They have large hooked beaky noses, and long claw-like fingers. Their blackish purple hair reaches the floor. Hags meet up at various times of the year and like to sing. *(Not that you'd recognise it as singing.)*

Hamadryads – Are the **Dryads** of any oak tree. Unlike other dryads, if the oak tree dies, the Hamadryad also dies. They are part of the tree and are unable, like other Dryads, to move from tree to tree. All Hamadryads began life as an acorn from the **Mother Oak** in **Annwn**. They grow and develop rapidly and once fully grown, they give their protection to all the trees and **Dryads** living in their forest.

Herborium – This is a special room at **Ewell House** where **Nora** keeps all the ingredients for her potions. It's also where she keeps her herbarium, a collection of dried herbs and pressed flowers that have been studied, labelled and written about in one of her many books. Nora also has books about plants, spells and potions in the herborium. *(I'm not always allowed in the herborium but Jack is.)*

Hudlath – A magic wand transformed from a **lath**. Once the wand has been empowered it will appear smooth. You have to be very careful how you use a magic wand. Sparks can erupt from the end. *(Jack singed my tail feathers the first time he used his wand but I got my own back when I used mine for the first time.)*

King of Annwn – The rightful king of **Annwn** is buried deep with **The Mound**; he chose mortality instead of eternal life. **Velindur** is the self-appointed King in Annwn.

King of the Forest – Jack Brenin is to be crowned King of the Forest when the new **Hamadryad**s are grown as foretold in the last two lines of the **Prophecy**:

When all is equal, all is done,
And joy is brought to everyone,
The Brenin will be crowned again,
Over the Forests he will reign.

Lath – A wand. A lath is a twig with magical properties that can be transformed into a **hudlath**. To empower the lath it has to be taken to one of the sacred wells where the keeper of the well, a special kind of **Water Nymph** called an **Undine** chooses your magical symbol. Once you have touched the symbol with your right hand it glows and becomes very hot, the symbol then appears on your fingertip. When you take your wand in your left hand it appears as a twig. But after you've been given your symbol, if you put it in your right hand the wand will transform into a **hudlath** (a magic wand).

Mother Oak – This is the oak tree on which **Hamadryad** acorns grow. The Mother Oak will shake her branches and grant the **Druid** some of her acorns. She is called: Sylvana, Mother of all **Hamadryads**, Guardian of the Oaks and Bearer of the Sacred Mistletoe. The **Druid**s in **Annwn**, and two **Dryad**s, called **Fernella** and **Fernilla**, care for the Mother Oak.

Night Guard – A band of eight rats, led by Motley, who keep watch over Glasruhen and report to Nora. The rats in the guard are: **Motley**, Podge, Midge, Lester, Morris, **Raggs**, **Fergus** and **Berry**.

Not So Fair Folk – These are usually the little people of this world and some of the larger people of **Annwn**. They are unable to fly, they don't have magical powers and they can't shape shift. They may be vindictive and don't mind causing harm. Unless you have special sight you'd find it hard to see any of the not so fair folk.

Nymphs – There are lots of different kinds of Nymphs. Some inhabit the trees and are called **Dryads** or **Hamadryads**. Others inhabit the hills and meadows. **Undines** are a type of **Water Nymph** and the Nymphs of the air are called Sylphs. They have the ability to fly and shape-shift.

Oak Well – This was the well tended by **Gwillam** in the centre of the **Sacred Grove**. The oak **cauldron plate** used to hang on the branches of the oak tree next to the well. *(This was my home before the Romans came.)*

Oracular Frogs – Only found in **Annwn**. The males predict the weather but female oracular frogs have other prophetic abilities. *(**Gavin** bought one as a present for me.)*

Otherworld – Another name for **Annwn**.

Prophecy – this is the prophecy, which Jack Brenin is destined to fulfil:

A Brenin boy you'll need to find
Born at Samhain of humankind.
The One you seek is brave and strong
And his true heart will do no wrong.
The Golden Acorn he will see
And listen to the Dryad's plea.
Underneath Pengridion Hill
He'll make a promise he'll fulfil.
When all is equal, all the same
That which was lost is found again.

Queen of Annwn – Her name is **Coragwenelan** and her full title is: Queen of the **Fair Folk**, Guardian of the **Gateways of Annwn**. She is also an immortal **Nymph** and **Shape-Shifter**.

Raven Boy – I'm a raven boy and have been for most of my life. Nora and I helped **Jack** to become a raven boy too. When we touch foreheads he transforms into a raven. Jack needs to touch foreheads with me again to change back into a boy. *(Being a raven boy has its advantages: you can fly and eat as much as you can get.)*

Romans – In AD 61 the Romans were ordered to kill all the **Druids** in Britain. The Romans at the **Viroconium** camp were the XIV Legion. Quintus Flavius Maximus was the Camp Prefect, in charge of the camp when the main body of the XIV Legion were away. Titus Antonius Agrippa was a Centurion in charge of a marching party of eight soldiers. Marcus Cornelius Drusus was a soldier. Gaius Rufus Octavian was the messenger who brought the news from the XIV Legion to Viroconium. *(I don't like Romans.)*

Runes of Annwn – The ancient writing of the Fair Folk of Annwn.

Sacred Grove – A forest of oak trees, which used to cover the whole area around **Glasruhen, Newton Gill** and beyond.

Samhain – One of the four main festivals, celebrated on October 31ˢᵗ, which was the beginning of the Celtic New Year. *(It's also Jack's birthday.)*

Seanchai (pronounced *shawn ack ee*) – A Druid who remembers and keeps important information safe. *(Nora knows just about all there is to know.)*

Shape-Shifter – Someone or something that can change its shape at will. It is different to transformation, which needs a spell or potion. *(Nora and Elan can shape-shift and so can the Dorysk. Jack can only transform.)*

Spear of Justice – One of the **Four Treasures of Annwn**, it is needed for the ritual to open the northern gateway. It was used to determine if someone was speaking the truth.

Spriggans – These tiny men (about 60cm tall) live underground. They are miners and think that everything that comes from the Earth belongs to them. They must always be roped together because a loose Spriggan can grow into a giant.

Staffs – Druids in **Annwn** carry staffs of power. They use them to perform magic.

Stone of Destiny – One of the **Four Treasures of Annwn**, it is needed for the ritual to open the eastern gateway. Some say that if you look into the stone you will see your future.

Sword of Power – One of the Four Treasures of Annwn, it is needed for the ritual to open the southern gateway. The sword would protect anyone using it for good from harm.

The Blessed Council – Those who were left live together in the **Druid's Village**. Thirteen of these Druids, who make up the Blessed Council, were chosen to work alongside the **Queen of Annwn**. Gwillam was unanimously voted their leader. They meet together in the Council Chamber, which is on the ground floor of one of the circular turret rooms in the **Glass Palace**. Each member of the Blessed Council has his own seat at a semi-circular table. The thirteen members of the Blessed

Council are: Gwillam, Nesta, Berwin, Elgan, Geraint, Nerys, Tirion, Gunnoda, Tegwen, Brid, Maddock, Gwenda and Kireg.

The One – Jack Brenin is the chosen one who is expected to help the inhabitants of Glasruhen. He's not sure why he's been chosen, how he can help or if he really wants to. *(There is a **Prophecy** about Jack and how he will save everyone.)*

Undines – A type of **Water Nymph** that likes to live in ponds, lakes, waterfalls, springs and wells. Several Undines live in the **Glasruhen** region. Their names are **Jennet**, Isen, Nymet, **Myryl**, Kerrin, **Coriss**, **Uriel** and Lucie. *(Make sure you take a gift with you if you need help or information or they won't even talk to you.)*

Uriel's Well – A well inhabited by a **Water Nymph** called **Uriel** in a desolate place on the south side of **Glasruhen Hill**. *(This place makes all my feathers stand on end.)*

Wands – The greatest wands are the ones from the **Hamadryad** oak and contain a special magic from **Annwn**. A wand is gifted to a new **Druid** by a **Dryad** or **Hamadryad**. Acolytes need a lot of training to be able to master their wands. *(Jack got me my wand but I keep getting it confiscated, apparently I'm not using it responsibly.)*

Water Nymphs – There are different kinds of water nymphs. All of them are great collectors. They love shiny objects and will trade information or grant a favour to obtain a special gift. Never give a water nymph a reflective surface or they might see themselves in it. They would be very angry if they saw their reflection, they consider themselves very beautiful, which they aren't. They are incredibly strong. *(An angry water nymph is something to be avoided.)*

Westwood Roost – Was once home to a family of **dragonettes**. It used to be at the back of the cave where **Finnola Fytche** now lives. *(It's the worst place I've ever been, a total mess and smells revolting.)*

WHERE IS IT?

The Map of Glasruhen – (pronounced *glass-rue-hen* meaning *ancient green hill*) From *The Golden Acorn* – *The Adventures of Jack Brenin* Book One.

Back Lane – This is a short cut from Forest Road to the market town of **Newton Gill**. It's a footpath and not a road. **Brenin House**, and the back gate of **Ewell House**, can be reached by going past the playing field.

Brenin House – The house where **Grandad** and **Jack** live. It's been in the Brenin family for generations.

Ewell House – Where I live with **Nora**. I have my own loft above the attic with my own window. **Elan** and **Jack** have their own rooms here too for when they stay. The house is very big and surrounded by trees and bushes. There are lots of statues in the garden and it's got a lake which is where **Gerda** and **Medric** live. Nora has herb, flower and kitchen gardens. There's a secret entrance at the bottom of Nora's garden which leads up to **Glasruhen Hill** or along to the bottom of **Sam Brenin**'s garden.

Forest Road – If you follow Forest Road it joins Salchester Road. **Salchester** is the modern name for **Viroconium**, which used to be the fourth largest Roman city in Britain.

Glasruhen – A small hamlet in the shadow of Glasruhen Hill. The two main houses in the hamlet are Ewell House, where Nora lives, and the Brenin House, where Jack lives with his Grandad.

Glasruhen Cricket Club – This is where **Sam Brenin** used to play cricket and now looks after the grounds and pitch.

Glasruhen Forest – An ancient forest mainly of oak trees, in the middle of which lives **Arrana**, the last **Hamadryad** left on Earth.

Glasruhen Hill – A large hill that looms above the hamlet of Glasruhen. The ancient Celtic Cornovii tribe constructed a settlement and hillfort on top of the hill.

Hawthorn Well – Can be found above **Ewell House** on the slopes of **Glasruhen Hill**. **Jennet**, a **Water Nymph** lives in the well. The hawthorn **cauldron plate** once hung on the hawthorn tree next to the well.

Hillfort – At the top of **Glasruhen Hill** there was once a fortified hillfort. It was built by the Cornovii tribe. The **window in time** can be found at the exact midpoint above the hillfort.

Newton Gill – A small market town at the foot of **Glasruhen Hill.**

Newton Gill Forest – Once a great forest of oak trees but now most of the trees have become **Gnarles.** The **Dryads** no longer live in the trees and the whole forest is slowly dying.

Playing Field – If you turn off **Forest Road** and walk along the back lane you come to the playing field.

Raven's Bowl – Located on an outcrop of rock at the summit of **Glasruhen Hill** is the Raven's Bowl. There are lots of legends about the place but this is where **Nora** performed the ritual to make **Jack Brenin** a raven boy, just like me.

Salchester – The modern name for **Viroconium**, which used to be the fourth largest Roman City in Britain. A few ruined remains of the once great city can still be seen in the fields around Salchester.

Standing Stones – These stones form a circle. The tallest stone in the middle has a hole near the top, big enough to put your arm through. They are hidden by deep magic and you can only enter the area with permission from **Arrana**.

Viroconium – A small fort in AD 61 which went on to become the fourth largest Roman City in Britain. It was the Latin name for what is now the small hamlet of **Salchester**. A few ruined remains of the once great city can still be seen in the fields around Salchester.

The Map of Annwn – (pronounced *an-noon* also known as the *Otherworld*). From *Glasruhen Gate – The Adventures of Jack Brenin* Book Two

Amphitheatre – A semi-circular stage at the foot of three hills near the **Eastern Portal** of **Annwn**. Seating has been cut into the hillside and the inhabitants of Annwn meet there to celebrate together.

Annwn – A land in another world, sometimes called the **Otherworld**. It's a place of peace and happiness, where it's always summer. There used to be portals on Earth, secret gateways, which could only be opened in certain ways at special times of the year. Only Druids had the knowledge and skill needed to perform the rituals that opened the gates. Mortals were only allowed into Annwn at **Samhain**.

Caves of Eternal Rest – When the **Romans** invaded Britain, they had orders to kill all the **Druid**s, some managed to enter Annwn through one of the gateways, but most were slain. Those that died were transported to **Annwn** where they had eternal life and could choose to live amongst the peoples of **Annwn** or go to a special place in the mountains, the **Caves of Eternal Rest**, and sleep in peace for eternity. Most of them chose to go into the caves.

Citadel – The fortress that surrounds and protects the **Glass Palace** was built after a band of men from Earth invaded **Annwn** and tried to steal its **Treasures**.

Clearing – A wide, open space to the east of the **Glass Palace** where the people gather together. The **Monolith** stands in the middle of the clearing.

Crannog – A village built on stilts in the middle of wetlands in the south of **Annwn**.

Druid's Village – Can be reached by travelling northeast from the **Glass Palace**. **Gwillam** lives here along with all the other members of the **Blessed Council**. The village is close to the **Mother Oak** and the **Mountains of Annwn**. The **crochan tree** grows in Gwillam's garden.

Eastern Gate – Marks the eastern boundary between **Annwn** and Earth. The treasure needed to open this gate is the **Stone of Destiny**. Two sentinel oaks guard this portal.

Glass Palace – The four glass turrets of the palace can be seen for miles around. It is situated in the middle of a lake in the very heart of **Annwn**. The Queen's garden is close to the water gate. The Glass Palace can only be reached by boat, unless you can fly.

Monolith – A large standing stone, found in the middle of **The Clearing**, to the east of the **Glass Palace**, where the people of Annwn meet.

Mound – A burial chamber in the southwest above the swamp. It's the resting place of the former **King of Annwn** who chose mortality over eternal life.

Mountains of Annwn – Can be found in the northeast. The entrance to the **Caves of Eternal Rest** is high in these mountains.

Northern Gate – Marks the northern boundary between **Annwn** and Earth. The treasure needed to open this gate is the **Spear of Justice**. Two sentinel oaks guard this portal.

Southern Gate – Marks the southern boundary between **Annwn** and Earth. The treasure needed to open this gate is the **Sword of Power**. Two sentinel oaks guard this portal.

Western Gate – Marks the western boundary between **Annwn** and Earth. The treasure needed to open this gate is the **Cauldron of Life**. Two sentinel oaks guard this portal.

The Map of Beconbury. From *Glasruhen Gate – The Adventures of Jack Brenin* Book Two

The Gelston River – This is the longest river in the county.

The Mere Pool – The home of **Coriss**, the **Water Nymph**.

The Mound – **Myryl** lives in one of the springs near the Mound.

The Map of Silver Hill and the Crags of Stonytop Ridge. From *Silver Hill – The Adventures of Jack Brenin* Book Three.

River Stype – Named after **Stype Tor**. It flows around **Westwood** and past **Winberry Hill** and **Silver Hill**.

Silver Hill – A large hill, Winberry Hill is its twin peak.

Stonytop Ridge – A long ridge of strange jagged rock formations. There's Shepherd's Rock, Scattered Rocks, **The Devil's Chair**, Manstone Rock, Cranberry Rock, Hagstone and **Stype Tor**. Some say the stones come to life on stormy nights and become **Hags**. There's an old rhyme about Stonytop Ridge:

When lightning flashes in a thunderstorm,
On Stonytop Ridge a Hag is born.

Stype Tor – The **River Stype** takes its name from the last rocky outcrop on **Stonytop Ridge**.

The Devil's Chair – There's an old rhyme about the Devil's Chair too:

Sit upon the Devil's Chair,
Sit upon it if you dare,
But if you do you must beware,
For you might vanish into thin air.

Westwood – An ancient woodland at the bottom of which used to be the **Westwood Roost**, a cave now inhabited by the **Hag**, **Finnola Fytche**.

Winberry Hill – A large hill, **Silver Hill** is its twin peak.

for more information visit

www.pengridion.co.uk

ACKNOWLEDGEMENTS

I'd like to thank
everyone at Infinite Ideas
for all their help and support.
My friends and family for their
encouragement
and invaluable contributions,
and a special thank you to Ron for
his support and veracity.

52222317R00211

Made in the USA
Lexington, KY
20 May 2016